Renee,

There are few things
in this world more
beautiful than a woman so
in love with her family!

God Bless

Jeanne A Kroger

JEANNE KROGER

STALKING CAMDEN

A NOVEL

Edited by Belinda Koch @ Lexicon Softworks

Cover photograph by Vicki France
Author photograph by Tim Courtney

ISBN-13 978-0-5780-0808-0
ISBN-10 0-5780-0808-0

Printed in the United States of America

For Holly, Jack, and Mary Jane.

To all of life's questions,

you are my answer.

PROLOGUE

The size eleven and a half hiking boot rested on the side of the now lifeless body. The boot was too big for the foot inside it but then that was the point wasn't it? An extra pair of socks and tight laces took up most of the slack. The boots would be disposed of soon anyway. They had served their purpose and it wouldn't do to keep them around. Keys, wallet, laptop, and any other items that could identify the poor schmuck would be deposited in a plastic trash bag and dropped in the dumpster behind a fast food restaurant a few exits down the interstate later today.

One strong shove to get it started moving down the hill and the body began to pick up speed. The incline at this part of the trail was particularly steep. This spot had been carefully chosen because it was not visible from either up or down the rest of the heavily wooded trail without bracing oneself against a tree to look down over the side of the path. Leaning over the edge, the killer watched the body as it slid and thumped its way down the hill finally coming to rest at the base of a large sycamore tree. The torso laid contorted half wrapped around the trunk of the tree with arms and legs splayed at odd angles. The neatly pressed plaid shirt and pleated khaki pants that had been put on with care this morning were now disheveled and smeared with dirt and debris. The freshly washed and combed hair was smeared with blood and mussed with leaves and twigs. With a last look up at the sky the killer was satisfied that the late summer thunderstorms promised by the local newscaster were on the way and what little forensic evidence there was would soon be washed away. With a slight smile of satisfaction the killer continued on along the path enjoying the fresh New England air and the beauty of the woods.

1

Holly knew she should have left earlier. Eric had just seemed so agitated that she hated to leave with all that silence between them. Mentioning his family, or lack of, was what had set him off. She should have learned this by now. Any reference to his past had this same conversation ending effect. Waiting around hadn't helped either. He had said almost nothing during dinner and while she pretended to be interested in the movie they had rented for this evening he read a magazine and eventually got up and went to surf the net on his computer. He was still sitting there when she finally gave up and decided to go home. By the time she had packed up her things, said goodbye over her shoulder, without any obvious response, and left the little cottage the sun had already started its descent. Choosing to ignore the diminishing light she opted to take the walking trail home instead of the main road. This was the route she used most often when visiting Eric, which she did fairly often because it allowed them more privacy than her living arrangement. This path was wider than many of the other trails, so she could easily maneuver her bike along all but the steepest parts where she had to get off and walk. She had never, however, attempted this so late in the evening.

The main road from the Wilkes estate to town was paved but the many twists and turns through the wooded hillside led farther away from town before meandering back in the right direction again and added about fifteen minutes to the ride home. Eric's cottage was part of the estate and was situated off a branch of the main drive leading to the large and almost always empty mansion. The path was one of several trails snaking through the woods outside of Camden, the small town where she had lived and worked since she fell in love with it during visits here with her roommate from college in Ohio. It hadn't taken long before she knew she would pursue her graduate studies here instead of Miami University in Oxford where her parents had wanted her to stay.

While the paved road was a safer bet, especially with limited daylight left, the path was faster and more peaceful. She had enjoyed many quiet walks along the cool mossy trail that wound its way through the New England woods situated between the town and the coast. You rarely met anyone on this trail because it led so far away from the park that served as the entrance to the various trails from the edge of town.

"Why didn't I put a light on this bike?" Holly asked herself out loud. Walter Johnson, her employer, had suggested this on several occasions, but she had put it off saying she would get around to it eventually. There was still a dusky light that would get her through the steepest part of the approaching down slope. After that she would probably have to walk until the lights from Camden were close enough to light her way along the remainder of the path that snaked its way toward town.

She swore under her breath as she hit a rut in the path that jarred her bike hard. The handlebars started to feel loose and vibrate. "You've got to be kidding," she muttered to herself. Fighting to keep the bike under control, she attempted to slow her descent by braking but nothing happened and the shaking got even worse. She swerved the front wheel of her bike to avoid hitting a large rock jutting out of the dirt path and the jolt which would have been harmless under normal circumstances was enough to cause the tire to separate completely from its frame, sending both the bike and Holly sharply forward and to the left. Too far to the left.

She watched helplessly as the wheel of the bike started to drop straight down the jagged slope, crying out as she followed the mutinous tire rolling and bouncing its way down the hillside. Tumbling over the front of the handlebars she crashed onto her right shoulder and continued to roll using her forearms and hands to try to protect her head as the hillside spun past her.

She came to an abrupt stop at the base of a large and very unwelcoming shrub. The wind had been knocked out of her and the sharp branches of the shrub were poking her in the back and sides. She fought the panic of not being able to inhale. Her lungs finally relaxed, she inhaled and began to gasp, then automatically turned her head and looked up toward where she had left the path. She hadn't really expected to see anything, so she was surprised and initially relieved to see the shadowy dark form of a person move along the edge of the path and then disappear. She hoped whoever it was had a flashlight.

"Hey!" she called in a weak, breathless voice. "I'm here. Hey! I could use some help." Nothing. She stared hard at the spot where she had seen the shadow, trying to focus through the darkness. There was nothing there. She quickly pushed aside the fleeting thought that she had imagined it. She had definitely seen someone at the top of the hill.

"Help!" she cried, louder this time. Still nothing. With the exception of her own heavy breathing, the woods were silent. She pushed up onto her left elbow and slowly rolled onto her back. *"Great. Dangerous bike crash followed by close encounter with creepy stranger."* She looked around trying to get her bearings but it seemed to be getting darker by the second. She guessed she had landed toward the bottom of the hill about thirty-five feet down from the path. She knew from the numerous hiking trips she and Eric had taken through these woods that there was nothing but rugged forest between her and the coast. If she closed her eyes and concentrated she could hear the water breaking against the rocks of Long Island Sound in the distance, but nothing else.

This area outside of town was a solitary place. Most of the time she thought this was a good thing. It was one of the reasons Eric had chosen to live here. He was by nature a bit of a loner. Eric Copeland was also a very talented artist who valued his privacy. The property where he lived and worked as a sort of caretaker was a large estate that was owned by the Wilkes family. The main house was closed up most of the year. Eric lived in a cottage that sat off to the left of the main drive and back into the woods a bit. There was also a shack just behind the cottage that he had converted into a studio where he spent many solitary hours painting beautiful landscapes. The Wilkes family owned several homes and rarely came out here, which suited Eric just fine. They thought it was chic to have an artist as a caretaker and gave Eric a free hand when he suggested converting the dilapidated outbuilding into a studio.

Holly liked the remoteness of the place also, unless of course she was knocked on her butt in a ravine with any number of potentially serious injuries. The most concerning of which at present was the gash in her hairline that was pouring blood down the right side of her face. There were tissues in the satchel that she had stuffed in the basket on the front of the bike, but that wasn't going to help her now. After taking a quick inventory of all of her moving parts to check for broken bones or something else equally serious she started to feel around the immediate vicinity for her bag.

She winced as the palms of her hands slid over the ground. She couldn't see very well but she was pretty sure there were some fairly nasty scratches from her attempts to protect her body during the fall. No bag. *"It has to be here somewhere,"* she thought to herself in vain, knowing full well the bag could be anywhere between her and the top of the incline.

It would be foolish to try to make her way forward through the woods from down here. There could be any number of obstacles in her way that could cause further injury. It would be easy to get lost in the dark, especially with her nonexistent sense of direction, and end up wandering around all night. The best way out of here was to make her way back up the hill and follow the path to town. It really wasn't more than another quarter of a mile or so to the entrance of the path in the park across from the end of the main street in town.

She had been hiking these trails with Eric all summer and was in great shape. Despite some painful scratches, a throbbing lump on her head, and one very sore shin, she started to feel her way up the side of the hill. She walked bent over and felt her way with her left hand while she tried to staunch the blood flow from her scalp with her right. It took her a good ten minutes to reach the top as she slowly picked her way among the rocks and shrubs, sometimes gaining one yard and losing two on the steep slope. She groped her way past the numerous menacing obstacles growing out of or embedded into the hillside and was amazed that she hadn't been more seriously injured.

Considering the lack of response to her calls for help, she hoped whoever had been up on the path when she went over the side was long gone. She was not feeling particularly brave and didn't need a run-in with some creep hiding in the woods. She made her way up the dark hillside, stumbling occasionally and then tripped over the frame of her traitorous bicycle, causing her to utter a few choice swear words. Once she reached the top of the slope, she carefully navigated her way down the rest of the path moving slowly and feeling in front of her with the toe of her shoe so she wouldn't take another trip down the hillside. She kept the heel of her right hand pressed tightly to the gash in her head. The blood flow had slowed, which was good, but the wound stung from the contact with her dirty hand.

She looked up at the sky, scowling at the dark thick clouds that blocked any chance of moonlight. After another twenty minutes of feeling her way down the path she felt the rise in air temperature as she stepped out of the cool dark woods into the warm September air of the park. Situated at the end of the main street of town and scattered with various pieces of wooden playground equipment, the park was also the entrance to several climbing trails. With the light filtering over from across the road she was able to look down and take stock of herself. The palms of her hands had angry red scratches on them that were smeared with dirt. Her right hand and forearm were streaked with blood that had run through her fingers, down the back of her hand and to her elbow. Her head pounded where it had been banged and bumped down the hill. As she looked down at her bloody dirt-streaked clothes she saw a rip in the front of her polo shirt that exposed a nasty scratch on her stomach. There was also an egg-sized knot on her right shin. Pretty.

She limped down two blocks and over two blocks to Sixteen Terwilliger Place where she rented a couple of rooms on the top floor of Beatrice Kingsley's Victorian style house. Mrs. Kingsley was going to have a heart attack when she saw Holly. There was no chance of sneaking upstairs and cleaning herself up because Beatrice Kingsley spent every evening in her front parlor listening to music or watching a program on the television set. Mostly she liked to sit near the window and keep track of the neighbors. She wasn't the gossipy type though. You would rarely hear more than a "Hmmm" out of her when a comment was made about one of the residents of the small town, located between Almsley College, where Holly was a grad student, and Long Island Sound. There wasn't much that went on in Camden, Connecticut that Beatrice Kingsley didn't know about.

As Holly climbed the steps to the front porch she realized that her keys were in her satchel along with everything else she carried around with her on a daily basis. Oh well, she would just have to find them tomorrow morning during a post wreck scavenger hunt for her personal effects. She rang the doorbell and tried pointlessly to rearrange her torn shirt while she waited for her landlady to leave her post by the window and open the door.

"Did you forget your keys honey?" Mrs. Kingsley called as she flipped on the foyer light and put on her glasses. The older woman, clad in her tidy housecoat and small ballet-style slippers worked the various locks on the heavy door while the bruised and battered Holly could only wait for the inevitable shock and exclamations of concern before she could step inside and begin the explanations and assurances that she was fine.

"Holly! My goodness, what happened? Are you all right? Here, sit down and I'll go get a towel and some ice." Her questions were all rhetorical of course and Holly, relieved and exhausted, didn't attempt to reply to any of them. Visibly shaken, Mrs. Kingsley rushed from the foyer to the kitchen to retrieve a damp towel and an ice pack and was shuffling back down the hall toward her within seconds. She gently pushed and pulled Holly into the living room and into one of the matching wingback chairs placed strategically next to the front window so that when she sat in here in the evening she could see both the street out front and the small television set that sat on an antique table in the corner. Rattled, Mrs. Kingsley perched herself on the edge of an ottoman covered in a heavy fabric that complemented the chair and started to take stock of Holly's injuries to see where she should begin.

"You fell off that bicycle didn't you?" and before Holly could answer, "I saw you come walking down the street and I wondered where your bike was. Of course I couldn't tell that you were hurt from my chair." When the weather was nice Holly rode her bike everywhere. The town was so small it wasn't more than a few blocks in any direction. It was one of the reasons she had chosen to live here instead of on campus. She'd had her fill of campus life during her four-year stint as an undergraduate at Miami.

"It probably looks worse than it is," Holly assured her as she sucked in air through her teeth and held her breath. Beatrice was blotting Holly's hands with a clean wet towel and the fresh wounds stung and started to bleed again.

"Come to the kitchen, the light is better," Mrs. Kingsley said, leading her battered charge out of the front room.

Holly followed her down the hall into the bright kitchen and settled herself onto one of the old ladder back chairs at the big scrubbed oak table. Beatrice Kingsley's kitchen always smelled of delicious home-cooked food. She was the first person Holly had ever met who still made and baked her own bread. Quite often Bea would make Holly dinner and bring it down to Johnson's Hardware where Holly worked part time in the evenings and on Saturdays. Holly secretly wondered if there wasn't another reason Mrs. Kingsley visited her at the store so frequently. She could easily have packed Holly a dinner and sent it with her when she left if it was proper nutrition Mrs. Kingsley was concerned about, but then she wouldn't have run into Mr.

Johnson and been able to let him know in person that she had packed more than enough in the basket for him as well.

"Ouch!" Holly yelped as Mrs. Kingsley dabbed antibiotic ointment on her hands.

"Now, stop fidgeting and tell me how this happened," Beatrice instructed as she continued to wipe and dab gently at Holly's tender forearms and elbows, causing her eyes to sting with tears.

"Well, I was coming back from Eric's on the trail through the woods when I hit a rut in the path and the tire came off of the bike." She didn't describe the subsequent trip down the hill. The mere sight of Holly had already visibly upset the poor woman. There was no need to send her over the edge with the scary details. It was hard for Holly to believe it herself. Her bike was very well cared for. Even if she hadn't looked after it herself, which she did, Mr. Johnson was always reminding Holly to put air in her tires, oil the chain and all the moving parts. He had tightened the nut that held the wheel on the frame himself a few weeks ago when Holly said it was starting to wobble.

Mrs. Kingsley didn't say anything but as she listened to Holly tell her about her long slow climb up the hill and hike back to town her face seemed to set in a concerned frown.

"You'll have to stop by Doctor Lerner's office in the morning and have him look at your head, but I think that these little clear strip things will hold the cut together pretty well." Bea applied several clear steri-strips to the gash. Holly's eyes watered as the initial shock of the accident wore off and her body started to ache all over. Mrs. Kingsley gave her some aspirin and sent her up to bed. She would have loved to soak in a hot bath but with dozens of jagged scratches all over her body she thought that might not be a good idea.

As she lay between the cool cotton sheets on her bed in the dark and exhaustion started to wash over her she wondered why she hadn't called Eric and told him what had happened. Wouldn't that be the normal thing to do? Their fight, if you could call it that, wouldn't have mattered. If Eric knew she was hurt he would have come straight over. She knew this. They had been spending all or most of their free time together for months now. No doubt Mrs. Kingsley had noticed that Holly had not attempted to let her boyfriend know about her accident. She didn't want to think about that right now. Sleep overtook her as her mind drifted back to the top of the dark hillside and the shadow that had watched her fall and left her there.

2

The next morning as she walked toward the hardware store where she worked Holly's entire body ached. She had taken a few more aspirin before she left the house but they hadn't started to take effect yet. In the light of day she looked worse than she had imagined. Her long brown hair was pulled back in its usual ponytail revealing a scratched chin and a neatly bandaged gash high on the right side of her forehead. She was wearing a different polo shirt, this one the color of her light blue eyes. Her long athletic legs were still tanned from the summer, but between the lower hem of her khaki shorts and the top of her Nikes were many raw scrapes and scratches. Long pants would have concealed these, but her legs were still too sensitive this morning. A few nasty blue bruises had started to appear on her knees and halfway up her thigh. For a girl who could usually turn a few heads with little or no make-up, she was turning more than usual today and not because of her beauty. Holly just smiled and said hello to the residents she had come to recognize. Mercifully, she didn't see anyone who knew her well enough to stop her and inquire about her injuries. She was headed to the hardware store because she needed to pick up some tools to get the tire back on her bike so she could at least push it home. First, however, she stopped into Dr. Lerner's small office to ask his nurse Angie if he could see her today. She didn't really think a trip to the doctor was necessary but it was a less daunting choice than returning to face Mrs. Kingsley without having done so. Dr. Lerner was coming out of the back where there was a narrow hallway with three examination rooms and a small laboratory. His office and storage rooms were at the top of the staircase just past Angie's desk.

"Good grief! What happened to you?" Angie exclaimed. This outburst got the doctor's attention. He had a tendency to pretend not to notice people in the reception area so as not to get drawn into social conversations during office hours. The doctor didn't echo Angie's question but he did cross his arms and peer over his bifocals at Holly, waiting for an explanation. She looked around her at the empty waiting room and then back at the two people waiting for her answer.

"Oh, you know, same ole story," said Holly lightly. "Girl visits boyfriend, girl rides bike home in the dark, girl crashes bike down steep rocky hill into shrub."

"That's not funny Holly," Angie chided. "You could have been seriously injured." They were on a first name basis. Angie doubled as Dr. Lerner's nurse two days a week when Cheryl, his regular nurse, was off. Holly had been coming in for allergy shots weekly since she moved to Camden and she found that Angie could administer the shot with virtually no pain, while Holly was convinced that Cheryl was something of a situational sadist when left alone with a needle and a vulnerable patient, so she made sure to get her shots on Angie's days in the office. Over the past year they had gotten to know each other pretty well. Mrs. Kingsley had warned Holly to take care what she discussed with Angie as anything she heard that wasn't in someone's medical chart was regurgitated in one form or another throughout town by the end of the day. Holly thought Angie was funny, but she was careful to keep her personal life to herself and give vague answers to any questions that didn't relate to her reason for visiting.

"I was just going over to the bakery for a cup of coffee before the first patients arrive," volunteered Dr. Lerner, finally breaking his silence. "Angie, why don't you grab us both a cup and I will take a look at Ms. Miller here." Recognizing that this was not a request, Angie grabbed her purse and started for the door while Dr. Lerner showed Holly to the closest exam room.

Holly showed him the gash on her head and he told her that Mrs. Kingsley had done an excellent job and that she should continue to put antibiotic ointment on it. He probably would have put a stitch or two in it last night but it had already started to heal and her hair would cover most of the small scar that would be left. After looking at her other cuts and bruises and checking to make sure she didn't have any pain or complaints that would cause him to suspect internal injuries, he told her she was good to go.

"How's the Copeland boy doing?" asked Doctor Lerner. "I saw him last night when I was over at Rosa's picking up my dinner after I closed up the office."

"Fine. Great really," she replied. "He's still painting. He never seems to run out of new material up at the Wilkes place. When did you say you saw him?" Holly asked, slightly confused.

Dr. Lerner didn't immediately answer, probably regretting the question already. He didn't like to get involved in people's personal lives in town. Angie had confided this to her one day. Apparently to Dr. Lerner, keeping a professional distance from his patients was important. Finally he said "Around eight o'clock I guess. I stayed late to update some records."

"Oh, he must have come to town just after I left," she mumbled more to herself than to the doctor. "Well, thanks for taking the time to see me this morning," Holly said while gathering her bag. "I have to go back to the scene of the crime and collect my bike. It was too dark to deal with it last night." She quickly left the office and headed in the direction of Johnson's Hardware Store.

As she walked further down Main Street toward the store she wondered about what Dr. Lerner had said. Eric hadn't said anything about coming into town last night. He must have left just after she did. He probably took the main road, having been smart enough not to try the path that late. It wasn't unusual for Eric to come to town for dinner. He often did so on nights when Holly was working. She would take her dinner break and go eat with him. On these occasions she would let Mrs. Kingsley know so that she didn't show up at the store with supper. But he hadn't mentioned it last night. Of course, he hadn't said much at all after Holly had brought up his family. She was working on framing some old black and white family photos of her grandparents for her mom and dad for Christmas and offered to do the same for Eric. He told her all of his family photos were in storage somewhere in Virginia. Holly volunteered to take a road trip with him to go look for a few, saying it would give a more personal touch to the little cottage he lived in. He didn't answer her though. In fact he didn't say anything else all evening until she told him she was leaving.

"You're awfully early." Holly was yanked out of her thoughts by her boss' voice. He was sitting in his usual morning spot on the bench outside his storefront.

"So this is what you do when I'm not around," Holly teased, giving him a bright smile. There wasn't a lazy bone in the man's body. Walter Johnson was a retired Marine who still kept his rigid schedule. Up at dawn, had toast and juice for breakfast, and then walked the entire town before heading to the store an hour before it opened. Only after he had performed his morning ritual of checking each shelf for stock and tidiness and set up his cash register did he come outside and allow himself a cup of coffee and a few minutes to read the paper.

"I hope the other guy looks worse than you do," he said with a half smirk.

"There were three of them and they were all over six feet tall," she retorted laughing and then winced. The cuts and scratches on her chin, cheek, and forehead all hurt when she smiled.

"Well, go on," he urged, crossing one leg over the other and shifting himself in a position to watch her while she explained. "I heard you fell off your bike out on that trail in the middle of the night."

"It wasn't the middle of the night," she defended weakly.

"I guess we'll be putting that light on your bike now." He sighed dramatically, shaking his head. "Some people have got to learn everything the hard way."

"Before we can put a light on it, I have to get it back here. I need some tools to fix it first though."

"Did it get damaged in the fall?" he asked. She hadn't thought about any damage the bike might have sustained during the crash.

"I'm not sure about that. It was too dark to see. But before I fell I hit a rock in the road and the front tire came off." She was looking down at the toe of her tennis shoe. When she finally looked up at him there was a stunned look on his face.

"You mean you had the accident because your bike fell apart?"

"Uhm, yeah." Holly felt terrible. Her boss and friend looked pained. He had promised her parents, especially her father, that he would look after her. In truth he had. He was never nosy, but he looked out for her interests. And he was particularly careful with her bike.

"I don't understand it," he said to himself. "I tightened that nut myself. I know I didn't strip it. And the brakes were fine."

Holly would have rather swallowed her tongue than to confirm this to the man who took so much pride in everything he did. "Well, the handlebars started to get wobbly and started to vibrate as I went down the hill on the path. I tried the brakes but then I hit a rock and the next thing I knew the front tire was going over the side and the bike and I just followed it down."

Poor Mr. Johnson looked positively gray. He was standing now; had been since she mentioned the damaged bike. "I'll just get my hat and some tools and we'll go see about that bike."

"You can't leave the store," she reminded him. "It's not a problem, if you'll just give me the things I am likely to need to get the tire back on the bike long enough to walk it back here. I can go and back in an hour." She said all this to his back as she followed him around the store. He put on the Marine Corps ball cap he always wore, and proceeded to fill a small canvas bag with a few tools and some hardware. Her attempts to convince him to let her go alone were futile. He wasn't listening to her.

His face was set in a determined frown that she had never seen before. It was the first time since knowing him that Holly could really picture him in the military. She would not like to be on the receiving end of that look.

He asked her where she had gone off the path and she told him as he locked the door and put out the CLOSED sign. More guilt. Even with her long legs, Holly had trouble keeping up with him. Walter Johnson was in great shape. He didn't say anything, just walked purposefully straight down the street and across to the park. There were several different trails that began and ended in this park and Holly pointed to the trail that led to the Wilkes estate before he asked her. She jogged along behind him not attempting to break his silence. Were all men like this? The male psyche was such a fragile thing.

As they got about midway up the long steep hill where she had crashed the night before, she started to look for any signs of the accident. As she peered over the side of the narrow path she caught her breath. It had been impossible to see anything last night and the shock of the fall had kept her from thinking of anything but getting up the hill and out of the woods. Now looking down the hill she realized how truly fortunate she had been. There were large and small rocks jutting out sharply all over the hillside. Bushes, sticks, and other vegetation covered the sharp drop that was in fact much farther down than she had thought.

"Well I'll be damned," Walter said, shaking his head. "Holly, you are one lucky girl. I don't know how you managed to fall down that hill and climb back up in one piece." He looked away from her and started to busy himself with finding the safest way down the hill. They walked up a little further and were able to spot the bike frame and about fifteen feet away from it, her satchel. Several of her books had slid out of it and lay scattered just beyond the bag. Thank goodness it hadn't rained last night.

They worked their way down to the bottom of the hill and found the tire. Mr. Johnson carried it back up to where the bike frame was and Holly gathered up her belongings. She carried the tire and her bag while Mr. Johnson carried the frame and they struggled back up the hill. When they reached the path again Holly held the frame while Mr. Johnson used the tools from his bag to put the tire back on the bike. Once that was accomplished, he proceeded to roll the bike back and forth. Satisfied, he made a grunting sound. Next he squeezed the brakes several times and as Holly had described nothing happened.

"Maybe the wire wore through somewhere," she suggested as he squatted down to follow the brake wire down from the handlebars and underneath the bike. Where the small plastic tubing that encased the brake wire ended at the back of the bike there should have been a single piece of wire that continued on but there wasn't. At least it wasn't attached. Hanging loose at the back of the bike was the broken piece of wire. "Well," she said, "there it is."

"Except it didn't break from wear. Look closer." He held out the wire and she leaned in to get a closer look at it. "The wire isn't frayed or even worn at all. The other end is still inside the tubing but it probably looks just like this," he offered in a flat quiet voice.

"Well, what caused it to break? Did I step on it or something? Or maybe a stick got caught in it?"

"No, I don't think so," he said. Then after a few seconds he took a breath and said, "Holly, it's possible someone cut it."

Holly didn't reply right away. She knew Mr. Johnson too well to think he would joke about something like this. She also knew he wouldn't have said it if he weren't pretty sure about it. So she waited.

"The end of it is cut clean and pinched together a little bit. It looks like it's been cut with wire cutters. You rode the bike to the Wilkes place yesterday? You didn't walk it up the hill?"

"I walked up the hill and rode on from there. The brakes worked fine. There is a small slope that leads down to Eric's cottage. I have to use my brakes going down that hill and I lean the bike against his wood pile." Holly's mind was struggling to catch up with Mr. Johnson. Was he saying that at some point between the time she arrived at Eric's and the time she left somebody had cut her brake line with wire cutters? That was impossible. There was no one on the Wilkes property but her and Eric. She said this to Mr. Johnson but if he heard her he didn't answer.

Holly stuffed the rest of her dirt-covered belongings back into her equally dirty bag and started down the path toward her boss. He had already started gathering his tools and putting them back into the canvas bag. Mr. Johnson handed her the bag of tools and proceeded to walk the bike back down the hilly trail. Holly stayed just behind him as the path wasn't wide enough for them to walk side by side. He turned his head back toward her and said that he could have the brakes fixed by this evening when she came to work and she could have her bike back as long as the frame wasn't bent. He could check that when he got it back to his workshop in the back of the store.

While they were walking Holly rummaged through her satchel to make sure she hadn't lost anything. She looked over her shoulder to check the path behind her. They had traveled too far down the path to see the spot where she had crashed and all she could see was a steep incline dotted with brush and trees toward the bottom. The sun was higher in the sky and warming up the woods around them. Her attention was drawn to a place further up the path where the sunlight glinted off of something down the hill. She glanced ahead at Mr. Johnson who was shaking his head and mumbling something to himself as he carefully guided her bike along the trail. She set the tool bag and satchel down and started to make her way down the hill toward whatever it was that was reflecting the light. The hillside was much steeper here and she reached out for any root or rock sticking out of the ground that would keep her from sliding. She put her shoe on a clump of dirt to help balance herself but the dirt crumbled and she began to slide down the hill. She tried to slow her descent by digging the heels of her sneakers into the dirt and sliding on her backside. She grabbed at whatever she could to slow herself down but she was headed right for a clump of brush and whatever was reflecting the sun on the other side of it.

She stopped suddenly, catching a small tree trunk with her shoes and keeping herself from sliding into the bushes beyond. Her eyes were riveted to the sight a few feet to the left and a little further down the hill. As her brain tried to come to grips with what she saw she was suddenly overcome by the horrific odor given off by the decomposing body in front of her. The reflection had been coming from the face of a watch attached to an arm sticking up at an impossible angle. Back pedaling up the hill and holding her breath Holly was just able to let out a short scream before the smell overwhelmed her again. The sound of flies buzzed in her ears as she fought the urge to vomit. Crying and clawing her way up the hill she was startled when a firm hand grabbed her arm and jerked her upright.

"D-Dead," she stuttered. It was all she could say as she leaned away from Mr. Johnson and started to dry heave.

"Are you sure?" he asked, starting toward the body.

She grabbed his arm and nodded emphatically. She caught her breath and together they climbed up the hill. Neither one spoke on the way back. Holly was struggling to maintain her composure and Mr. Johnson didn't want to interrogate her. They would alert the sheriff as soon as they got back to town and he would have plenty of questions of his own.

Sheriff Matt Butler was patient and allowed Holly to take her time describing what she had seen as they sat back in Walter Johnson's office. He had already been to the site where the body was found and he assured them both that the body was being removed and the woods combed for evidence.

"Do you know how he died? Who he is? Uh, was?" Holly asked the sheriff.

"There's nothing I can tell you right now, but we should know something soon," he told her. She knew that he couldn't discuss the case with her anyway so she didn't ask any more questions.

He asked her if she recognized the man in the woods. It would have been difficult due to the short amount of time she had seen him and the condition of the body for Holly to tell for sure whether the person in the woods was anyone she had met, but there was nothing about him that was familiar to her. His clothes - khaki pants and a striped button-down collar shirt combined with some sort of loafers for shoes - could have belonged to anyone. The park and trails were open to the public so everyone could use them. She hadn't seen a backpack and he wasn't wearing hiking boots so it was unlikely he was there for sport. She said she guessed he could be just some guy who decided to take a walk.

The sheriff offered her a ride home but she told him she wanted to walk. She was sure Mrs. Kingsley had heard of the body found in the woods by now and she wanted to calm down before relaying the events of the morning to her landlady.

Holly thanked Mr. Johnson for helping her. "I'm sorry you had to close the store. I hope you didn't lose much business."

"Don't worry about that. The only people that come by this early are some of the old timers that come to get a cup of coffee and talk about the weather and the baseball game. Nothing I didn't hear yesterday."

Holly knew he was just trying to make her feel better. Johnson's Hardware was one of the busiest shops in town. All the locals preferred to use the town shops to support the local businesses. Many college students chose to come over to Camden because it was closer than the nearest Super Wal-Mart and the prices were cheaper than those at the campus shops. He had a buzzer that rang in the back when the front door opened and the wall between the workshop and the store had a large picture window in it with one-way glass so he could keep an eye on things from the back. There were also security cameras with television screens that he could see from both the front register and the shop area.

She said goodbye to Mr. Johnson who was already wheeling her bike back into his workshop. As she left the store a tired-looking mother came in carrying an infant and was followed by a complaining toddler. Holly gave them a wooden smile and wondered how much of the town already knew about the body in the woods. If Angie had heard, which was almost certain as Dr. Lerner handled the local coroner duties unless the county coroner was needed, then some version of the story would have circulated through the small town by now.

She knew that she needed to study for a few hours and get some laundry done before her shift started at Mr. Johnson's at three o'clock. It was important that she concentrate on mundane things to keep the horrible picture of that poor dead man out of her head.

She wanted to press her white blouse and her new tan slacks because she was meeting her friend Megan for lunch tomorrow after class. Megan never appeared to go out of her way to dress up, but even in her khakis and low heels she had a way of making Holly feel plain. Holly was a better athlete though. She and Megan had donned hiking boots, packed water bottles and taken on the many trails in the New England countryside when Eric was too deep into another painting to be bothered. Although Megan struggled to keep up with Holly she did always manage to look clean and fresh at the end of the day. Holly, on the other hand, generally ended up sweaty and with some sort of foliage in her hair. Megan Saunders was a fierce competitor though. She always knew what she wanted and worked hard to get it. She had beaten out several students with more experience to get her position as Assistant to the Head of the Psychology Department. She went over or through anyone who got between her and what she wanted and Holly respected her for that. Eric thought Holly was crazy for feeling inferior in any way to Megan. He told her she was worth ten Megans and she knew that he meant it. Whenever they were out together he never paid attention to other women. They certainly paid attention to him though. Holly remembered dates in college and high school when a beautiful girl would walk by and her date's eyes would wander. But not Eric Copeland. From their first date he had only had eyes for her.

3

The leaves were changing and the air was fresh and clean. Connecticut was beautiful in the fall - in all of the seasons really. Holly had fallen in love with the East Coast when she had visited over the holidays with her college roommate, Sarah. They had spent a couple of long weekends here and it hadn't taken Holly long to decide where she would move after graduation. Her roommate unfortunately, had followed her fiancé to California after graduation, but Holly didn't care. She hadn't cared then that she didn't have any friends or family here; she just knew she wanted to live here. Of course now she was so ensconced in the little town she couldn't imagine living anywhere else. The lawns of the houses that skirted Main Street, the main thoroughfare in Camden, were old but well kept. The streets were lined with tall trees, the kind that had been here for generations. The majority of the residents were retired, but according to Mrs. Kingsley more young families were moving here every year. There were also a few families of professors from the college and some of the employees of the larger businesses that were within commuting range. Camden had one elementary school, one middle school, and one high school. There were a few private schools close by that were affiliated with various churches and some very expensive boarding schools within a hundred miles for those who could afford it.

Holly was just a few houses away from where she lived when she noticed the familiar figure of Eric sitting on the top step of the porch. He hadn't seen her yet and she slowed her pace and took the opportunity to study him. He was handsome in an unshaven handyman sort of way. His dark brown hair always looked as if it needed a trim. But at just under six feet tall and with green eyes Eric Copeland was very handsome. His build and good looks would lead you to believe he was an athlete, but Eric, while fond of any outdoor activities, was first and foremost an artist. He painted landscapes that were breathtaking. There was a gallery owned by a man called Hugh Mason about an hour away from Camden that had sold several of them.

Eric was by no means a starving artist. He had money that he had inherited after his parents' death and also when his grandmother who had raised him afterward had died. Holly had managed to get this much out of him over the last year, but little more. He could have afforded a nice apartment or house off campus and spent his time socializing with the other students while he pursued, at a snail's pace, a master's degree in art history, but he was content to spend his spare time hiking, cycling, and touring the various parks and historical sites up and down the coast with her. There was something very sad about him at times that Holly felt was more than just the death of his parents and grandmother. There was always something vulnerable just below the surface. Whatever it was though, he was not willing to share it with her.

He noticed her walking toward him at last and stood up as she waved and picked up her pace. Moving up the walk to the steps, she noticed that his expression changed, causing his brow to furrow. It only took her a second to realize that she must look pretty scary with all the cuts, scrapes and bruises.

"I heard you had an accident. I didn't realize it was that bad." His face registered shock.

"Thanks," she said with a smile. "You look great too."

"That's not what I meant. Why didn't you call me? Are you OK? What did the doctor say?"

"I see you have been talking to Mrs. Kingsley."

"Angie, actually. I went in to town to get breakfast and a paper and she was picking up coffee. I have to admit, I felt a little stupid hearing about my girlfriend crashing her bike from the locals in town."

He hadn't mentioned the body. She was certain that if he had spoken to Angie he had been given all of the gory details whether he wanted them or not. It occurred to Holly that he was angry. Hurt at least. Now she felt like a jerk. She should have called him. She had never played games with him before and she didn't know why she had hesitated to confide in him now. Truthfully she knew that she blamed him a little for being such a baby last night, causing her to be late. But that wasn't all. Nothing about last night made sense yet, not the accident and not the creepy person in the woods. Really, she just wanted to forget about it.

"I haven't had time yet. I left early to go and get my bike and my things that I couldn't see to pick up last night. I was going to call when I got back but I had to spend some time with the sheriff. I'm glad to see you now though," she said, knowing how pathetic an excuse that was. "It looks worse than it feels, anyway." Another lie. She felt terrible.

"Angie said you rode your bike home in the dark and went off the trail. I can't believe you would do something so dangerous. I left just after you but I took the road. I thought I might see you. I wanted to apologize for being such a jerk. I figured I missed you so I got something to eat and went home."

"Thanks Angie," she said sarcastically. "Half the town must think I'm a complete moron by now. I didn't ride home in the dark. I had an accident with my bike. I went over the side of the hill. By the time I climbed back up it was dark."

He dropped his head and sat down. She knew he must feel guilty. "Are you OK?" he asked her again.

"Yep," she said, smiling at him lightly. Sometimes he was such a boy. "No stitches, no internal injuries. Just a few scratches and a damaged ego."

"It's not funny," he said. "You could have been really hurt. There are some nasty hills on that trail." Holly changed the subject. "I was just about to make something to eat. Are you hungry?"

"Nah, I had breakfast late and I have to drive out and drop off a canvas at Mason's this afternoon. I'll stop by the store on my way back this evening and we'll have dinner if you like," he said, moving closer to her.

"Great!" she smiled. "I'll let Mrs. K know not to make dinner tonight. I think she'll be disappointed though. It's crab cake night and Mr. Johnson loves her corn relish." They both laughed at this. Holly's feeble attempts at matchmaking were an ongoing joke between her and Eric. She moved against him and took a deep breath. He smelled like laundry detergent, sweat from the morning bike ride, and his sporty cologne. He wrapped his arms around her and buried his head in her neck. He too took a deep breath and held it. "I'm glad you're all right," he whispered into her hair. They stayed that way for a long tender moment, arms wrapped around each other; she could feel their relationship mending. Eventually he moved his head back and looked for a place on her face that it wouldn't hurt to kiss and gently kissed her upper lip. "I have a few other places that are safe to kiss if you'll just step inside," she teased him. He groaned.

"I'm late already. I'll collect tonight when old man Johnson isn't watching," he said hugging her.

"Mr. Johnson is always watching," she cautioned with a grin. "He is a very devoted protector of my virtue."

"We'll see." He kissed her head and pulled his sweater on over his head.

"Did you uh, want to talk about this morning?" He asked with his hands on the handlebars and his left foot idling on the bike pedal.

She shook her head no and looked directly into his eyes. She wondered what his reaction would be if she had said yes to his question. But she didn't think she wanted to talk to Eric about this morning. She didn't really want to talk about it at all, and she could tell by his demeanor that he didn't really want to discuss it.

"I'll talk to you later," she said with a forced smile and watched him wheel his bike out to the street.

She realized after he left that she had been holding her breath. She was grateful that he hadn't grilled her about her grisly discovery in the woods. It might seem strange to anyone else that Eric would not be interested in talking about the body in the woods but Holly instinctively knew that he would not want to talk about it and for once she was happy about his aversion to any conversation about death. His past was riddled with it.

Later that evening they shared a pepperoni, tomato, and green olive pizza at Rosa's. These were the only ingredients that they both agreed on. Holly was allergic to mushrooms and Eric didn't like green peppers or anchovies, but they liked sharing so they compromised. Eric got there early and ordered so Holly could sit and eat with him and not be late getting back to the store. Mr. Johnson wouldn't have cared if she took a little longer but she only worked for a few hours as it was, so she hated to bail for long periods of time. Besides the store was buzzing with people looking for gossip about the events of the morning. She was grateful no one had bothered them during dinner with questions.

The hardware store was actually where they had first met. He had come in several times for things he needed for himself or for a simple maintenance job at the Wilkes place. There were contractors to handle anything difficult. After weeks of random and some not so random encounters Eric finally asked her out to dinner. They had been attached at the hip ever since.

After dinner he walked her back to the store, waved hello to Mr. Johnson and went back to Rosa's to get his car. Aside from his occasional moodiness, Eric was always very attentive and generous. Holly decided to forget about the other night and chalk up the evening to lessons learned. After her discovery in the woods this morning it seemed petty to hold a grudge about a moody boyfriend.

She passed the next hour inventorying paper products on a spreadsheet attached to a clipboard that her boss had prepared. Every evening whoever was working out front inventoried one commodity when there were no customers to wait on. It didn't take long and kept shelves stocked without building large amounts of inventory on the shelves in the back. Walter Johnson was nothing if not efficient.

As Holly locked the front door and returned to the register to batch out the credit card machine and count the till, Mr. Johnson wheeled her bike out of the back room.

"Good as new," he said proudly.

"Thank you, I wish you hadn't stayed late to fix it. I could have gotten by without it for a while," she said, feeling guilty.

"Wasn't any trouble. I was going to listen to the ball game anyway. I probably would have just tinkered with one of my planes tonight." Mr. Johnson was a World War II airplane enthusiast. He had detailed models hanging from the ceiling throughout the store. In fact, it was that very subject that started the friendship between Holly's father and Walter Johnson when her parents had visited last summer. Holly and her mom were shopping for supplies and getting to know the town when Mr. Miller noticed the model airplanes. Mr. Johnson approached him and a lengthy conversation ensued about the merits of the individual planes. The two men disappeared behind swinging doors into what Holly later discovered was the owner's workshop where he built and fine-tuned his models when business was slow. It had taken Holly and her mother almost an hour to separate the men and by that time they were bonded through their common interests. Holly's father was an avid reader of all things military. He loved military history, but he especially loved aircraft.

Joe Miller found several more excuses to visit with Mr. Johnson during their stay and by the time the family was ready to go back to Ohio, Holly had a job in the store and Joe had a friend who would keep an eye on his precious daughter.

Brought out of her thoughts by the sound of Mr. Johnson clanking the safe shut behind her, Holly quickly straightened up the counter area and grabbed her bag from under the counter.

"Ready?" she asked.

"After you." As he held the door she pushed her bike out and started down the sidewalk. Smiling to herself she reached down and switched on the shiny new light on her bike.

"You be careful now," he said. His face had been set in a concerned frown all day. She hoped that the sheriff would come tell them soon that the poor soul in the woods was just a stranger who had suffered some sort of accident, was being sent to his family and could rest in peace.

"I will, thanks again." She waved and he turned and headed for his own house.

Holly was anxious to get home. She was still feeling sore and achy from her accident and had to get up early in the morning. She was looking forward to a hot shower and her warm bed. Sleep would not come easily tonight though as visions of the morning forced their way into her thoughts when she was alone.

4

Holly walked out of the lecture hall in the Arts building looking forward to her lunch with Megan. She made her way down the long corridor to the large front doors and out onto the steps. She raised her face to the warm sunshine. There was a breeze blowing and the campus was alive with students moving back and forth across the lush green lawns from building to building. There was an outdoor café on the small street that served as town for the college students living on and around campus. There were several bars, gift shops, bookstores, and the requisite pizza place. Holly had loved going uptown with her friends at Miami in Oxford. But after four years of long days of classes, late nights out with friends, and all night study sessions, she was happy to have a little distance between herself and that life.

Megan, however, still lived just off campus in a small cramped apartment with another girl named Kathryn. It was more convenient for her as she worked on campus as the assistant to the Dean of Psychology, Dr. Simon Fiennes. She also tutored undergraduates for extra money, so it was important for her to live close to the students and her work. Her roommate paid half of the rent to save face with her strict Catholic parents but lived with her boyfriend at his apartment. This arrangement worked out well for Megan as she could afford the apartment and still have her privacy.

Holly got to the café a few minutes early and got a table out on the sidewalk. It was too beautiful to be inside. This was actually where she and Megan first met. She had made it a habit of eating here once a week as a treat to herself when she first moved here. On several occasions she noticed the same girl eating alone and they would occasionally exchange comments about the weather or a particularly bad server. It wasn't long before they started arranging to meet and have lunch together. Lunch turned into the occasional shopping trip and regular phone calls and soon they were good friends.

"Earth to Holly," Megan teased as she lowered her elegant form into the green plastic chair. "What were you thinking about?"

"Nothing, just how beautiful it is here in the fall," Holly said. She marveled at how cool and beautiful her friend looked.

"OK spill," Megan said, pointing to Holly's hands and face. "Fall out of a tree following that social introvert you call a boyfriend around the woods again?" At this they both laughed.

"No, Miss Know-It-All. It was not a tree. I fell down a hill, and I was alone. At least I think I was alone." Megan gave her a strange look and fondled the silver charm bracelet she always wore on her right wrist. She didn't get a chance to question Holly further because their waiter had arrived and was rattling on about the soup of the day.

Megan ordered chowder and iced tea, Holly ordered a salad and tea and they got into their usual routine of updating each other on the past week's events.

"What did you mean when you said you thought you were alone?" Megan asked with a concerned look on her face.

Holly told her the story starting with her argument with Eric, if you can call being ignored for an hour an argument, and ending with her fall. She did not tell Megan about Mr. Johnson's concerns regarding her brake wire. It was not a concept she could come to terms with yet. She believed that there had to be some other explanation that just wasn't yet obvious.

"Why didn't you go back to Eric's instead of going home?" Megan asked the question that Holly had been avoiding asking herself. That's what you get for having a best friend who was a Psychology major.

"I don't know really. I guess I was exasperated with him for being petty and I blamed him for keeping me late. He probably would have liked me to leave earlier. I was just hoping to get past the silence before I left. I should have known better. Eric needs a full day to recover from anything. It wasn't his fault anyway. I am the one who waited around and then took the trail home instead of the road."

"You already know what I think. But I care about you so I will say it again. Date other people. There are some great guys around here that aren't harboring deep dark family scars."

"Yes, Mom. And we don't know that Eric has 'deep dark family scars'. For all we know he still misses his parents and has trouble dealing with family topics. But, hey, who better to help him with that? I am all about family. I just have to find a way to get Eric to open up."

"I just don't want to see you throw away this time in your life when you should be having fun instead of trying to fix some guy with a permanently broken heart."

"I'm not trying to fix him. I just want to know more about him. I like him just the way he is. End of story."

"Change of subject then. How about that body found in the woods yesterday? You live near there; what's the scoop?"

Holly's face drained of color and her mouth was suddenly dry. She had hoped Megan hadn't been paying attention to the news, and she wasn't prepared to discuss it yet. She had managed to avoid answering any direct questions in the store last night and apparently Mr. Johnson had phoned Beatrice Kingsley to insure there were no interrogations at home. But Megan was her best friend.

"Holly, what's the matter? Was it someone you knew?" Megan asked.

"No, I uh, don't think I know…knew him. Of course his face… I couldn't tell." Her voice was shaking and she felt tears in her eyes. She hadn't cried yesterday at all. Why did she have to be such a baby now?

"What do you mean his face?" Megan demanded. "How did you see his face Holly?" Megan had reached over and grabbed her hand and the look on her face was harder than Holly had ever seen.

"I...I found him." Holly whispered and her voice cracked. A single tear rolled down her face.

"It was you? The paper didn't identify who found the body. How...?" but she didn't continue. Her face immediately gained its normal composure and she released her grip on Holly's arm, taking her hand in a gentle motion.

"It must have been terrible for you," she said quietly, almost mechanically. "When you are ready we will talk about it. But I can tell that you are not ready now."

Holly bobbed her head up and down, too emotional to answer and took a deep breath.

"You know you can always talk to me about anything, right? What's the use of being best friends with a psychology major if you can't get a free head shrink now and then?" She said this with a playful smile on her face and Holly started to relax.

"Enough about that then. Are we still on for shopping today?" Megan easily changed the subject.

"You bet. I need new sneakers. I ruined my other ones climbing trees." They both smiled at this and Megan began to update Holly on the status of her roommate and students she tutored, half of whom were sophomore boys who had a crush on her. Holly drove them to the outlet mall about twenty miles away in the Volkswagen Jetta her parents had given her as a high school graduation gift. The two girls made this trip at least once a month. It was nice for both of them to get away and be able to buy something that didn't have the college mascot on it.

They passed the rest of the afternoon companionably and with no mention of Eric or the dead person in the woods. They both knew that their efforts at friendly banter were forced at times but they were also both happy to go along with the ruse. Holly needed time to come to grips with her shocking discovery and Megan was kind enough to give it to her.

They hadn't ended up buying much but they tried on everything. Holly could afford to shop since she had few expenses and saved all of her money, but she knew Megan lived on a shoestring and suspected that most of her elegant clothes came from a secondhand store. Today however, she wondered if she had been wrong. Megan had purchased an expensive pair of designer shoes and a piece of jewelry, definitely not costume.

"Did you win the lottery and forget to tell me?" Holly joked, drooling over the new bracelet.

"I have just been working so hard I decided to treat myself," Megan answered nonchalantly. For the rest of the afternoon they talked, window shopped, and tried on cool things they would someday buy when they had made their fortune. Later that evening they stopped for ice cream and then Holly dropped Megan off at her apartment.

On her way home from Megan's she drove by the only hobby shop around and asked the proprietor to help her pick out a gift for Mr. Johnson. She knew he came here for some of the things he didn't carry at the store or for specialty parts for his planes or other projects. Mr. Sampson suggested a brass fuel tank that was the right model for a plane Mr. Johnson was building. He had ordered it for another customer but that customer wouldn't be in for another week or two and there was plenty of time to order another one. Holly was happy with this suggestion. It was difficult to buy something for her boss. He was so organized and had every detail so well planned that it was almost impossible to find something he needed. She bought the fuel tank, thanked Mr. Sampson and drove home feeling pleased with herself.

5

It was the first week of October and the air was crisp in the morning. Holly was looking forward to a visit from her parents the following weekend to celebrate her birthday. They had planned to stay in a hotel off campus but Mrs. Kingsley was having none of that. She had one guest bedroom besides the rooms occupied by herself and Holly and she insisted that the Millers stay with her. Holly's parents agreed and her mother and Mrs. Kingsley decided to make a family dinner together. Mrs. Kingsley said she would make Holly's favorite carrot cake ahead of time since the Millers would be coming in on Saturday and there wouldn't be enough time to do everything and have a proper visit as well.

Eric was invited for the festivities of course and volunteered to bring a good bottle of wine. He was planning on cooking dinner for Holly himself on Friday night as a sort of private celebration between the two of them. It was no surprise what he would cook. Eric only knew how to make pasta. He made the sauce himself though, slow cooking it all day. He had seen it on a cable TV show and decided to try it. It was so much work however, he only made it for special occasions and vowed never to learn to make anything else.

Holly had made a hair appointment for Friday and decided to get her nails done as well. This was partly to treat herself but mostly because between working at the store and spending weekends hiking and biking with Eric her nails were bound to draw negative attention from her mother. That was still a week away though and she had a project due soon for school. She was sitting in the porch swing trying to get something intelligent down on paper when she noticed the sheriff making his way up the walk. Her heart started to pound in her chest. Holly hadn't talked to him since the day she had found the body in the woods. He stopped in the store to visit with Mr. Johnson, and he would smile or wave but to Holly's relief he had never brought up the subject. Angie updated her with the current gossip on the subject whether she wanted it or not. Apparently the man had never been identified and the cause of death was still in question. The poor man had died of a head injury but it wasn't clear whether he fell down the hill and hit his head on the way or whether he was struck on the head and then fell down the hill. Considering Holly's own fall the night before both of these options gave her chills.

"Good morning," he said coming to stand in front of her.

"She put her hand up to shield her eyes from the sun and smiled back in answer.

"You've probably seen me a time or two lately at Walter's store, but I got the feeling you weren't anxious to talk, so I didn't approach you. Walter tells me you seem to have gotten over it all pretty well." She nodded her head still wondering why he was there.

"Well I can see you are busy so I won't beat around the bush. I wanted to stop by and let you know we are closing the case on that young man in the woods. Turns out he was visiting up here from down south. He apparently had a crush on some girl he used to know from back home, and came up to plead his case. Unfortunately the young lady didn't feel the same way so he was planning to head back home the day of his accident, according to his family."

"What was he doing alone in the woods?" Holly asked.

"I'd like to know that myself Holly. The young lady goes to school over at the college. One of my deputies talked to her and some of her colleagues and all of her time is accounted for. Seems the young lady goes to school and holds down a job as well. Anyway she appears to be his only contact up here and all of her time is accounted for during the timeframe of his death. Who knows, maybe he was just takin' a walk to clear his head. Damn strange business if you ask me. The county coroner is determined to rule this as an accident. That old fool is retiring at the end of the year and doesn't want to leave any open cases on his desk. Carl, Doctor Lerner, well, let's just say he and I have our doubts about the whole thing, but - well, there's nothin' to be done about it now. I just wanted to let you know that it's over. The papers will carry the story tomorrow and in a day or two this will settle down and it will be behind us."

The sheriff stood and put his hat on. Holly could tell by the way he smashed it on his head that he wasn't at all happy about having to close the investigation into the man's death. She was looking forward to putting it behind her and she hoped the coroner was right and that it was all a terrible accident.

"Sheriff? Does his family know?" She asked as she followed him across the porch to the steps. He stopped on the top step and turned to look at her.

"Yes, I spoke to his mother this morning. That woman was beside herself. Damn sad business." He shook his head, gave her a little hand wave and continued down the path to his car that was parked at the end of the drive. Holly waved good-bye, pulled her sweater closed and crossed her arms. It seemed colder now and she felt a shiver as she watched the sheriff's car pull away down the street.

The next few days were busy with classes and work and the next week flew by pretty quickly. She hadn't had a chance to see Megan this week but she was coming to dinner on Saturday and Holly was looking forward to having everyone she loved together in one place. It would be interesting to see how Megan behaved around Eric. They had only met briefly once and both had of course, been polite. Holly was a little worried about any questions her parents might ask Eric about his family but she had already told them that his parents were dead and she had been vague in response to further inquiries. Anyhow he was a big boy; he was going to have to field these questions sooner or later.

6

Friday morning Holly went straight from campus to the beauty salon to get her hair conditioned, trimmed and blown out. Her long brown locks were thick and had a natural wave that would have been curls if her hair were shorter and not so heavy. It had been a while since it was last trimmed and she wanted to have a moisturizing treatment put on it so that it would shine tonight for her special evening with Eric. She was also getting her nails done. What there were of them anyway. She had never bitten her nails, thank goodness, but she was a bit of a tomboy, and keeping them long was something she had never been able to do. She had been taking special care lately so that for one weekend at least she would have both hair and nails looking special. So far so good.

An hour and a half later with shiny hair and red nails Holly was headed home to once again try on and discard everything in her closet before settling on a navy Ralph Lauren jersey dress and flats. A spritz of *Happy* perfume and she was off. She drove her car through the car wash on the way and was feeling pretty good as she drove to Eric's. Salt N Peppa's "Schoop" was playing on the radio as part of a special flashback program and Holly sang along when she knew the words and made up the ones she didn't. She parked her car in the small space next to Eric's old two-door BMW and smelled pasta sauce as soon as she opened her door.

"Hide all the presents, the birthday girl is here!" she called as she came in the front door. Eric was setting the table. He looked up and smiled.

"You're early."

"No I'm not. Smells great. I'm starving."

"Happy Birthday," he said as he wrapped his arms around her and kissed her long on the mouth. "I have been looking forward to having you to myself all week."

"I know I have been busy lately, but I'm yours all night. I just have to get home in time to shower and meet my parents in the morning."

"Deal." He let her go and returned to his table setting.

"Do you need any help?" she volunteered.

"You could pick some music. I only ask that it not be rap."

"Spoilsport." Holly laughed. She went through Eric's CD collection and found *Eric Clapton's Greatest Hits*. She loved "Wonderful Tonight". She thought this would make good dinner music and turned it on while she found a lighter and started lighting the candles Eric had on every surface.

"Madam." Eric had a dish towel draped over his arm imitating a formal waiter. He made a sweeping gesture and pulled out her chair for her.

"Why thank you, kind sir." She sat down. He lowered his head down into her hair and whispered, "You look beautiful."

"Thank you," she blushed. He kept his head where it was and asked softly. "Are you sure you're hungry?" Her stomach growled in response and they both laughed.

"I went right from class to the salon and then home to change and I didn't have time to eat," she explained.

"Well then my lady, let me wait on you." He poured her a glass of merlot then tossed the salad and put it on their plates.

"Mmmm. Eric, this is heaven."

"Wait till you try my sauce, or as the Italians call it, my gravy. I have been working on it all day. I left it for a while when I had to run to town for butter. Can't serve margarine to my best girl on her birthday. Anyway, other than that I have been slaving in that kitchen all day."

"What do you mean your *best* girl?"

"Uh, did I say best girl? I meant only - yeah that's right - only girl," he teased.

"That's better." She smiled at him and picked up her fork. The salad was crisp and soon devoured.

He cleared the salad plates and started to ladle out the pasta and sauce.

"It looks delicious," she told him. He refilled her glass and as he set it down by her plate he also set down a small square leather box.

"Happy Birthday Holly," he said, sitting down across from her.

"Can I open it now?" she asked excitedly. He nodded, looking proud and embarrassed at the same time. She opened it to find a beautiful gold necklace with a heart pendant on it. There was a diamond at the center of the heart.

"Oh Eric! It's beautiful. It's so beautiful," she said with tears in her eyes. She truly hadn't expected anything more than dinner and maybe flowers for her birthday. Eric had never been demonstrative before. This was a big step for him and it meant a lot to her.

"Will you help me?" she asked as she unfastened it. She handed it to him and held up her hair while he hooked it behind her neck.

"Well?" she asked. "How does it look?"

"Great. Go look in the mirror." He motioned to the small mirror over the hall table by the front door. Holly turned on the lamp on the little table and looked at her reflection in the mirror. The necklace was indeed beautiful. Her birthday could not have turned out better.

They sat down to eat and chatted happily. The sauce was indeed delicious but Holly found she was not as hungry now and frequently reached up to touch the little heart at her throat. Eric was telling her that the gallery in town had sold another one of his paintings and that the buyer wanted to meet him.

"That's great. When do you meet him?" she asked scratching her upper lip with her lower teeth. He answered her question but her mind was suddenly occupied with an all too familiar itching sensation in her lips. She looked at Eric to see if he had noticed anything yet but he was busy eating. She prayed that it was just a spice or seasoning that was irritating her skin but within a few seconds the itching sensation had moved to her throat as well.

"Eric." she said, but her voice didn't sound like her own. Her tongue and lips were swelling too. Her heart was pounding. How could this happen? Why? Eric glanced at her and for a moment looked puzzled, then he jumped out of his chair and landed by her side on his knees.

"What should I do?" She was starting to have difficulty swallowing now and she tried to tell him to get her bag but what came out of her mouth was gibberish. He looked panicked and got up and ran to the bathroom. He came back a few seconds later holding a bottle and started yanking open kitchen drawers. She watched him helplessly as tears rolled down her face. He dropped to his knees at her side and his hand shook as he poured Benadryl into a big spoon. He poured it down her throat but not all of it went down. He tried to get more onto the spoon but it kept spilling over the side. Holly was starting to have trouble breathing and could only look pleadingly at Eric and point toward the door. He looked in the direction she was pointing for a second before jumping up and running the short distance to the door. She felt herself slipping off the chair and knew she was losing consciousness. She felt him return and lay her on the floor. Holly felt a stabbing pain in her leg. Her heart started to pound and she passed out.

7

"Holly, can you hear me?" A man's voice was talking to her but she couldn't see him. "Holly, open your eyes." Someone was rubbing her hand. A bright light shone in her eyes. "I'm Dr. Carson; you're in the emergency room. An ambulance brought you in after you had an allergic reaction and went into anaphylactic shock. Your boyfriend gave you a shot with your EpiPen and they gave you more epinephrine in the ambulance. Your heartrate is probably pretty fast but that will slow down. You're going to be fine. I'm giving you some Atavan to relax you and you can sleep if you want to. The swelling will continue to go down over the next twelve to twenty-four hours, so you just relax now and you'll be good as new in no time."

She drifted in and out of consciousness and could see various people standing over her but Eric was always there on the perimeter or holding her hand when they were alone. He looked miserable. She felt miserable. What could she have been allergic to? Her whole life she had only been allergic to one food - mushrooms. Eric knew this and had never used mushrooms when he cooked. Eric almost never cooked. He had saved her though. He had seen the EpiPen in her bag when they had first met and she had explained to him what it was for and how it was used. Thank God he had remembered and known that when she was pointing at the door she was actually pointing at her bag.

Her beautiful birthday dinner was ruined though. She thought of her necklace and reached up to feel for it. It was there. She smiled but felt her strange swelled contorted lips and started to cry. Eric bent close to her and kissed her forehead. "Don't cry Holly. You're still the most beautiful girl in the ER." He handed her a tissue and she blew her nose. They didn't have time to discuss the events further because Mrs. Kingsley came rushing into the room followed by Mr. Johnson.

"Oh, Holly! You poor dear. My goodness, what happened?" Beatrice Kingsley was patting Holly's hand and pushing her hair out of her face and Walter Johnson was staring at Eric.

"Ahng awurgik koo shungking," Holly said through swollen lips and tongue. This only made Mrs. Kingsley's anxiety worse. Holly looked pleadingly at Eric. He cleared his throat, stepped closer to the bed and picked up Holly's other hand.

"We were having dinner when Holly started to have an allergic reaction to something," he said. "I gave her some antihistamine she keeps at my place but she was already having trouble breathing, so I used the epinephrine shot she keeps in her bag. I didn't know what else to do so I called the paramedics." This was more than either Mrs. Kingsley or Mr. Johnson had heard Eric say in the entire time Holly had been dating him.

"What were you eating?" asked Mr. Johnson.

"I made pasta and salad," volunteered Eric. Holly nodded her head in agreement.

"I know you're aware Holly's allergic to mushrooms. Is there any way there could be some in the sauce you used? Did you use jar sauce?" asked Beatrice.

"No," he answered. "I make my own. But I have made it for Holly before and she never reacted to it."

"What about the dressing on your salad?" she asked still trying to figure out what could have caused the reaction. Walter Johnson listened but didn't say anything.

"I made it using vinegar, oil and sugar," Eric said. "I really only know how to make a few things and I always make them the same way. I don't know what happened." At this point the doctor came back in to check on Holly. He said she was doing better and could go home in a few hours if the swelling continued to go down and there were no complications.

"Excuse me doctor, but we are trying to figure out how this happened. Holly is only allergic to mushrooms as far as we know, and according to Eric there weren't any mushrooms in what she ate." Mrs. Kingsley patted Holly's hand again, determined to get to the bottom of things.

"Mrs. Kingsley is it? I have seen you around here before haven't I?" asked Dr. Carson.

"Yes, I volunteer on Tuesdays. I deliver toys to the children waiting with their parents. And you may call me Beatrice."

"That's right, I knew I recognized you. Well, Beatrice, people with food allergies rarely have just one allergy. From looking at Holly's chart I can tell that she also suffers from some indoor and outdoor allergies as well. The truth is that she is probably mildly allergic to other foods and allergens. People can develop new allergies at any age. Mild allergies can turn severe after years of little or no history of reaction. When Holly is feeling better she should see her allergist and probably undergo some blood work that may identify some new areas to steer clear of. With foods you can also eliminate everything but fruits and vegetables for a day or two and slowly start introducing different foods into your diet one at a time and watch for side affects like headache or upset stomach, etc."

"So you're saying Holly could be allergic to something else and mushrooms didn't cause this?" said Mr. Johnson.

"I'm saying Holly could be allergic to something else and mushrooms still may have caused this." At this the doctor smiled, promised to check in on Holly again in an hour or so and left. Everyone was quiet for a few seconds then Mrs. Kingsley looked at Holly and asked, "Would you like me to call your mom and dad?"

"No!" Holly said. "Gon't wurwy gem." She looked miserable and closed her eyes.

"Do you want us to wait until they release you Holly, or do you want to sleep and we can come back and pick you up when you're ready?"

"You go hone," she said through thick lips. It was almost nine-thirty by the clock on the wall and Mrs. Kingsley was usually in bed by now.

"If you could drop me at my house, I can bring Holly's car back here and drive her home in it when she is ready," Eric said to Walter.

Mr. Johnson hesitated and then asked, "That sound OK to you Bea?"

Beatrice looked at Holly who nodded at her and she said "Good idea, Eric. That way I can tidy up Holly's room and make sure everything is ready for her parents in the morning."

"Ged frum freep," Holly mumbled to her landlady.

"Don't worry about me dear. I'll put my feet up in the front room until you get home and settled and I'll catch a few winks." They said goodbye and Holly drifted into a deep sleep thanks to the shot of Atavan that Dr. Carson had put into her IV.

8

Holly looked into her mirror and dabbed a little more concealer under her eyes. Her hair was still shiny from the treatment and cut yesterday. A long hot shower had felt good this morning and she tried to put last night out of her mind. The swelling on the right side of her upper lip was still visible but other than that and a general puffiness around her face she looked OK. Certainly nothing that would scare her parents. She would of course tell them what happened last night but without any of the drama. Mrs. Kingsley, while full of motherly instincts was not the gossiping sort and could be counted on to recount the events of the evening modestly. Mr. Johnson would not say much either, but something about him worried Holly. He had said almost nothing in the hospital last night. She knew he wasn't angry with her and he couldn't be angry with Eric. It must be a male macho protection thing. Holly had been in some way left in his care by her father and in the last couple of weeks she had suffered a dangerous bike accident and had a life-threatening allergic reaction.

Mrs. Kingsley was busy tidying up her already perfect house. Having another woman come to stay was intimidating to any perfectionist. The two women got on well though and Holly didn't have anything to worry about on that front. She was looking forward to tonight and couldn't wait to show her new necklace to her mother. Her father would like it too but would worry that she was getting serious with Eric. Joe Miller wanted his daughter to be independent and travel. He wanted her to experience her own dreams before she started chasing someone else's. He also wanted her to live closer to home.

Her parents had called once they had arrived at the airport and picked up their rental car. They never wanted anyone to come and pick them up as Joe Miller always had to have his own transportation and her mother loved the scenery along the east coast almost as much as her daughter did. They were talking on her parents' cell phone while they were driving. Her father had the speaker button on so they could both hear her. Holly told them about her trip to the emergency room the night before but she kept her voice light and reassured them that she was fine.

"My goodness, Holly, what do you think caused it?" her mother asked.

"I'm not sure Mom. The doctor said it could be anything. Possibly a new allergy or maybe an old one that just got worse. He suggested I see my allergist and get tested again soon. Until then I just have to be careful."

"We'll make an appointment for when you come home at Christmas, because they won't be open on Thursday or Friday of Thanksgiving week. And for heaven's sake don't go anywhere without your EpiPen."

"OK Elizabeth, that's enough," her father interrupted. "I'm glad you're OK sweetheart. We will be there in about forty-five minutes and your mother can see for herself that you're fine."

"That's not funny Joe. We'll see you soon honey."

"Bye guys; drive careful." They hung up.

With that out of the way Holly set off to town to collect a few last minute things for Mrs. Kingsley. She was pretty sure she would be back later with a list of her mother's requests but she would bring her father with her on that trip to visit with Mr. Johnson. It was chilly out this morning and she decided to drive instead of ride her bike. There was too much on her list to carry back on her bike anyway. As she backed her car out of the narrow driveway she started to let the events of the previous evening sink in. The dinner had been truly romantic and the necklace was a surprise, but the rest of the night had been terrifying. She knew very well that if Eric had not understood that she was pointing to the bag with the injection in it that she probably would have died last night. There were butterflies in her stomach and her hands started to shake a little. She had been brave and put on a strong face for everyone and would continue to do so because that is who she was, but right now she would allow herself this moment. She pulled over in front of the post office, took a deep breath and leaned her head against the steering wheel. She wasn't stupid. She knew that Mr. Johnson had some reservations about Eric. He didn't know him the way that Holly did though. Eric had issues; that was true. Holly wasn't even sure what they all were. But she was sure that he would never do anything to hurt her. The accident was just an accident. And Holly didn't carry an EpiPen around for no reason; she had allergies. She was lucky, she told herself. She had a boyfriend who was crazy about her and had saved her life. End of story.

Her moment of anxiety indulged, Holly pulled back onto the road and moved up and across to the little grocery store on the corner. This store was a little larger than Mr. Johnson's but the two owners had always respected each other and didn't carry too many of the same items. Their produce was mostly from local farmers and was always fresher than she remembered the produce being in the large chain grocery stores back home. The other things on her list could be purchased at the hardware store and she would stop there next.

As she came through the door to Mr. Johnson's she saw her boss on a ladder twisting hardware into the ceiling. "Putting up the Mustang?" she asked.

"Getting the spot ready. I figured I would show her to your dad before I put her up." She could tell he had filled the plane's miniature bombs with baby powder by the white dust down the front of his black zip-up jacket.

"Planning on bombing anyone?" she teased. He smiled a little, knowing he'd been caught.

"Just that Zipfer kid," he replied in an unusual dose of sarcasm. The Zipfers let their precocious son run up and down the aisles of the store unchecked while they shopped. Whenever they came into the store when Holly was working Walter Johnson always made a beeline for the back of the store and stayed there until they were gone.

Walter Johnson was in rare form today. His play buddy Joe Miller was coming to town. They would swap military information they had read in the latest issue of Jane's or some other periodical devoted to their favorite topic, compare Joe's beloved Air Force to the Marines, talk baseball and above all drool over every detail of Walt's World War II plane collection.

Holly realized that her parents would be arriving at the house any minute and quickly gathered the supplies on her list, stuck the money in the register and bolted out the door leaving her boss whistling and getting his plane ready for its debut.

Holly came in the kitchen door with a bag in each arm greeted by the delicious smell of carrot cake baking in the oven.

"I'm in heaven," she said.

"Did you get everything on my list?" Mrs. Kingsley tried not to look too pleased. But she winked at Holly and handed her a spoon with homemade cream cheese frosting on it while she reviewed Holly's purchases.

"Hello! We're here!" they heard from the front hall. Holly was just about to take another lick from the spoon when Mrs. Kingsley grabbed it and tossed it into the ever ready tub of hot soapy water in the sink and started to hustle Holly down the hallway.

"Come in, come in. Oh, you must be tired. Here, let me take your things," Mrs. Kingsley fussed. Joe fumbled with jackets and luggage and Elizabeth and Beatrice exchanged hugs. After the initial niceties Elizabeth sought out her daughter's face and with her mother's eyes scanned every inch. This only took a few seconds but Holly knew that her attempts at making the events of the previous evening less dramatic hadn't fooled her mother. Elizabeth reached out and brushed a stray strand of hair out of Holly's face and lightly touched her swollen lip with her fingertip. Then she folded her daughter into her arms and took a deep breath. Holly felt tears stinging her eyes and noticed that her father and Mrs. Kingsley were no longer in this part of the house. Mother and daughter moved into the front parlor and settled themselves on the sofa.

"Tell me," her mother said.

"I'm OK really. It didn't hit me till this morning. I took a few minutes and dealt with it, and now I'm OK," Holly confessed. Her mother smiled.

"You're so much like your father. He is always so strong through any crisis. Nerves of steel. Then when everything is all over he goes off by himself, has a stiff drink allowing himself a few minutes of weakness, and then it's done. But you don't have to be tough all the time Holly. Nobody expects you to. What happened to you must have been terrifying." Holly could see her mother was fighting back tears.

"I'm not being tough Mom, just practical. I am going to get retested at Christmas just like you suggested. I have gotten replacement EpiPens and have left a few extras in strategic places like work and Eric's house, and I am being careful about what I eat. That is all I know how to do. Dad always said the best way to deal with a problem was head on. So, that's what I'm doing." Holly hugged her mother and asked, "Is it too early for a glass of wine?"

"I knew you got something from me besides your beauty." Arm in arm they set off down the hall in search of the others and some refreshment.

The rest of the afternoon was spent with Mrs. Kingsley and Elizabeth Miller bustling around the kitchen cooking their favorite dishes and occasionally taking iced tea breaks and talking at the big table. Whenever they needed something Holly was dispatched to go to the store to pick it up. On the first of these trips her father went along willingly, happy to escape any possible kitchen duty. Their first stop was at Mr. Johnson's for another measuring cup so the two women wouldn't have to share. They weren't over the threshold of the door before Walter Johnson and Joe Miller were rushing off to inspect Walt's P52 Mustang. Holly watched the two men bent over the plane spewing facts about the plane's history and capabilities. She did get a little feeling of pride when she heard Mr. Johnson point out the brass fuel tank Holly had bought him. Her father looked over at her and winked. It was at this point that she realized that Joe Miller would not be returning with her to Bea's house yet. She collected the measuring cup and went back to the house to lay out her outfit for dinner. She also wanted to call Megan to make sure she was still coming.

9

Holly was just fastening her new necklace and checking her reflection in the mirror one more time when she heard the doorbell ring. The first guest had arrived and by the sound of it, was being welcomed in by her father. She could hear the voices of her boss and her father move down the hall and then get louder again as everyone said hello in the kitchen. Confident that she looked great Holly turned out the light in her little dressing room and made her way down the small flight of stairs leading to the large second floor and then down the main staircase. She was just about to turn and go down the hall to the kitchen to join the others when a shadow approached the front door. The doorbell rang just as she opened it.

"Hi handsome, you better get out of here, I'm expecting my boyfriend," she teased. He smiled and stepped into the front hall.

"Well he's out of luck because I'm not going anywhere." He leaned in and gave her a long kiss.

"Was that the door?" she heard Mrs. Kingsley call from the kitchen.

"Take your jacket off," she said eyeing the flowers he had in his hand. "Should I put those in water?"

"Nah, Mrs. Kingsley will probably want to do that herself." He gave her a crooked grin and handed her the bouquet. She kissed him again, took his hand and led him down the hallway to greet the rest of the party.

While Eric was shaking hands and saying hello to everyone Holly went over to retrieve a glass vase from under the kitchen sink. She was filling it with water when she saw headlights shine down the small driveway. *"Megan"*, she thought. She dried the dripping water off the vase and carried it out to the front room to claim a place of honor. Just as she set the flowers on the table in front of the picture window, the doorbell rang. She walked to the door checking her reflection in the little hall mirror on her way.

"Happy Birthday" Megan said, smiling as Holly pulled her into the house. "You look terrific."

"Thanks. So do you," Holly said. And she did. Megan was wearing a simple but clearly expensive lightweight wool sweater set the same green as her eyes, with tan slacks. Around her neck lay a strand of simple but elegant pearls. Megan wore her long blonde hair down, held back by a thin tortoiseshell headband. The look was typical Megan, understated but beautiful. Holly was proud of her friend. She took Megan's arm and together they went to join the party.

Dinner was an eclectic mixture of East meets Midwest. Mrs. Kingsley had made the crab cakes that Holly had come to love. Joe Miller agreed that they were the best he had ever tasted and admitted that you just couldn't get anything like that back home. Holly noted when Walter volunteered that in all his years on the east coast he had never had crab cakes as good as Bea made, her landlady blushed and looked quite pleased. Holly had long suspected that while Mrs. Kingsley kept herself busy with her house and volunteer work, she was secretly very lonely.

Eric sat next to Holly's mother and talked about his paintings and her store. There was a brief moment of tension when Megan and Holly walked into the dining room and she waited for Eric and Megan to greet each other. There was the briefest pause before Eric reached out his hand and told Megan he was glad to see her again. She returned his greeting and the moment passed. Holly noted that with their matching height, good looks, and green eyes these two strangers could have passed easily as brother and sister. Megan sat between Holly and her father but since Joe spent most of his time talking to Walter, Holly and Megan spent the dinner hour catching up. Mrs. Kingsley looked quiet and very content. Holly knew she was happy to have her house full again. She had lost her son in a car accident ten years before and her husband had died of heart problems less than a year later. There were no grandchildren and her daughter-in-law had moved back to Atlanta with her family. Now there were only distant relatives and rarely any houseguests. Holly leaned over to where Beatrice sat at the head of her table and said quietly "Thank you, dinner was wonderful."

"Thank you dear," whispered the old woman with the glimmer of tears in her eyes. "This house was made for a family."

The rest of the evening passed without incident, which considering recent events, was a blessing. Holly and Megan cleared the table while Eric washed dishes. Elizabeth and Beatrice sat at the big table in the kitchen drinking tea and instructed them where to put things. Megan claimed to have an early morning lecture and had to leave. She thanked Beatrice for inviting her and said goodbye to Holly's mother. Her goodbye to Eric was brief and Holly couldn't help wondering at the quiet animosity between them. Holly walked Megan out to her car. "Thanks for coming." She hugged her.

"Your family's great," Megan said. "You're very lucky."

Feeling a little guilty, Holly said "You and I are going to have to take a road trip to Florida and visit your parents. I could use a little sun and sand."

"Sure. That sounds like a great idea." Megan's mouth was saying the words but her body language was saying it was never going to happen. Holly felt suddenly very grateful for her close family. Holly hugged Megan again and waved as she drove away. She did indeed feel very lucky. It was a beautiful night and she thought it would be a great night for a walk with Eric. Her parents wouldn't mind. She was sure her mother was tired after the long day and anxious to lie down. Her father would fall asleep reading in the nearest chair. She went back inside to find a jacket and her boyfriend.

Holly walked around to the front steps and as she climbed them she spotted her father and Mr. Johnson huddled together talking quietly. She approached them and said, "You two are looking awfully serious."

"Just catching up, sweetheart. I'm so full of cake I can hardly breathe." Her father smiled and gave her hand a squeeze. Mr. Johnson echoed that sentiment adding that Bea's carrot cake was the best around. He sat back in his seat and puffed his pipe, pretending to look at the stars. Holly was pretty sure she had interrupted a serious conversation and she was also pretty sure it was about her. However, to ask would be giving them permission to discuss her private life openly and she was not willing to do that. As an only child it had taken a long time for Holly to separate herself from her protective parents and she wasn't going to give back any of her decision making prerogatives now. She leaned over, kissed her father on the head, told the two men to enjoy themselves and went off in search of Eric.

She found him seated at the kitchen table having coffee and talking to her mother and Mrs. Kingsley about the different places he had visited along the east coast. Holly rescued him from the probing questions of the two women. They found their coats and went for a long stroll down Main Street in the direction of the park that contained the entrance of the path that led to Eric's house.

"You think anyone will notice if I drag you back to my place for a couple of hours?" he asked wrapping his arms around her. "You know there was a little more romance planned for last night than dinner, necklace, and an ambulance."

"That's not funny. I feel awful ruining your plans like that. I can't imagine what I reacted to. I love that you went to all the trouble of cooking." She leaned against him and kissed him. "I haven't thanked you though for saving my life. You're my hero." She batted her eyes dramatically. His face clouded over.

"I thought you were going to die," he said bluntly. "I didn't know what to do. I gave you the antihistamine but it seemed like there wouldn't be enough time and you were pointing to your bag. I can't believe I remembered what you told me. When you showed me that injector last year I was a little freaked out. Then last night I kept trying to remember what you said to do with it. I didn't want to mess up." She realized he was shaking. His eyes were watering. "Everyone I love dies," he said. His voice was almost a whisper. "I thought you were going to die too."

Until now she hadn't realized how traumatic the whole event had been for him. She had been unconscious, but he had been trying to save her. He must have been terrified. Now here she was making light of it. She slid her arms into his unzipped jacket and wrapped them around him, burrowing in.

"It's going to take more than some funky cooking to get rid of me Eric Copeland. You got that?" She stood with her head lying on his chest, listening to his heartbeat, wishing she could go back to his place and show him just how much she cared for him.

They stood there holding each other and watching their breath in the cold October air until the emotion had passed, then walked back toward the house holding hands in silence.

10

Sunday morning Holly, Mrs. Kingsley, and the Millers had an early breakfast and went into town to the Presbyterian Church. They filed into a pew in the middle of the light-filled sanctuary and immediately spotted Walter Johnson a few rows ahead of them. Upon sighting him Holly noticed Bea reach up and touch her hair and generally fidget with her outfit. Holly smiled to herself and looked at her mother who looked beautiful. While all of Holly's friends' parents seemed to be getting older, Holly's mom seemed to be in some sort of time warp. The only way you could tell any difference in her now and ten years ago was to compare pictures and look closely. The hair might have changed a bit in style, as had the clothes, but she still looked young and had more energy than most women half her age. Holly was glad to see her mother. She had never regretted her move east, but she missed the companionship she and her mother always shared at home.

After church Joe and Walter set out to make some needed repairs around the Kingsley place and Holly went out to lunch and shopping with her mom. They drove north to an indoor shopping center that had several nice restaurants and dozens of upscale stores. They had a nice lunch at an Italian restaurant and shopped until their feet were killing them. Shopping marathons were another thing Holly had missed about home. Her trips with Megan were mostly gal pal time. Megan's funds were usually limited - until recently it seemed. The two girls were usually content to look around and occasionally purchase an accessory item or a necessary article of clothing. But today was all about unnecessary pleasure. The mother and daughter team moved from one shop to another, collecting shopping bags as they went. Elizabeth purchased a beautiful china teapot for Mrs. Kingsley as a hostess gift. Holly knew that it would take a place of honor in the front parlor as soon as the Millers had gone home.

Exhausted from their contributions to the Connecticut economy, Holly and her mother loaded their packages into the Miller's rental car and started their journey back home.

"Can I ask a question about Eric?" Elizabeth said.

"Sure Mom, Eric's not a secret."

"Are you two serious, or are you still open to seeing other people."

Holly considered this for a moment and then said, "We haven't made any declarations one way or the other but I know for a fact that neither of us is seeing anyone else or has any immediate intentions to for the time being."

"Your father says you had an accident on your bicycle a couple of weeks ago."

"I see Walter ratted me out. It wasn't too bad. I lost a wheel coming down the path in the woods between the park and the Wilkes place and went over the hill," Holly explained.

"You do seem to be having a run of bad luck," her mother said hesitantly.

"Are you going to get to your point soon or are we going to dance around like this all the way home?" Holly asked.

"Don't talk to me like that Holly Miller. Your father and I are very concerned. You could have died last night and Walter is convinced that someone tampered with your bicycle. Do you know how that makes me feel as a mother about to get on a plane and leave you here?" Her mother's voice was definitely stressed, possibly close to panic. Holly knew her mother had missed being involved in her life and had worked hard not to interfere.

"Mom, we've known since I was a kid that I could and probably would have a severe allergic reaction at some point. The good news is that the safety system that we put in place works. I survived because you taught me how to be prepared and how to prepare the people around me. And as for my bike, all I can say is if someone didn't tamper with it then it must mean that Mr. Johnson stripped the nut when he put it on last time. He can't face that he might have done that and caused the accident. Frankly, I would rather he believe someone else did it than blame himself. So now, can we just move on to the part where you remind me not to get pregnant and go see what Mrs. Kingsley has made for dinner?"

Elizabeth Miller stared at her daughter in amazement, then gave a little laugh and nodded her head. Holly of course, was right. They had trained her well - drilled her is more like it - and she had survived without them. As for the bike she was probably right about that too. Holly had never made an enemy in her life. Walter's concern about Eric seemed to be unfounded. He was a little quiet but Elizabeth couldn't see him harming Holly. He did genuinely seem to care about her. It was time to trust her daughter to make her own decisions and she was going to say exactly that to Joe tonight after dinner.

11

The following week life got back to the normal routine of school, work, and cruising the countryside with Eric with the occasional unplanned stop so he could make a quick sketch of something that caught his eye. They were headed north on I-95 toward New Haven. There were several historic homes that dated back to the eighteenth or early nineteenth century Holly was dying to see. Some of them belonged to families of some of her favorite authors. Several of the homes that were open to the public had gardens and private cemeteries that Eric would disappear into to gaze at and draw until Holly dragged him away. They had packed a picnic lunch, with some generous contributions from Mrs. Kingsley, and told her not to wait up for them.

They took Holly's Jetta because she loved to drive it whenever she got the chance. Living and working so close together she only got to drive to class and back a couple of days a week. The autumn in New England was unbelievable. Holly had always loved the change of season in Ohio, but there was something about the reds, yellows, and oranges in New England that seemed to be brighter and warmer. The air was that clean fall air, still comfortable but crisp and promised cold weather soon. Holly took a deep breath and wished there had been time to bring her parents up here to see this part of her adopted state. Eric was reclined with his eyes closed. She knew he had been up late painting. He was working on a commission that was meant to be a Christmas gift. She though it was odd that he had taken the job but when she mentioned it to him he just shrugged and changed the subject. Eric generally painted for his own pleasure. He had sold several paintings but he had always decided what and when and how he would approach a new project. He was very particular about his work and frankly she had been surprised when he had agreed to put his work in a local gallery. He was private about everything in his life, especially about his family and his life before Camden.

"Did you ever come up here as a kid?" she asked and made a point to keep her attention on the road and the beauty around her. He opened one eye and looked at her. Satisfied that this wasn't heading in a more personal direction, he closed it again and said, "No." But it wasn't long before he had fished his iPod out of his bag and put his headphones on ensuring the conversation would go no further.

She sighed, irritated by his short answer and his obvious attempt to shut her out. She reached over, snapped the radio on and surfed the stations for a song she liked. A little while later they pulled over at a scenic spot meant for travelers to stop and take pictures. There were a few parking spaces and off to the side there were two picnic tables. They ate their lunch and stretched their legs, taking in the fresh air. They had left early so they would arrive in New Haven just after lunch and would have plenty of daylight hours for exploring. Holly had called ahead to make sure the different houses and gardens they wanted to see would be open today. Armed with their sketch pads and full stomachs they made their first stop at Trowbridge Square. The hours passed as they explored the Prince Hall Masonic Temple, and the Hannah Gray House. Holly was fascinated by the homes and the families that had lived in them, while Eric was interested in the artwork and the gardens. They stopped at the Grove Street Cemetery where several famous abolitionists were interred and Eric drew several sketches while Holly explored and took a few rubbings of the headstones. They decided to head south a few miles and stay at a bed and breakfast they had passed on the way in. Holly was looking forward to a hot shower and hoped there was some place near by that delivered, because she was exhausted. They had packed overnight bags and told Mrs. Kingsley that they probably wouldn't be back until the next morning. Once they were checked in and found their room, Eric started studying the selection of menus provided by the local establishments for pick up and delivery ordering. Holly made a beeline for the bathroom to inspect the water pressure.

"Pizza or Chinese?" Eric asked poking his head into the steamy room. "Or we could forget it and I could supervise your shower."

"How about you feed me and I won't make you sleep in the car," she said smiling at him from around the edge of the shower curtain.

"Ouch. OK, I see how you are." He slumped his shoulders in exaggerated dejection and started out the door.

"Eric?" she called to him in her sweetest voice.

"Yes?" he answered hopefully.

"Chinese." Holly shut the shower curtain and smiled to herself although she hadn't forgotten being brushed aside when she had asked Eric about his childhood vacations. She finished her shower in peace and when she got out he was gone. She pulled on a cream nightgown that she had bought during the shopping trip with her mother. Elizabeth had actually picked it out although Holly didn't think this was exactly what she had in mind. She was towel drying her hair while rummaging through her backpack for a brush when she knocked over Eric's sketchbook. She found the brush and pulled the book up onto her lap. She sat on the end of the Queen size bed pulling the brush through her hair and slowly turning the pages of Eric's book. It always amazed her how they could both be looking at exactly the same view and see something completely different. The first sketch was of a pitcher on a table in one of the houses they had toured. Holly vaguely remembered the table and possibly the pitcher, but in the sketch the pitcher was beautiful. The lines and details were lovely. It was clearly one of the treasured yet necessary possessions of the household at one time and it had caught Eric's attention. He had also drawn the fireplace. The scale was much larger than she remembered. The way he had drawn it you could walk right into it and there was a blazing fire in his sketch. There had been no fire at the house.

His fire seemed to reach out into the room. She turned the page and saw the first of several sketches of the Grove Street Cemetery. These were all very dark; however, the afternoon light had been very sunny and bright. There hadn't been a cloud in the sky, but the sky in the sketches was dark and ominous. The trees were barren of leaves altogether and seemed to be leaning as if being pushed by a strong wind. The sketches made her feel cold. He had spent a long time working on these while she had busied herself examining the old headstones and eventually gone in search of some soft drinks for them. Eric had obviously been very involved in his drawing and she wanted to leave him alone. Now that she saw what he drew, she got a chill. She knew that he was an artist and inclined to take artistic license with his work, but it bothered her that his perceptions could be so completely different from her own. *"Maybe,"* she shrugged, *"or maybe that's why he's selling paintings and I'm still writing papers on other people's books instead of writing my own."* The click of the door and the smell of food got her attention. She tucked his sketchbook back into the pile of jackets and other things brought in from the car and went to help him unload his loot.

They ate hungrily, talking about what they had seen and about other trips they would like to take. They broke open their fortune cookies and laughed at their fortunes. Then they made love and fell asleep in each other's arms and Holly happily forgot about the sketchbook.

12

Megan was waiting at a table inside the café as it was a little chilly outside and the sun kept hiding behind one cloud after another. She was dressed in her usual slacks and sweater but in spite of her perfect complexion her cheeks were flushed and she looked a bit anxious. Holly shrugged out of her jacket, and hung it on a nearby hook. "Hi, I'm glad you called. After spending the weekend with Eric it will be nice to talk to someone who doesn't put up so many emotional stop signs." She felt guilty for saying something so disloyal about her boyfriend but she had to have someone to talk to.

"Well, like I said, Professor Fiennes has that guest lecture up at Yale tomorrow and I have to cover for him here. I didn't want to miss all the steamy details of your weekend, so today it is. You know I don't have time for a life of my own so I am living vicariously through you." Megan's conversation seemed over-animated for her and her smile too bright. She had also ignored the perfect opportunity to take a pot shot at Eric. Holly was wondering if everything was really going OK with her friend when the waitress came to get their drink order.

"Hot tea with lemon," Megan ordered. She was always careful about what she ate and drank because she had been diabetic since childhood and took insulin injections daily to control her blood sugar.

"I'll have tea too, no lemon, and make it Earl Grey," Holly said. They went ahead and ordered salads since they knew what they wanted and were anxious to spend some time together catching up without interruption.

"Is that a new necklace?" Megan began, eyeing the heart Holly had worn every day since Eric had given it to her. "Must be nice having a rich boyfriend shower you with gifts." Megan was smiling but there was an edge in her voice that Holly had never heard before. Something was definitely bothering her. The pale mauve cashmere sweater she wore looked like it had been made for her. The only jewelry she had on was a simple pair of diamond studs and her mother's charm bracelet. Another expensive designer outfit. Holly couldn't help but wonder where Megan had suddenly come across the money for such luxuries, but since she wasn't volunteering and Holly had been taught as a child that it was rude to ask people questions about money, she would just have to wait until Megan decided to confide in her. Maybe she had a new boyfriend. Holly secretly hoped it wasn't the professor.

"Hey" she said, "Is everything OK?"

"You mean besides the fact that I am tutoring fifteen hours a week, teaching three classes, grading papers, and writing my thesis? No, everything's great." Megan looked surprised by her outburst and quickly reached across and put her hand over Holly's. "I'm sorry. I haven't been getting much sleep. And I have a research project I have been working on that isn't going as well as I would like. I'm just a little frazzled right now."

"I'm sorry to hear that. It's funny you always seem so together while I am always chasing my tail. I always feel like a total schlep next to you. Is there anything I can do?" Holly asked.

"Yes, you can distract me with tales of your trip north with that dark artist of yours." Megan gave her a half smile and pushed her lemon around in her tea with her spoon. This was the smooth controlled friend she knew.

Holly recounted the drive north and the beauty of the countryside. Megan had never been north either, having come from somewhere in Georgia. Her parents were much older than Holly's and were living in a retirement community in Florida. Holly had never met them and Megan rarely spoke of them.

With a slight twinge of guilt Holly confided in Megan about the different views Eric had taken on the sights they had seen. When Holly described the graveyard and fireplace sketches to Megan she listened and seemed to be thinking very deeply about something because Holly had to repeat her name several times to bring her back to the conversation.

"Did you ask him about them?" Megan asked looking concerned.

"No, I didn't want him to think I was snooping or judging. He's the artist after all. People are actually paying for his work, so who am I to judge?"

At this Megan just nodded her head and played with her salad. They talked for a while about Holly's party and her parents' visit. Megan grumbled about her students and about the amount of work she was doing for Professor Fiennes. Holly knew that Megan really liked working for him though. She had talked about him a lot when they first became friends.

"You know I spoke to Professor Fiennes briefly about Eric. Don't look so appalled. He doesn't know him and he is an interesting case study. He is apparently an orphan, refuses to speak of his past or his family, chooses to live in a remote setting, and is a tortured artist." Holly didn't say anything. She waited for Megan to continue.

"Don't look at me like that. You're my best friend and I work for an expert on behavior. I might as well tell you that I mentioned to him your bicycle accident and your allergic reaction as well." Holly's mouth dropped open but she quickly closed it, squared her shoulders and interrupted her friend.

"Megan, you know very well that Eric had nothing to do with either of those things. How could you imply to anyone that he did?" Holly felt anxious and she could feel the heat coming from her flushed cheeks. She didn't want to hear that Eric could have anything to do with what had happened from her, even if the opinion did come from the renowned Dr. Fiennes.

"Holly," Megan continued calmly," the truth is, no one knows what happened to that bike or what caused your allergic reaction. I simply related them to him as factual events. If it makes you feel better the Professor said they were both likely coincidences," Megan said, clearly not finished.

"Go on," Holly said crossing her arms.

"Well, he suggested therapy for Eric of course, to deal with his past. But Holly, you can't force Eric to deal with anything without pushing him away from you. How can you be happy and build a relationship with a man who doesn't trust you with his broken heart?" There it was. The question Holly had been carefully walking around for months. This wasn't a case of jilted love or the child of divorce. This was a dark pain starting with the death of beloved parents at a young age and ending with who knows what? She felt there was more but she couldn't confirm her suspicions because Eric wouldn't talk about his past at all.

"I can't just scrap a relationship that in all respects makes me unbelievably happy because Eric has a sad past. Right now I can live with what I don't know." Holly knew this was a lie even as she said it.

Megan reached across the table and said, "I just want you to be happy. And I can see that you are, so I will leave it alone." Megan awkwardly changed the subject. "Now, are there any eligible bachelors for me over there in that one horse town you live in?"

"Sure. They all keep their teeth in a glass next to the bed at night, but other than that there are a couple of real hotties." Megan choked on her salad and Holly laughed. The tension between them was broken by Holly's dry sense of humor and they relaxed into their old comfortable routine.

"You never know, one of those smitten young students of yours just might turn out to be Mr. Right," Holly teased. Megan didn't reply to this, just raised her eyebrows and gave her friend a half smile. Holly wondered if she had struck a nerve but she knew Megan wouldn't lower herself to sleeping with an undergraduate. She was far more likely to fall for her professor.

"How is the professor anyway?" Holly asked.

"Great!" Megan beamed at the introduction of one of her favorite topics. She had a serious case of hero worship where her boss was concerned. "He's certainly keeping me busy. Between him and the students I barely have time to sleep. Speaking of which," she said checking her watch, "I have to go." Suddenly she was gathering her things and reaching for her jacket.

"You didn't finish your lunch," Holly complained but Megan was already out of her chair. She leaned over and gave Holly a hug.

"I'm glad we got to meet today. Take care. See you soon," Megan whispered into her friend's ear as she gave her another quick hug. A second later she disappeared into the bustle of students coming and going. Holly sat back in her chair and finished her tea, wondering about the strange lunch. She was suddenly sorry she had confided so much about her relationship with Eric to Megan. She supposed good friends always worried about each other, but she thought she should definitely be more careful in the future about what she shared about her boyfriend.

13

Tuesday turned out to be a beautiful day and Holly spent the morning bundled up on the porch swing working on a paper for school. She had her laptop resting on her knees as she gently swayed to and fro in the big comfortable swing. She had Googled Eric Copeland on the internet but hadn't come up with anything. There were a few references to a Judge Charles Copeland but they were the wrong age to be Eric's parents. She admittedly wasn't getting much work done and Eric wasn't helping. He kept instant messaging her that she should give up and come over to go out with him. She had been getting behind lately and needed to start working every day to catch up. She promised herself she was going to get her laundry done and finish some of her research before she went to work at the store. Mrs. Kingsley was volunteering at the hospital and Holly had the house to herself. She liked to do her laundry on Tuesdays so she wasn't in the way. She checked her watch. Just enough time to clear her things away and have a sandwich before leaving for work.

There weren't any customers in the store when she entered and she walked to the back to stow her bag and her jacket. As she walked through the swinging door she heard voices and realized that her boss had company. The sheriff turned and smiled as she put first her bag then her coat over it on the hook behind the door.

"Hi, Guys, what's up tonight - planes or poker?" she asked smiling.

"Dinner first; then we might see about a friendly game of cards," Sheriff Butler answered her.

"I'm having dinner with Matt tonight over at Rosa's in case you need anything," Mr. Johnson informed her, nodding his head in Sheriff Butler's direction as he walked toward the door. "I'll stop back to help you close up before we head over to Bill's place." Mr. Johnson gathered his coat and hat. "Mike Hinson is coming in for some needle nosed pliers. I set them on the counter by the register."

"Have fun you two." Holly smiled and waggled her fingers at them. She was glad to see her boss enjoying himself. Aside from his work at the store and church on Sundays his bi-weekly poker night was the only place she knew of that he ever went.

She went to the front desk to retrieve the clipboard that held the evening's inventory items on it: Cleaning supplies. She moved to the aisle with the cleaning supplies and started with the first item on the list. For each SKU number of dish detergent she counted and put down hash marks on the spreadsheet, straightening the bottles as she went. She was kneeling at the bottom of the row of shelves when she heard a tiny ping. She looked down at the immaculately clean floor and saw a tiny screw. She picked up the little screw between her fingers and held it in the light, then realized where it had come from. Reaching up she pulled her glasses off of her face. The wind on the porch had dried out her contacts today and she was giving her eyes a rare break by wearing her little wire-framed glasses. The screw had indeed come from her glasses. As she held the two pieces of her eyewear and the small screw in her hand, she walked back to the front desk and looked around. She knew they didn't carry any of those little eyewear repair kits in the store but she had seen one here somewhere several months ago. Mr. Johnson wore glasses and it had probably been his. She remembered seeing it in a drawer somewhere. She was checking the drawers up front when she remembered a few months ago she had been looking for a highlighter and he told her to look in his desk drawer in his office in the back. That's where she had seen the little repair kit.

It was a slow night and she'd had only one customer since she got here. There was no one in the store now and she would know by the buzzer if someone came in, so she went back through the swinging door and through the back room and workshop to the small office. The door was shut but not locked. Everything inside was just like the rest of the store, clean and tidy. Holly pulled the desk chair out and pulled the drawer open. She saw the little clear plastic tube with the red cap that held the repair kit and picked it up. Startled by the ringing of a phone, she grabbed for the handset but before she picked it up she realized that it had been the double ring that was for the fax line. The fax machine started to groan. Holly put her glasses up to her face and watched as the little screen on the machine read first "CONNECTING" then "RECEIVING". Just then she heard the buzzer acknowledging a customer coming into the store. She quickly grabbed the repair kit, shut the drawer, and left the office. She walked back to the front desk greeting the customer as she approached and proceeded to repair her glasses while she waited for the lady to make her choices. She didn't like to ignore customers but she wasn't going to be able to see to ring her up without her glasses, so she worked as quickly as she could. She got the screw back into the frame and put the small screwdriver back into the kit. She set it aside to put away later as another customer had come into the store. Business picked up and she worked steadily for the next twenty minutes or so.

When the store was empty again she took the opportunity for a quick bathroom break. She grabbed the repair kit and retrieved her purse from the hook behind the door. She brushed her hair and applied a fresh coat of lipstick in case Eric decided to drop by. As she left the bathroom she remembered the glasses kit and went back to Mr. Johnson's office. There were two pages in the fax tray. The header was on the bottom and had been put in reverse order by the sender so the information page was on top. It was an employment application that had been filled out. As she looked closer she saw it was dated almost two years ago and the applicant was Eric Copeland. Holly's heart started to pound and she knew she should leave but she reached out and picked up the application. It was for the real estate company that managed the Wilkes estate while they were gone. They hired the gardener, the pool man, and Eric. The fax had come from Sam Waterson who owned the agency. Sam had helped Walter Johnson acquire his business years ago when he moved here and they had remained friends. Since Waterson didn't get along with Sheriff Butler for reasons her boss had never told her, he was never included in the regular poker night. But why was he faxing Eric's application here? Holly didn't know what to do but she couldn't stand there holding the application all night and she couldn't ignore it either. She went to the copier in the corner and turned it on. It took forever for it to warm up and finally she made a copy of the application. She turned the copier off and replaced the original in the fax tray the way she had found it. Pushing the chair back into the desk the way she had found it, she glanced at the room to make sure nothing else was out of place then turned off the light and shut the door. The buzzer rang as she stuffed the copy down into her bag behind the door. With a mixture of guilt and anxiety she took a deep breath and walked out onto the sales floor.

14

Later that evening when Holly was alone in her room, she sat on the little sofa across from her bed and wondered about the fax she had copied. She had already figured out why it had been sent to Mr. Johnson. He could get the favor more easily than the sheriff could because of his friendship with Sam Waterson. It was probably Walter Johnson who had started the inquiry into Eric's past anyhow. The two men were probably waiting for that fax when they decided to go to dinner. Holly wasn't angry with Mr. Johnson for being concerned as long as it didn't get back to Eric that he was checking him out. Her boss just couldn't get past the whole bike thing. Unfortunately he had found a willing ear in his friend the sheriff. Holly leaned over, pulled the application out of her bag and smoothed it out. She recognized Eric's handwriting with his long slanting lines. He had listed his information at the time as his address off-campus at Columbia. His father and grandfather had gone to school there and he had gotten his undergraduate degree there as well. Under emergency contact he had listed a law firm in Chesterfield, Virginia. That must be the town where he had been raised. Holly realized how sad it was for Eric that at his age he had no relatives and his emergency contact was his lawyer. *"Well, he has me now,"* she thought. She scanned the page for any other details and put it back in her leather satchel. The bag had been a graduation gift and she took it everywhere. She rarely carried a purse unless she was going out to dinner or somewhere equally formal. The smell of fresh baked cookies wafted up the stairs to her room and Holly thanked God for her landlady as she pulled on her terry robe, jammed her feet into her fluffy slippers and flip-flopped her way down to the warm kitchen for a snack.

Beatrice Kingsley had just settled herself into the overstuffed armchair by the fireplace in the kitchen. There was an oval woven rug under her feet and she had her slipper-encased feet crossed on it. Holly pulled out one of the chairs at the big kitchen table and lifted a cookie off the plate.

"Did you eat any supper?" the tired older woman asked without opening her eyes. Holly smiled.

"Yep. Mr. Johnson brought me back half of his steak hoagie from Rosa's," she answered with half an oatmeal raisin cookie in her mouth. She stood up and opened a cabinet to get a glass for milk and asked, "He doesn't like Eric, does he?"

For a moment there was no answer, then "Walter knows I don't stand for gossip so he's not likely to share his opinions about town folk with me one way or the other, Holly. But I can tell you that he cares for you an awful lot."

"So does Eric."

"Well then, sounds like you're a lucky girl."

"What do you think about Eric?"

"I think he's a nice young man. What do you think about him?" she asked, her eyes still closed.

Holly picked up cookie crumbs with the tip of her finger and said, "Most of the time I think he's great. It's just that you have to be careful not to talk about things with him that you would with other people." She thought for a second and continued. "I want to know what his parents were like. I don't even know their names. But he pretends like he never had a family. And I know his grandmother raised him but he doesn't speak about her either. I wonder if he will ever feel comfortable talking about them with me." Holly looked up from her glass of milk to find her friend staring at her. She was a little unnerved.

"How long are you going to wait?" Bea asked, leaning forward in her chair. "You're a smart girl Holly Miller and you need to start using that head of yours. That boy has some problems, everyone does, but they are his problems and he needs to deal with them. Are you going to spend the next few years walking on eggshells so he can hide on that hill pretending his life didn't happen? Life goes on after death Holly. People move on." After this uncharacteristic outburst she settled back into her chair and closed her eyes again.

Holly poured more milk and broke another cookie in half. She thought about what Mrs. Kingsley had said. Of course she was right; Eric had built this invisible wall between himself and his past and he lived with it. Holly was a fool if she expected that one day he would just volunteer to take it down. Holly didn't tell her about the faxed application that she had copied and taken from her boss' office. She knew her landlady would not approve. She cleaned up the cookie crumbs and covered the cookie plate with plastic wrap. After washing out her glass and setting it in the drainer she quietly left the kitchen. She knew that Mrs. Kingsley would wake up in an hour or so, turn off the gas logs and go to bed. She liked her chair and her fire before bed so Holly left her to it.

15

Holly didn't have to worry about the right time to raise the subject with Eric. It came up a few days later while they were having dinner together at Rosa's. Holly was talking about going home for Thanksgiving and suggested they fly in a few days early so she would have time to show him around and introduce him to her friends. She was telling him how beautiful the campus at Oxford was and how she wished he could have seen it with all the leaves on the trees, when she noticed he was staring at her.

"What's wrong? Would you rather drive? It will take a day off our trip each way but I guess that's OK."

"Holly..." He seemed at a loss for words. "I can't come home with you for the holiday." He looked deeply uncomfortable.

"Why not? Surely you can get away from the Wilkes," she argued quietly. "And you said you're almost finished with the commission work you accepted. Did you make other plans?" she asked. But she already knew why not. Eric didn't do family. He had been fine at her birthday party because it was only a few hours and he knew no one was likely to grill him about his family.

"I just can't. I'm sorry. I didn't realize you were planning on us both going. I just assumed that you would go and I would stay here."

"Why? Why would you assume that I would leave you here alone and go enjoy Thanksgiving without you?" she demanded in a sharp whisper. There were enough people eating dinner in the restaurant that combined with the old Sinatra recording coming from the jukebox in the corner, she was unlikely to be noticed, but she kept her voice low anyway.

"Well, I can't very well expect you to stay here with me and miss the holidays with your family can I?" he asked, looking her straight in the eye.

"I guess I don't understand why it has to be either/or," she said.

"No, you don't," he answered. "But I can't come home with you Holly. I won't. So drop it, OK?" He picked up his fork and twirled his spaghetti. They had both decided to try something other than pizza tonight.

"How long?" she asked, thinking about her conversation with Beatrice by the fireplace a few nights before.

"I don't know what you're talking about." He sounded puzzled.

"How long are you going to let your past interfere with our future?" she demanded in an even voice. She knew he wouldn't answer her. Any reference to his past brought on complete and unrelenting silence. She reached for her bag and slid out of the booth. He didn't make any attempt to stop her. She walked down the street, careful to avoid the front of the store where she worked. Mr. Johnson would be closing out the register now and might see her and she would feel obliged to stop and say hello and right now she just wasn't up to it. Besides, she knew her boss had a real problem with her boyfriend. He didn't trust him and regardless of their current situation she wasn't about to give him any more reasons to dislike Eric than he already apparently had.

16

Holly stayed busy on Tuesday morning and pretended not to care that Eric hadn't called. It was Mrs. Kingsley's day to volunteer at the hospital and Holly had a list of errands to run for her. She was on her way back from the cleaners when she heard a whining noise. She couldn't tell if it was coming from her car or not so she opened her window and listened while she drove slowly. Yep! That was her. She was thinking that she would have to have that looked at when the noise stopped. She listened for it intermittently as she went about her business but she didn't hear it again. When she returned home she hung the various articles of clothing she had picked up in the front closet and went to the blinking answering machine. It was Eric. He had left a message telling her he was going to the gallery to see the manager about a possible show but would call her later. His voice sounded dull and even. Still, he had called first. That was a good sign. She went about the rest of her morning listening to Cheryl Crow on her headphones and dancing around the house with a vacuum cleaner. Just as she was winding the cord up the phone rang.

"Hey," he said when she answered.

"Hey yourself!" she replied, smiling to herself.

"Did you get my message?"

"Yep. Are you going to get your own show?" she asked him.

"Looks like it. Early spring," he replied sounding a little more enthusiastic.

"Congratulations. You deserve it," she said honestly.

"Look Holly, I talked to my old roommate from Columbia yesterday and he invited me to come visit. I think now would be a good time for a lot of reasons. Once I get started on this show there won't be time for a trip to New York." She couldn't remember him ever mentioning wanting to take a trip to New York. She had often suggested it because she loved the museums and the busy streets. Everything was so alive. But Eric had always preferred their trips to more quiet spots, like the trip they had just taken to New Haven.

"When are you leaving?" she asked, realizing that he had already accepted his friend's invitation.

"Thursday. I'll be gone less than a week," he added.

"Well, I hope you have a great time with Mark. It's been a long time since you have seen each other," she said lightly.

"Holly, I'm not running away from us. I just want to think about what you said. OK?" She still thought it sounded like running away but all she said was, "Sure, Eric. Take whatever time you need."

They talked for a few more minutes before she told him she had to get ready for work. It was true, but she was also feeling a little emotional and she didn't want him to know it. She was packing some study materials in her satchel in case the store was quiet again tonight, when she came across the employment application she had stashed in her bag. She looked it over again and noted that the town where Eric had listed a summer internship before college was the same as the location of the law firm listed as his emergency contact. She decided that this was probably the place where he grew up. She went to her computer and looked up the Virginia town. She was surprised to find that while it was somewhat larger than Camden, the towns were very similar.

Sometime between packing her things and heading in to work Holly made the decision to take a road trip of her own. She knew that Mr. Johnson would be willing to give her a few days off and she could use the time to do a little soul searching, although whose soul she was seeking was a different question altogether.

She planned her trip in her head throughout her shift and got more excited all the time. There was no need to tell Eric she was going anywhere. She couldn't tell him the truth and didn't see a reason to lie if it could be avoided. Mr. Johnson said she could have Saturday off and she knew she could miss class on Friday without any problem. She would work Thursday night and leave Friday morning. She would return Sunday evening and make her class on Monday morning. Mr. Johnson asked her where she was going so he could pick up some maps for her and help plan her route. She told him she was going to Williamsburg, Virginia. It wasn't too far from where she was actually going. And she told him she had always wanted to go there, which was true. She would have to remember to try to get to Williamsburg on the way down or back to get a souvenir and lessen the lie. Luckily the towns weren't too far apart so it shouldn't be difficult.

"Well at least you and Eric can take turns driving. That's quite a trip you've got planned," Walt commented.

"Actually Eric's not going," she said with more conviction than she felt. "I'm going alone." He looked at her for a moment and then said "Williamsburg." He repeated it more to himself than to her. "OK then." He went back to his office and stayed there for half an hour before coming back out. It seemed his relief at her not going away with Eric had tempered his concerns about her making such a long drive by herself. Holly felt excited. She loved road trips. Even as a child her parents would pile in the car on the weekend and head off to some not too distant landmark or museum. She and Eric had taken several weekend trips since they had started dating. Mr. Johnson's store wasn't open on Sunday and she never worked on Fridays anyway so it wasn't a major inconvenience to him. The store was unusually busy for a Tuesday evening and the rest of the evening passed relatively quickly. Holly was anxious to get home and start packing for her trip. She wasn't sure what she would be able to find out if anything, but she could at least see where Eric had been raised and maybe talk to someone who knew the family. Holly was sure she was in love with Eric Copeland and she wasn't going to lose him without at least trying to find out why.

.

17

Wednesday morning Holly spent most of her time in class making lists. She had inherited this trait from her father who planned every task or event down to the letter. She was walking toward her car when she pulled her cell phone out of her pocket and habitually checked the screen. She turned the sound off during classes. Actually her phone was on silent most of the time. Holly hated the constant intrusion of cell phones. She liked being unavailable. There was a sense of control in deciding when you talked to other people and having time to think about what you wanted to say to them. When she had told Eric this he had laughed at her and told her she thought too much. He hadn't even had a cell phone until they had started going out. He really hadn't needed one. He didn't have many close friends and anyone who wanted to reach him could leave a message at the cottage.

There were two messages on her screen. There was one from her mother, which she would return later, and one from Eric asking her to meet him for a beer tonight. He wanted to see her before he left town. *"Sure"*, she thought, *"I'll have a beer with you. Then I'm going to drive to Virginia and find out what happened to you."* She called and left him a message that she would meet him at the time he had mentioned in his message and drove the few blocks over to the café to meet Megan for lunch. She had considered canceling her lunch but had decided at the last minute that she should tell someone where she was really going. Her mother had told her to always make sure someone knows where you are. Unfortunately, if anyone asked Mr. Johnson or Mrs. Kingsley they would send a search party to Williamsburg. Her parents would worry all weekend about her, so she wasn't telling them anything until she got back. That left Megan. She arrived early, ordered some tea and started going over her lists again.

"Nose to the grindstone I see," Megan said as she slipped into the seat across the table. Holly had managed to snag a table next to the window and the sunlight shone on Megan's long blonde hair. She wore it down and parted on the side with her long bangs tucked neatly behind her ear. Her pearl earrings were simple and understated but she looked beautiful. Holly subconsciously reached back and ran her hand down her French braid. She had sidestepped her usual ponytail for the more formal braid but she still ended up feeling shabby next to her cool friend.

"List making actually," Holly corrected her once Megan was settled in her chair.

"Is this a shopping marathon you're planning?" Megan inquired, waving at the waiter. She didn't have any trouble getting his attention and quickly ordered a diet Coke. She turned back to Holly who was nibbling the end of her pen.

"No, actually, I'm road tripping by myself this weekend and it's sort of last minute so I want to make sure I don't forget anything." This got Megan's attention.

"Why by yourself? I thought you and Eric were destined to explore every inch of the east coast together." This was normal sarcasm from Megan and she barely looked up from her menu when she asked.

"Eric is going out of town to see his college roommate this weekend," Holly said, also staring at her menu. Two could play this game.

"Since when? You didn't mention it last week. Now he's going off to hang with the guys and you're going...where are you going anyway?" The waiter set her drink down and asked them if they were ready to order. Holly was relieved by the temporary distraction and ordered a club sandwich. She always ate a lot when she was nervous. Megan already thought she should give up on Eric and find someone else.

When they had both ordered Megan turned her attention to Holly and waited for a reply.

"Well, to tell you the truth I'm going to Virginia. Chesterfield, Virginia to be exact." Holly was picking at a thread sticking out of a button on her sleeve. "It's where Eric was raised. At least I think it is." Megan still said nothing; she just listened in her calm cool manner. Holly explained, "Eric and I had an argument. I don't have to tell you about what. Anyway, he accepted his old roommate's invitation to drive north for a visit and I decided to take the opportunity to get out of town and spend a little time on my own."

Finally Megan said, "Holly, I'm not sure I understand why you feel you need to go all the way to Virginia."

"I asked Eric to go home with me for Thanksgiving and he refused. He can't or won't even try to allow himself to be part of a family, and I can't see a future with him unless he can. I just can't give up on this relationship without understanding why he won't talk about his past. For some reason Eric either can't or won't tell me about his family." She felt her resolve starting to ebb but she was not going to be bullied out of going by Megan or anyone else. With more confidence than she felt she said, "I know I probably won't find out anything down there. He has been gone from there for a long time. Who knows if anyone will remember him, but I'm just not up to sitting around here all weekend waiting for my relationship to fall apart."

Megan had sat very still and listened while Holly talked. Finally she said. "I can see your mind's made up." Holly nodded, stunned that Megan had gone along with her so easily. "So, when do you leave?"

Holly hesitated out of a mixture of surprise and relief. She had truly expected Megan to argue with her about the rationalization of such a trip. Without saying another word however, Megan picked up her spoon and dipped it into her soup.

"Well, I was going to pack tomorrow after work. Then I can just load my car Friday morning and make an early start of it." Megan listened as Holly detailed the rest of her plans. After lunch they hugged goodbye. Megan told Holly to be careful and to call her and let her know what motel she was staying at. Holly was glad she had confided in her friend. She had been worried about Megan's response to her plans but she had remained the calm confident friend Holly had come to rely on.

Holly had a few stops to make on the way home and she wanted to have time to shower and do her hair before meeting Eric. She might be mad at him but she wasn't sending him off to New York with his bachelor friend without looking her best. She conditioned and blow dried her hair then brushed it until it was glossy. She applied some light blusher to her cheeks and a little mascara to her lashes. With some lip gloss and a little perfume she was ready to go. She had worn a pair of jeans that fit her long legs well and a top that she had bought when she was shopping with her mother. She stepped back to look at her reflection and smiled. She grabbed her keys and headed down the stairs calling to Mrs. Kingsley not to wait up on her way out. She was a few minutes late but that was OK, she didn't want to look too anxious. The argument was after all his fault and he had yet to apologize, but Holly knew not to hold her breath waiting for that to happen. He was unlikely to even bring up their argument at all. Eric never discussed anything personal that was unpleasant.

She entered the little pub that was down the street and around the corner from where she worked. They had only come here a few times together before. Eric probably wasn't anxious to go back to Rosa's right away, afraid that they might have to pick up their conversation where they left off.

"What's a girl gotta do to get a drink around here?" she said, smiling at him as she approached. She felt a little guilty inside like she was betraying him somehow by going to the place where he grew up. Maybe that's why she was being so nice to him when she ought to be strangling him. He looked handsome in jeans and a rugby shirt. Both of them had holes in them that designers would have charged and arm and a leg for. She knew Eric's had come from hiking but he still looked like he ought to be in a magazine.

He ordered her a Corona with lime and moved down a bar stool so that she would not be forced to sit right next to anyone. Most guys she had dated in college had never been as thoughtful as Eric. It was one of the things that had attracted her to him. He was a gentleman without making an effort to be. His manners were casual, not grand gestures meant to impress her. She guessed you could call it breeding. She had always thought that was a funny word. It seemed to be the snobby kind of word that belonged in old books and movies. But on Eric it was comfortable and complimentary.

"Thanks for coming," he said, looking at her apprehensively. She knew that was as close to an apology as she was likely to get and for now she let it go.

"I see you drove the truck," she commented. He kept an old Ford pick-up in a shed up at the Wilkes place to haul around materials for any repairs he might need to make. She had only seen it once or twice and was surprised to see it parked outside the little bar.

"I'm having the Honda tuned up before I leave." He tossed a piece of popcorn into his mouth. The pub kept coffee cans of spicy popcorn out for the patrons. Holly helped herself to some and looked around the room. There were a few people she recognized that came into the store from time to time but overall it was a quiet night.

Eric was wearing the Gucci *Envy* cologne she had given him for his birthday and he smelled great. She fished around for something to talk about so she would stop thinking about climbing onto his lap right there.

"So, uhm, do you and Mark have any particular plans for the weekend?" She took a long drink from her bottle of Corona and licked the bits of lime off her lips with the tip of her tongue. She knew he was watching and she hoped he was feeling as tortured as she was. She saw him look down at his hands and smile before he said, "You know; the usual. Strip clubs, parties; it's always the same thing when us guys get together." She knew he was teasing her and she flushed. Holly never did hair and makeup to go out for a beer. She suddenly felt obvious. She didn't say anything; just picked at the label on her bottle and pretended to pay attention to the television silently broadcasting one of those national twenty-four hour news programs.

Eric placed some money on the bar and stood up. He picked up her jacket from behind her stool and held it out for her. She waited for him to say something but he didn't. He guided her out of the bar by her elbow and led her directly to the passenger side of his truck. They drove back to his place in complete silence. Holly's heart was pounding. The truck smelled like beer and popcorn and cologne. He pulled up to the door and stopped the truck, not bothering to park it in the shed where he kept it. He opened the door for her and led her to the front door; key already in his hand. No sooner were they over the threshold than he kicked the door shut behind him and started to pull her coat off of her. He covered her mouth with his own with an urgency that she had never known from him. Her heart was beating so heard she was sure he could hear it. He kissed her while he undressed her in his living room. His hands were determined and needy and when he had taken the last piece of clothing from her body he moved his strong hands over her skin with a fierceness that took her breath away. He separated himself from her long enough to remove the rest of his own clothes and then maneuvered her onto his sofa quickly covering her naked body with his own. He kissed her long and hard and she closed her eyes and opened herself to him. He took her with a passion and intensity that left them both breathless. Afterward he pulled a blanket down over them from the back of the couch and they lay there together and slept. He woke her sometime later and started to kiss her, more gently this time. They moved to the bedroom and he made love to her again; this time he was in no hurry. He kissed and caressed her body gently and for a long time. Their lovemaking was intense but gentle and he stared into her eyes as they both moved together quietly. Afterward when they were both physically and mentally exhausted she snuggled down into the soft clean blankets and fell asleep against him.

She woke up to the smell of sausages frying. She usually was a light eater in the morning preferring toast and juice, but the smell of maple sausage and coffee was making her mouth water. She pulled on an over-sized sweatshirt of Eric's and a pair of her sweat pants and shuffled into the kitchen. She poured a cup of strong coffee as he tipped the pan and tumbled a half dozen brown sausages onto a plate. Popping two pieces of toast into the toaster with one hand and pouring sugar into her coffee with the other, she leaned back and received a kiss on the head and a swat on the bottom.

"I'll take you back to get your car after breakfast," he said. She brought her toast to the little table and sat down.

"What time are you leaving?" she asked.

"I have a few errands to run this morning, and then I was going to come by here, pack a few things and leave around one-thirty. I have to stop by the gallery to drop off the agreement for the show so I won't actually get on my way until sometime after noon." He looked at her to see if she was going to argue with him about his trip but she just sipped her coffee and thumbed through a section of the paper.

"Sounds good," she said, still pretending to read the paper. Guilt washed over her but she managed to remain calm. After a few minutes she tidied up the paper, set her dishes in the sink and started to gather her clothes from the night before.

"Eric! Will you grab my makeup bag from my satchel?" she called to him from the bathroom.

"Sure," he replied. She heard him plop her bag onto the chair and start rummaging through it. "How do you find anything in here?" he asked.

"I happen to know where everything is in that bag," she retorted, wrapping her wet hair in a towel. She brushed her teeth with the toothbrush she kept at his place and started to pull on clean jeans and a sweatshirt. She always kept an extra outfit here and he just washed it with his own laundry. Thinking he still hadn't found her makeup she opened the bathroom door and started to go out to get it when she saw him standing there holding her makeup bag. He wasn't smiling though. He handed it to her and walked away without saying anything. *"Well, if he feels guilty about leaving this weekend let him,"* she thought. She hadn't mentioned their argument, partly because she was already determined to go to Virginia and if he changed his mind she would have to explain her trip.

She finished getting ready and turned the bathroom over to him while she finished tidying up. She opened her satchel to put the makeup bag away and there on top of everything else was the application. He must have found it when he was looking through her bag. Her heart sank. She wondered if he had also seen the notes and list she had written for her trip in her notebook. It wasn't opened but she couldn't be sure. She quickly put everything back in the bag and went about tidying the kitchen. She had just finished wiping down the counters and hanging up the dishtowel when he appeared again dressed and with his keys in his hand. She smiled at him but he had already started for the door so she picked up her bag and followed him. He turned the radio on in the truck when they got in and fiddled with it, changing first to one station and then to the next. They barely spoke and when she leaned over to kiss him before getting out of the car he just stared at her. She was too stubborn to give up now and beg him to forgive her for interfering. Besides if he had confided in her even a little bit about his past she wouldn't have resorted to snooping. She hopped out of the car and without looking back walked to her own car and got in. He watched her for a few moments and then pulled away. Once she was in her car she leaned her head against the steering wheel in frustration. Her mind was spinning at how quickly things had changed between her and Eric once again. How could she have been so careless as to carry that application around with her? With a heavy heart and a heavy sigh she put her car in gear and drove home. Eric would probably never call her again and she was glad for the distraction this weekend. A road trip was exactly what she needed and if she was going to lose her boyfriend because of his tragic past she could at least have the satisfaction of knowing what it was.

18

She was stacking light bulbs on a shelf when her boss came out of the back room.

"I got the maps you're going to need," said Walter. "I also printed a set of driving directions with alternates in case of traffic or weather." He handed her an envelope. She thanked him and started back to put the envelope in her bag when he asked, "Did you take your car in to be serviced?"

"No, you and Dad looked at it when he was here for my birthday and I am leaving it here to be serviced when I go home for Thanksgiving."

Walter put his hand out. She rolled her eyes and went to get her keys. Pulling on his trusty hat and jacket he went out the front door and disappeared. He was gone for about fifteen minutes when he came back in and asked her when her car had started making that noise.

"You mean that whining sound?" she asked.

"Yes, that one." He answered with the affectionate annoyance one usually reserves for small children and puppies. She was neither, but cared too much for him to be rude.

"I have only heard it one time and that was last week." she said to his back as he disappeared though the swinging door. She sighed and went to help a customer who was lugging a heavy carry basket to the front desk. He returned and waited for her to finish with her customer. He held out a key chain and she stared at it.

"That's not my key," she said.

"No, that's the key to my Pontiac," he answered. "If you're still planning on going to Virginia then you will need to take a car that will get you further than the state line."

"You really think there's something seriously wrong with my car?" she asked. She loved that car. Part of the joy of a road trip was driving her car. His Bonneville was spotless but it was far from cool.

"Are you sure you want to loan me your car?" she asked, hoping he might change his mind.

"Sure, go ahead. Just don't throw French fries all over the place. I could have had dinner from the food between your seats out there," he said and walked away. *"Great. No boyfriend and a road trip in an old guy car,"* she thought.

She was wiping off the front glass window of the display counter when he came up and said, "Why don't you take off early? I already ate and I told Bob Samuels I would help him with a framing problem he's having over at that house they're fixing up. So I was going to hang around here anyway."

She knew he could tell she was down, and he was right. She took him up on his offer, went out and got the CDs and other things out of her car that she would take with her and went home to pack.

An hour later she was packed and ready to go and it was only five o'clock. Mrs. Kingsley was filling in for a friend in a bridge game and Holly was restless. She left a note for Mrs. Kingsley saying she had decided to leave early and that she would call her when she got to Virginia. She checked her list to make sure she had everything then loaded up the car and headed south. Mr. Johnson's car drove pretty smoothly. She popped in her Alanis Morissette CD and turned the volume up. She wished she could talk to Eric but she also wanted to put some distance between them. Truthfully, she was avoiding him as much as he was avoiding her. She picked up her cell phone to call and let Megan know she was leaving early but the low battery signal beeped. She had put it on the charger at home so it should have been charged. She plugged in the car charger and it signaled that it was charging. She decided to leave it and let it charge for a while. Her spirits lightened as she put distance between herself and Camden, alone for the first time. Setting the cruise control she stretched her legs out as far as she could and headed down I-95 singing along to "Jagged Little Pill". She stopped at an exit in Maryland and filled up the gas tank on the Bonneville. It used considerably more gas than her Jetta but she was grateful to Mr. Johnson for lending it to her. The gas station attendant told her there was a terrific local restaurant near by and she decided to stop and have dinner.

The food was every bit as good as the clerk had told her and after talking to the waitress for a while she decided to stay in a motel about forty-five minutes south. She was getting tired and the waitress told her that motel was a clean well-run establishment in a safe area. Holly finished her dinner and checked her map. With luck she would be in Chesterfield before noon tomorrow as long as she got up and moving on time. Her cell phone was still saying there was no battery so she made a note when she got into town tomorrow to find a cell phone store and get a new battery. She could call Mrs. Kingsley in the morning from her motel room and let her know she was OK. Stuffed from the restaurant's "home cooked" barbeque she got back into her borrowed car and headed south toward her motel.

19

Friday morning Holly woke up late. She had tossed and turned most of the night and finally fell asleep around four in the morning. When she looked at the clock on the table by the bed it read eight-seventeen. So much for the early start. She stumbled into the bathroom to shower. Feeling a little more awake and desperately in need of caffeine, she quickly packed her belongings back into her bag. Before leaving the room she went to the phone and called Mrs. Kingsley's house. There was no answer so she left a message that she was fine and would call later when she had acquired a battery for her phone. With the obligatory phone call made Holly got a to-go cup of coffee from a self serve area by the motel's front desk, paid her bill and got back into her car. She crossed the Virginia state line just before noon and couldn't ignore her stomach any longer. She got off at what appeared to be a busy exit and pulled into a small strip mall that offered a sandwich shop. She sat on a bench outside the shop, ate her lunch and enjoyed the warm sunshine on her face. She was comfortable with her light jacket on. She people watched while she ate and despite herself she wondered what Eric was doing. She was suddenly glad that her phone wasn't working. She didn't know what to say to him if he called and she didn't want to know yet if he hadn't called at all.

With a quick top-off at the gas station next door she was ready to get going. She was within thirty minutes of her destination and she was starting to get butterflies in her stomach. She turned the radio on and searched for a local station. She found one playing current hits and turned the volume up. Fifteen minutes later, she saw the sign announcing the exit for Chesterfield. She took a deep breath and let it out slowly to calm her nerves as she exited the highway and headed toward Eric's hometown. She traveled along a rural route road for about a mile before turning onto another similar road that led into the town of Chesterfield. It was larger and busier than Camden but there were many similarities. She followed her directions to the small chain motel where she planned to stay. Once she had checked in and put her things in her room she went out to see the town. She got directions from the front desk and drove past the various buildings, many of them very old. She made a pretty thorough tour of the town before stopping at her first destination, the Chesterfield Public Library. She spoke to the librarian at the front desk and was taken to a small room with computers on one side and microfiche machines on the other. It wasn't long before she found an old reference to a judge from Chesterfield with the last name of Copeland. This was the same judge she had come across when she had Googled Eric's name that day on the porch. Holly got out her notepad and began to take notes. She discovered from the newspaper articles that Eric's father had been an attorney and studied law at Columbia as had his own father before him. Eric's father had not lived long enough to become a judge but the reference could be to his grandfather or another relative. An hour later she found another reference; this one to a fire at the home of the late Judge Charles Copeland. Charles had been Eric's father's name and Holly had a feeling that the judge was definitely a relative. She approached the young librarian who helped her find some old newspapers on microfiche and she began to look through them starting with the dates referenced on the internet. She found several references in the local paper to Judge Charles Copeland. There were also references to his wife Eleanor.

Holly took a break and went out to a vending machine and got herself a diet Coke. She stretched her legs and finished her drink. She was heading back into the library when an older woman approached her with spectacles dangling around her neck by a beaded string. She had to be at least seventy years old but moved quietly and efficiently across the space between the front desk and the entrance where Holly stood.

"Hello dear," the woman said in a practiced library voice. "I'm Alice Fitzwilliams, the head librarian here. Maggie says you're looking for some old articles?" Holly moved with her while they spoke in whispers until they reached the computer room.

"I'm actually doing some research on a family that lived here several years ago," Holly answered.

"Which family would that be dear?"

"The Copelands. Did you know them?" Holly asked.

"Well, I moved here twenty years ago with my second husband. He grew up here as a boy and wanted to retire here. The judge died just before we moved here and I only met his wife on a few occasions. If you tell me what kind of information you are looking for I may be able to help you find something. I have to leave shortly because it is almost story time in the children's area." She listened as Holly told her the information she had found and that she was looking for family names and connections. Holly got the distinct impression that Mrs. Fitzwilliams knew a lot more about the Copelands than she let on. But she either wasn't interested in gossiping or she didn't want anyone to publicize anything potentially critical about her town and use her as a reference. She did lead Holly to some more articles about the judge and his more notorious cases and then left to read to the waiting children. Holly's back was stiff from sitting in the same position for so long so she printed out the rest of the articles and took them with her to read over dinner. On her way out of the library she asked Maggie where she could find a store that would carry batteries for her cell phone. She was directed to the office supply store at the end of the square. She thanked the young librarian and left.

Holly made her way down to the office supply store but they didn't have the right battery to replace her own. They referred her to another store a few miles out of town that might carry it. While she was there she picked up a highlighter and a folder to keep the information in that she had collected. Her stomach was once again telling her that she had skipped a meal and she hurried back to the motel to freshen up before heading out to find a place to eat. There was a diner on the main strip that was a local favorite according to the desk clerk at her motel. She took her notebook and folder of articles and went in to get a seat. The restaurant wasn't too busy since it was between lunch and dinner. Holly asked for a booth so she could spread out her papers. The last six years of college had taught her nothing if not how to do research. She opened her notebook and started to write down the names of people, places, and events that might be relevant to Eric's past.

A waitress rushed by with an armful of plates and promised to be back in a few minutes. She returned with a coffee pot and a menu and proceeded to pour Holly a cup of coffee and rattle off the day's specials. Holly's mouth was watering already. She ordered clam chowder, which was the soup of the day, and a club sandwich without even looking at the menu. The waitress informed her that her name was Millie if she needed anything else.

Holly thanked her as she poured cream and sugar into her coffee. She looked out the big plate glass window of the restaurant and wondered how many times Eric had eaten here. There was a sign near the entrance that read "Established 1957" and its windows looked out over the central point of the town. Eric and his friends probably came here after school or on weekends. The town itself was busy but tidy. There were enough people to make it appear prosperous but still small enough that as she watched, people frequently waved or honked at someone they knew. Holly smiled to herself. She had been raised in a large suburb with large shopping malls and Super Wal-Marts and schools with thousands of kids. It was what her father called "urban sprawl". You could drive around your hometown all day and not run into anyone you knew. It occurred to her that Eric must have some fond memories of his childhood. He had enough money that he could easily have gotten lost in a big city but he had chosen to live on the outskirts of a town that resembled the one he had grown up in. The one he never spoke of.

Her food materialized while she had been gazing out the window and she dug into it hungrily. Millie checked on her occasionally, removing her soup bowl and refilling her coffee cup and water glass from time to time while Holly read some of the information she had gathered at the library. There was one small article that had a picture of the judge and his wife and referred to a charity event. The small paragraph under the picture also mentioned the judge's sons Charles and Patrick. Holly made a note of this, suddenly disheartened. Eric had never mentioned an uncle. Maybe she had the wrong family altogether or a different branch of the family.

"You studying for a test or something honey?" Millie asked, bringing Holly's attention back to the diner.

"Well, sort of. I'm researching a family that used to live here."

"Which family?" Millie asked.

"The Copelands. Have you heard of them?" Holly put her hand over her coffee cup so Millie wouldn't fill it up again.

"Sure. Most people around here have heard of them. He was a judge here about twenty years ago. Why are you interested in them?" Millie asked cautiously. This didn't bother Holly at all. She had found that when she first moved to Camden the people were friendly to her but not necessarily open with personal information until they had become comfortable enough with her to consider her one of their own.

Holly reached around for a plausible explanation that wouldn't expose her relationship to Eric.

"I'm a student over at UV and I have selected the judge as the subject of a paper I am writing. I heard of him from a student there who used to live around here." It bothered her how easily she could lie these days, but Eric deserved a little discretion, she told herself.

"Well, I know that the judge was real popular around here for a long time and people were real sad when he died. I moved here with my family just after that so I can't tell you anything specific about him but if you come back in the morning Alice will be here. Alice was born here and knows everything about everybody," she said with a knowing wink and turned and moved away. A family that had come in for dinner flagged Millie down. Deciding there wasn't anything more to be gained here today Holly packed up her things, paid her check and went for a walk.

The town was quieter at the dinner hour on Friday than Holly would have expected. There was the usual traffic and several families and couples had come into town for dinner, but overall it was very peaceful. She crossed the street, walked up a few blocks and stopped in front of a large brick building. Outside was a marble plaque that read "Smith & Klein". This was the same law firm that Eric had referenced on his application. There were lights on inside but Holly didn't bother to go in. This was the last place she was going to get anyone to give her information about Eric or his past. Holly was pretty certain that any inquiries into Eric's background here would result in a quick call to their client, which was the last thing she wanted right now. Holly turned down a tree-lined street that was lit by streetlights meant to look like old-fashioned gaslights. There was just enough daylight to show off the beautiful lawns of the large well-kept homes. When she came to the end of the block she was standing across the street from a beautiful white Georgian manor house. The green lawns rolled up to a wide set of steps that ended at an august pair of black doors. There were six pillars across the front of the three-story house. Even if it hadn't seemed familiar to her this house would have stopped her. The estate was breathtaking, but there was indeed something about it that made Holly believe she had seen it before. The house itself didn't look as old as the ones around it but it was by far the most elegant home she had seen so far. Holly walked several more blocks but the light was fading fast and she needed to get back to her car. It was still too early to go to bed and she wasn't hungry so she drove up to the other end of town where she had seen an old movie theatre. There were only two shows playing. One was a remake of an old movie about aliens attacking earth. The other was a classic chick flick. It had been a long time since she had seen a movie. She used to go with her friends and sometimes with her mother back home. Holly decided that since she was on a semi-vacation she would treat herself to a night at the movies. She had all day tomorrow to think about Eric and the events that had compelled her to come here to his hometown.

By the time the movie let out Holly was ready to go back to her hotel room and crash. She picked up some snacks and a newspaper and headed back to her motel room. It was too late to bother Mrs. Kingsley. Besides, Holly was enjoying being out of touch. She valued her independence and didn't want to report in every couple of hours. She still hadn't picked up a battery for her cell phone but she would have to tomorrow. She made a list of the things she wanted to do the next day and snacked on pretzels and diet soda while she flipped channels. It was late when she finally fell asleep and she was proud of herself for not staying home in Camden and moping around while Eric was in New York having fun with his friend.

20

Saturday morning Holly woke up starving. She had eaten dinner early yesterday and the pretzels before bed hadn't done much to curb her hunger. Her father teased her that she ate like a football player. She was lucky she was athletic and had a naturally quick metabolism; otherwise she would be in real trouble. The waitress at the café yesterday had told her that if she wanted information on Judge Copeland she should come back in the morning and talk to Alice. Holly decided to kill two birds with one stone and eat breakfast in Alice's station at the café this morning to see if she could learn something. She showered and dressed in jeans and a sweater. After blow drying her long hair and pulling it up into its customary ponytail, she dusted her cheeks and her eyelids with a light color blush. A little lip gloss and a touch of brown mascara and she was done. Holly always thought that where makeup was concerned less was more. She had nice features but whenever she broke down and attempted to start putting color on her eyelids and cheeks she always ended up looking like she was ready for an audition as a circus clown. Friends had always been jealous of her creamy complexion and told her how lucky she was that she didn't need make up. Holly secretly agreed and was glad because she had never had the patience to spend long hours in front of a mirror. She looked at her reflection and gave herself a shrug of approval. Gathering up her bag and notes from yesterday she grabbed the phone book and looked up the number for the store the librarian mentioned where she might get a battery for her phone. She found it and called them for directions. Next she dialed the house in Camden and left another message for Mrs. Kingsley.

She left the number of the motel since she was still not available by cell phone and promised to call back later in the day.

Holly took the scenic route on her way to the diner and drove through some of the neighborhoods surrounding the town. There seemed to be a classic structure to Chesterfield; the old expensive neighborhoods on one side of the railroad tracks and the small inexpensive neighborhoods and trailer parks on the other side of the tracks that ran north and south a few blocks west of the center of town.

She parked in a park-like lot that served as a median across the street from the diner and crossed at the corner light. There were already several customers coming and going through the front doors of the busy diner and Holly held the door for an elderly couple before moving into the front area to wait for a seat. After a few minutes a tired looking hostess asked her how many. Holly told her she was alone but would prefer to sit in Alice's station if that was all right. The woman gave Holly a tight smile and told her she would have to wait a few minutes until a table opened up in that area. Holly located a spot on a bench near the front door and sat down to wait. The smell of coffee and eggs and bacon was making her mouth water and she realized she was staring at a young woman who was alternately talking to her boyfriend on her cell phone while she forked eggs and toast into her constantly moving mouth. Holly fought the urge to smack the girl on the back of the head for having such poor manners. She also thought it would be a good lesson if she shoved her over and showed her how to eat her breakfast properly. God she was hungry.

"Miss!" She looked up to find the hostess staring at her. Holly grabbed her bag and followed the woman to a table toward the back of the restaurant. She sat down and put her bag on the seat of the chair opposite her. When she turned to say thank you the hostess was gone. She looked around at the crowded restaurant and wondered which of the waitresses was Alice. She didn't have to wait long to find out because a big voice called "Comin' through!" and banged through the swinging double doors of the kitchen. The voice belonged to a stocky no-nonsense woman carrying a large tray loaded with plates on her shoulder. She quickly unloaded the tray onto the table next to Holly then turned around and tucked the tray under her arm while she retrieved the pen from behind her ear. "What can I get you honey?" she asked Holly.

Holly ordered enough food for two people and a pot of hot tea and handed Alice her menu. In a flash she was gone. Holly started to wonder if she would be able to get a few minutes to ask Alice about the Copelands. As she glanced around the restaurant she noticed that there were a few empty tables now, though there hadn't been any when she had arrived, and there wasn't a line at the front door waiting to be seated. This was good news. Maybe the breakfast crowd was dwindling.

Holly took her time eating her breakfast, which wasn't hard considering how much she had ordered. She was sipping her second cup of tea and feeling very satisfied when Alice walked over and started to clear the dishes away from her table. The tables around her in Alice's station were mostly empty by this time so Holly took the opportunity to raise the subject of the judge.

"Um, excuse me, Alice?"

"You can't still be hungry!" The older woman smiled at her and parked a dishrag-clad hand on her hip.

"No," Holly replied sheepishly. "I was just wondering if you might have a few minutes to answer some questions I have about Judge Copeland. I know you're working, but I promise not to take long."

"What do you want to know about the judge for?"

"I'm writing a paper on him for a class at UV and I have gotten a lot of information through my research on his cases but I was looking for some insight into his family life and the way he was viewed by his neighbors." Holly lied smoothly. Alice didn't say anything right away and just kind of stared at Holly for a few seconds, then she mumbled "Just a minute," turned and walked away. Alice disappeared behind the swinging doors and returned a few seconds later with a cup of coffee in one hand and a pastry on a plate in the other hand.

"I might as well take my break now. I got Lucy to cover that table over there." Holly moved her satchel to the floor beside her and Alice settled herself into the seat across from her and took a sip of her coffee.

"What's your name honey?" she asked.

"Holly. Holly Miller."

"Well, Holly, I can't say as I spent a lot of time with the judge and his family aside from when they was here in this restaurant seein' as how I'm from the west side and all," Alice said referring to the part of town Holly had driven through this morning.

"But I reckon I know as much about that family as anyone else round here that wasn't a close friend or employee." She winked at Holly and helped herself to another forkful of pastry. Holly had gotten out her notebook and a pen and was trying to look relaxed. Her stomach was suddenly full of butterflies and she was starting to regret eating both eggs and French toast.

"Could you describe the immediate family for me?" Holly asked.

"Well there was the judge, Charles and his wife Eleanor. Then there were the boys Charles and Patrick." Alice took a sip of her coffee.

"Were there any grandchildren, or other family members living around here?" Holly asked lightly. Alice's mouth set in a straight line for a moment, and then she frowned and shook her head. "That family never did have no luck." Holly waited for her to continue.

"The oldest boy Charles married a pretty girl named Kathleen. They had two sons, Eric and the younger one Lucas. I remember hearing Eleanor had a right fit when they didn't name Eric after the judge and carry on the name Charles, but Kathleen named him after a favorite brother who died as a boy." Holly's heart was pounding. She was finally hearing about Eric's family. They weren't ghosts after all but real people.

"Are any of them still living around here?" Holly asked allowing a little of the excitement that she felt to show in her voice. Alice looked at her, cocked her head to the side and sighed.

"I can't say as any of them are still living at all. Maybe Eric, but no one has seen him for years and I doubt he will ever come back here."

"I don't understand. What happened?" Holly asked.

"Same thing that always happened to that family. Seems like it was one terrible thing after another." Alice got up to refill her coffee cup and Holly silently prayed that no one would interrupt them before she found out more about Eric's past.

After Alice resettled herself in the chair she asked, "Where was I?"

Holly decided to ask about Eric's uncle "What about Patrick?"

"That boy!" Alice said in an exasperated tone, but her face was all smiles. "He was a trick. From the first time he set foot in this restaurant he was trouble. I was just a teenager then but I remember him clear as day. Always unscrewing the lids on the salt and pepper shakers. Loosening the top of the ketchup bottle. When he was a teenager the girls were wild over him. He acted cool but he was always just a big kid." Holly could tell Alice had a soft spot for Patrick like an aunt has for a favorite nephew. She also realized that Alice must be in her sixties, although she was certainly in good shape and kept busy running around the restaurant.

"I'll never forget the day he died. I couldn't believe it." Alice's voice caught and she paused. "A customer came in and people started to whisper from one table to the next. When the story made its way back to me I nearly dropped my tray. It was silly really. I barely knew him but I had watched him grow up. It's funny how you get involved in people's lives when you see them every day and watch them grow up." Alice had been talking more to herself than to Holly. She looked across at the confused girl and went on. "It was a motorcycle accident. He was driving that bike too fast like he always did and he hit a patch of gravel at an intersection just outside of town and slid in front of a truck. Well, there were broken hearts all over town on both sides of the tracks. Charles had just gotten married to Kathleen and they were expecting their first baby - that would have been Eric. Eleanor was devastated. You would never have known it to see her and she never came in here of course. The judge brought the boys in here when they were young and they came on their own later on, but Eleanor wouldn't be caught dead in a diner." Alice took a break from her tale and stared at her coffee. Holly noticed that the story seemed to tire her more than the hustle and bustle of the diner. After a few seconds Holly changed the subject from Patrick back to the judge.

"How long after, uhm Patrick's accident, did the judge die?" Holly didn't want to upset Alice even more, but she seemed to perk up at mention of Eric's grandfather.

"Well, the judge had a bad heart you know, and Patrick's death was hard on him, but he never missed a day on the bench. Not for illness or anything else. Right up until the day he died. He lived long enough to see both his grandsons." Alice smiled proudly at this. Holly thought it strange that anyone should feel so involved in the lives of a family so completely unrelated to them. But perhaps that was part of the charm of a small town. People involved in each other's lives. She was starting to get to know the people who came into Mr. Johnson's store and she could to some extent follow the various dramas being played out in Camden, thanks in large part to Angie.

"What about Charles and Kathleen?" Holly asked. "They can't be very old now."

"Well, they would have been right around fifty if they hadn't been killed in a car accident when the boys were young." Holly felt a lump in her throat. Eric had told her his parents had died in a car accident. That must have been devastating for him.

Alice's coffee had kicked in and she was finishing her story. "After that it was just Eleanor and the two boys. She wanted Eric to go into law like his grandfather and his father but he wasn't serious like his father or even Lucas for that matter. He was happiest camping and running around with his friends. He was good in school mind you, but he wasn't what you might call devoted."

Holly smiled and nodded her head. This boy that Alice described sounded very much like the man that Holly had come to love.

"He used to come in here after school and get a piece of pie and a glass of milk on Fridays, and he would talk to me just like his uncle Patrick had." Alice paused again. Then she said in a softer voice "I don't care what anybody says I can't believe Eric set that fire. He may not have seen eye to eye with the old woman or even Lucas for that matter, but I can't believe he would have harmed either one of them or anyone for that matter." Alice started to pick up her dishes and Holly panicked.

"Wait! Just a few more minutes Alice, please. What fire?" Holly's heart was pounding. She had read an article in the library that had referenced a fire at the judge's home.

"Lord, honey, the fire that killed Eleanor and Lucas. The one that burned the poor judge's house to the ground and killed what was left of his family. Eric wasn't home at the time and some say he set the fire, but I say that's a bunch of bull." Alice's cheeks had become a mottled red color. She took a deep breath and tucked a stray lock of hair behind her ear before continuing. "Anyway it doesn't matter, there wasn't enough proof to pin the fire on anyone and shortly after that Eric left town to live with a relative of his mother's and he never came back." Alice was standing now; clearly she had said all she intended to say on the matter. Holly stood and offered her hand.

"Thank you for taking the time to talk to me. I can tell this was very emotional for you. If I wanted to know more about the fire is there anyone you can think of that I should ask?" Holly hoped she wasn't pressing her luck but she had more questions and she didn't want to press Alice any further.

"Well, the old fire chief retired last year and moved to Florida. The police chief that was working then was Tom Sparks. He retired about five years ago, but he still lives here in Chesterfield."

"Could you tell me where I could find him?" Holly asked.

"Sure honey, he's sittin' up there at the counter."

21

Holly took in the group of men sitting at the counter up front. Chief Sparks, according to Alice, was the second from the end. Taking a final glance at Alice's form as it retreated through the swinging doors, Holly packed up her satchel, put a large tip on the table and headed up front to the cash register. She paid her bill and fumbled with her bag and her receipt, buying time while she made her way toward Tom Sparks. Now that she knew he was an ex-police chief she could see it in him. Perfectly ironed shirt. Short hair cut. Black shoes. You can take the man out of the job....

"Um, excuse me, Mr. Sparks?" He looked over his shoulder at her and then slowly swiveled around in his seat until he was facing her.

"Can I help you miss?" he asked politely, but he wasn't smiling. His friends gave her a cursory glance and went on with their conversation.

"I'm sorry to bother you but I was hoping I could ask you a few questions?" She had intentionally kept her voice low but looked him directly in the eyes.

"Well, now, that used to be my line," he said laughing "Questions about what?"

"Well, about the fire at the Copeland house to be specific. And about Eric Copeland." He looked at her for a moment and then turned back around in his seat. She thought for a moment that he was just going to ignore her, and she wasn't sure what she was going to do about it. He turned back around and handed her a napkin. She looked at it and there was an address on it.

"I'll be home by twelve o'clock. Come by then and we'll see if there is anything I can do to help you." With that he turned around and started talking to his friends again. Holly mumbled a thank you on deaf ears and walked out into the sunshine. It was just now eleven and she had an hour to kill before the meeting so she decided to drive out and pick up the phone battery. She needed to stay busy so she wouldn't go crazy thinking about what Alice had told her. She crossed the street and got into her car. When she had closed the door she leaned her head against the steering wheel and took a deep breath. Alice had been right; the Copelands had been the victims of every kind of bad luck. It was overwhelming, the loss and sadness that the family had suffered. Someone rapped sharply on her passenger window. Holly sat bolt upright and looked over to see Alice peering in. She was wearing a sweater over her uniform and had a purse over her arm. Holly turned the key in the ignition and started the car quickly pushing the button that lowered the passenger side window.

"I don't know who you really are and I don't really care," Alice said in a weak voice, "but if you see Eric, tell him Alice said 'Hi!' will you?"

Holly nodded her head dumbly. Alice turned and walked away and down the street. So much for the college student story. Holly put the car in gear and drove away paying attention to traffic and her directions and trying not to think about anything else.

She found the store on her second try and located the battery with the help of an eager sales assistant. With her purchase made she stopped at a filling station to get gas and have Mr. Johnson's car washed. She felt guilty for not being in touch with either him or Mrs. Kingsley for the last two days but she had needed her space and she was privately glad her cell phone hadn't been working. She didn't want to lie to them about where she was and what she was doing but she couldn't talk about Eric or his family until she knew more. There was already such a strong bias against Eric that this new information would only be seen as proof of his instability. She pulled the car out of the car wash and over to the vacuum and air compressor at the side of the lot. She quickly vacuumed what little dirt there was out of her boss' beloved car and checked the air in the tires with the gauge he kept in the glove box. Feeling a little less guilty after her maintenance efforts, Holly got back into the car, checked the clock on the dash and set off to find the address on the napkin that Tom Sparks had given her at the diner.

She recognized the street name as one she had driven past earlier this morning during her tour of the town. The streets in that neighborhood were all named after trees. It was on the east side of town but in a more modest neighborhood. She found the neighborhood and began looking for the street. It was a quiet street ending in a cul-de-sac. The houses were not large but they were not too close together and the yards were well taken care of. The trees lining the streets and driveways were big and old and beautiful. It was five minutes after twelve and Holly was reading the numbers on mail boxes when she saw Mr. Sparks sitting on a porch in a rocking chair watching her. She pulled into his driveway and walked up his front steps. He stayed in his chair and motioned her to an identical rocking chair. Holly sat, placed her satchel bag on the ground next to her feet and looked up at the ex-police chief. Before she could say anything he leaned forward with his arms resting on his knees and his hands clasped together and said, "Alice tells me you're a student writing a paper on Judge Copeland. She also said you were asking about the family's background."

Holly's mouth started to get dry and she hesitated to answer for a moment. She looked down at her tennis shoes and suddenly felt very ashamed. Alice had been very open and honest with her about events that were clearly painful to her and Holly had lied about everything but her name. She took a deep breath and looked directly at him and said, "Mr. Sparks...?"

"Holly, that's your name right? People 'round here just call me Chief or Tom."

She nodded at him and swallowed, her mouth drier than before. The chief, realizing her discomfort, said "Why don't I get us some lemonade and we can sit out here and have a nice chat."

He got up and went into the house, returning shortly with a pitcher and a couple of glasses. "Doc Simpson says I got to drink less coffee and I don't like soda so I drink a lot of lemonade." He smiled, obviously trying to put her at ease and handed her a glass. Holly drank half of it immediately then set it down.

"Thank you," she said. "My name is Holly Miller, Chief, and I am a student, but not at UV, as I told Alice. I am not writing a paper on the judge but I am here to research his family and past."

"Would you mind telling me why?" he asked. Holly knew her only chance of getting the chief to cooperate with her was to tell him the truth.

"I lied to Alice to protect Eric from gossip. I can see now that she would never do anything to hurt him but I didn't know that when I came here. You see, Eric and I have been seeing each other for about a year now." She went on to tell him about Eric's refusal to discuss his past or share any of his life with her. "I love Eric Chief, but I don't think we can have a future together until Eric can talk to me or anyone about his past. But I just couldn't walk away from him without understanding why."

"How does Eric behave around your family and friends?"

Holly hesitated. "Eric has always been a perfect gentleman on the few occasions when I have forced him to be social. My parents have met him twice and they like him." She paused, thinking. "My boss Mr. Johnson, and my best friend don't trust him, but they just don't know him like I do."

"May I ask why they don't trust him?"

She told him about the bike accident and the allergic reaction from Eric's dinner. She kept her voice light and unconcerned but she told him the truth. It felt good to be honest. She finished her story and reached for her glass of lemonade.

"Holly, you asked about the fire at the Copeland house and I honestly wasn't going to tell you much. But because I think it is important that you understand your situation completely I am going to be more specific." He sat back in his chair and crossed one leg over the other.

"Eric was fifteen when it happened. Lucas was almost thirteen. Eleanor and Eric argued a lot that summer, which wasn't unusual for a teenage boy and his parent - or grandparent in this case. Eleanor was extremely demanding. Eric looked so much like Charles she couldn't help wanting him to be like his father; but in fact he wasn't anything like his dad. She arranged a job for him to work in the courthouse as a low level clerk but he quit after about a week and got a job in maintenance at the park instead. Eleanor thought he did it to spite her. Lucas and Eric got along like most brothers, alternately playing sports and fighting. The arguments escalated when Eric told Eleanor that he had no intention of ever studying law. Eleanor was furious; she refused to let Eric take driving lessons for his license unless he agreed to quit his job and go back to work at the courthouse. As a punishment for disobeying her Eleanor went out of her way to favor Lucas and rode Eric about everything he did. The evening of the fire the girl who helped in the kitchen said there was a screaming match between Eleanor and Eric and he stormed out of the house around ten o'clock. He claimed he went to the park and hung out at a camp site he and some friend kept set up by the lake. The house caught fire around eleven-thirty. The fires started on the second floor in and around the bedrooms. Lucas and Eleanor never had a chance. They couldn't have gotten out even if the smoke hadn't disabled them. The house was old and all wood. It was engulfed in flames within minutes. By the time the fire department had the fire under control they were both long gone. Actually we thought Eric was in the house too. He came running up the street around one o'clock and had to be restrained by some neighbors from running into the house." The chief took a drink of his lemonade and stared out over the porch. He had the same pained look on his face that Alice had this morning.

Holly felt cold and sick to her stomach. She was stunned and couldn't even begin to digest what the chief had just told her.

"Eric didn't speak at all that night. One of his father's partners represented him while we questioned him the next day.

We located the spot where he had been at the park and it was clear that he had been there but he could have easily set the fire and returned to the park. We couldn't tie any physical evidence to him. There was an accelerant used to set the fire but we couldn't link it to Eric. There were no traces on his hands or clothes. We basically didn't have a strong case against him and he had enough support in town that we knew that without an eyewitness we could never get a conviction. So we dropped the charges and Eric disappeared." He shook his head.

"You can't believe Eric would do something like that Chief, can you?"

"Holly, if I've learned one thing in my life it's that people are capable of doing anything. I always liked Eric. He never caused any trouble and his parents were real good people. But who can say what makes people do what they do? Eric was the best lead we had in that fire but it was flimsy. If I had anything hard on him he would be in jail right now. As it was he inherited the entire Copeland fortune, and is, according to you off painting pictures in Connecticut somewhere." The Chief looked at a gold pocket watch he had tucked in his shirt and then took another sip of his drink.

"There were no other suspects, no angry employees, family members, no one?"

"Not at the time, no. Just Eric. There was a girl who came later and challenged the will. Claimed to be an illegitimate daughter of Patrick's, but the case was dismissed. She had no evidence except some old letters of her mother's."

"Do you have her name?" Holly asked.

"I have a copy of the Copeland file in a box somewhere. I kept copies of all my unsolved files. I'll have a look around and see if there is anything in there on her, but I wouldn't hold my breath. What is the name of the town you're from?"

"Camden," she answered. "And thank you for talking to me."

"Well, I can't see as I've been much help. My advice is to let that dog lie and find yourself a nice young man without a double murder investigation in his past." He stood up and shook her hand. Holly gave him a piece of paper with her address and phone number on it in case he thought of anything else.

"Holly, does Eric know you're down here snooping into his past?"

She shook her head reluctantly.

"Well, if I were you I wouldn't bring up to Eric this conversation or any other information you have picked up from your time here in Chesterfield. The truth is no one knows what he is capable of. I certainly don't. Maybe I was wrong not to pursue the case back then. I would feel responsible if anything happened to you because I let Eric go."

"Please don't worry. Eric doesn't know I'm here, and I am not going to tell him. Not right now anyway. But I have to tell you I think you're wrong. Eric couldn't have set that fire, and if you truly thought he had you wouldn't have let him walk away like you did."

"How long are you staying in town?" the chief asked.

"I'm going home tomorrow morning." Holly smiled at him.

"Well good luck to you." He shook her hand and watched as she got into her car and drove away. As he walked back into the house he decided to go ahead and look for the Copeland file. It would be one of the last things he did.

22

After such a large breakfast Holly was not ready for lunch so she decided to look for the Copeland house that had burned down. She opened the file of articles and looked for the one about the judge and his wife. She wished she had remembered to ask the chief where the house was. After thumbing through several articles she found the one she was looking for. She stared at the picture of the judge and his wife in front of their home. Of course; that's why the house had seemed so familiar. The big white house she had walked by on Friday evening was the same house as in the picture. She drove to that neighborhood and pulled over on the street to the side of the house. She got out of her car and began to walk around the house. It was as beautiful today as she had thought it was on Friday. It must have been restored exactly because Holly couldn't see any difference in the house from the picture, at least on the outside.

"May I help you?" A small woman of about sixty-five in a large gardening hat appeared on the other side of the wrought iron fence and surprised Holly.

"I'm sorry, I was admiring the house," she said.

"You're not from around here?" the lady asked.

"No, I'm just visiting. This was the Copeland house wasn't it?"

"Yes, dear, we moved in a few months after it was rebuilt. We always loved it and when my husband retired from the bench we thought it would be a great place for our grandchildren. We have eleven of them," she reported proudly.

"Did you have it rebuilt the same as the original after you bought it or did the owner do that?" Holly wondered if Eric or his representatives at the time had decided to rebuild the house.

"Oh no, we didn't buy it. The house was never for sale, just for lease. We would like to have bought it but the owner wanted the estate to stay intact. So we agreed to lease it. I know it's silly to lease a house this size for so long but the estate manager gave us a marvelous price and a long lease and we loved the house so much." She smiled proudly across the manicured lawns as she spoke.

"Does the owner ever come to see the property?" Holly asked.

"Heavens no! We haven't seen him in years. My husband worked with his father. But Charles has been dead now for almost twenty years. His son inherited the estate, but apparently has no interest in this property. I can't say I'm disappointed. We've come to think of it quite as our own. Well, it was lovely talking to you dear but I've got to get busy or I'll still be out here when Albert gets home from the golf course." She waved and moved back toward the rear of the house from where she had come . Holly continued to walk around to the front of the property along the tree-lined sidewalk and admired the home where Eric had spent so much of his youth. She thought about his brother Lucas for a moment. Eric had never even mentioned having a brother. How devastating to lose him after losing both parents. He was so alone in the world. Tears pricked her eyes and her throat felt tight as she started to imagine the terrible losses he had suffered. She stared at the house and her eyes traveled to the second floor. The bedrooms were up there - the rooms where Lucas and Eleanor had been trapped and died. Who could have set a fire like that? There had to be some other explanation. She still couldn't believe that Eric had had any part in the deaths of his grandmother and brother.

She walked a few blocks in a different direction than she had the other night, running through all of the things that Alice and the chief had told her. Eric's family life had been both charmed and tragic. She was suddenly grateful for the boring middle class life she had led growing up. It was sad that the dramas of everyday life of the Copeland family had been played out in front of and dissected by the town. She started to understand why Eric had not wanted to return to this town where so many bad memories were still alive in the memories of the people who lived and worked here.

Making her way back to her car Holly decided it was time to check in with Mrs. Kingsley. She drove through a hot dog stand in town, got lunch and took it back to the motel with her. Carrying her lunch and fishing in her satchel for her key she stumbled through the door and unloaded her burdens on the table by the window. She munched on a hot dog while she wrestled the battery out of its package, put it in her phone and plugged it in to charge. Holly undressed, got into the shower and stood under the hot water hoping it would relieve the tension that was creeping into her shoulders and neck. She had come here looking for answers and she had them. She also had more questions, but they weren't going to be answered here, not on this trip.

She stepped out of the shower and toweled off. With one towel around her body and another around her hair she sat down on the side of the bed to apply some much needed lotion to her legs when she noticed the message light blinking on the phone next to the bed. The bulb was very dim, which is why she hadn't seen the light when she entered the room. The sun coming in through the window had overpowered the dim little light. She picked up the phone and dialed the number to retrieve her message. While she was being connected she automatically reached in the top drawer of the bedside table for the pad of paper and pen that were always left for patrons to use. She had just pulled the cap off of the pen when she heard Mrs. Kingsley's voice. She was obviously trying to sound calm but Holly could tell that she was upset about something. Her message was simple; please call home as soon as you can. No "I hope you're having a good time." or anything like that. The next message was from Sheriff Butler. He had left his cell number and asked that she call him as soon as she got in. Holly's heart was pounding. She couldn't imagine what was wrong but it must be serious. As she was replaying the sheriff's message so she could write down his number she noticed her cell phone was vibrating on the table by the window. She wrote down the number, hung up the motel phone and slowly rose and walked over to her cell phone. There was a message on the screen telling her she had messages. There were also numerous missed calls from Mrs. Kingsley, the sheriff, and one from Megan. Nothing from Eric. Had something happened to him? She didn't trust the battery on her phone to hold up for an important call after such a short charge so she got her credit card out of her wallet and made the call to Mrs. Kingsley's house from the phone in her room. There was no answer so she hung up and dialed the number the sheriff had left her. He answered on the second ring.

"Sheriff? This is Holly Miller."

"Holly, are you all right?" he asked.

"Yes, I'm fine. I'm in Chesterfield, Virginia. What's going on?" she asked.

"Have you spoken to Mrs. Kingsley?" The sheriff was obviously trying do find out if she had been told anything already.

"No. Please Sheriff, what's wrong? Is Eric OK?"

"I can't tell you about Mr. Copeland one way or the other. I wish I could talk to him myself," he said. Then, "Holly, Walter Johnson has been in an accident. He's hurt pretty bad."

Holly's throat got tight again for the second time that day and this time tears formed in her eyes and fell down onto her cheeks.

"Is..., is he..., where is he?" she asked.

"He's at Memorial Hospital. He's banged up pretty bad. He's got a bad concussion and a broken arm. His left leg got pretty banged up too, but the doctor thinks he will heal OK as long as there are no complications."

"What happened?" she asked quietly, wondering what could have happened to have the sheriff wanting to look for Eric.

"Well, he was leaving the store Thursday night and got hit broadside by a truck. I can go into the details with you when you get back here. I assume you're going to come back soon?"

"I was going to leave in the morning but of course I will leave right away. I can be home in about six or seven hours if I have some luck with traffic."

"Walter's going to be fine and you getting yourself killed racing home isn't going to help things, so just take your time and drive carefully. Beatrice doesn't need anything else to worry about right now."

"Where is she?" Holly whispered, her voice strained and cracking.

"She's been at the hospital since it happened." Guilt overwhelmed Holly. She had been avoiding talking to them and they had needed her. Now the tears were flowing freely down her face.

"Will you tell her I'm on my way? My cell phone hasn't been working but I got a new battery. You can reach me anytime." She was rambling and crying.

"I'll tell her, Holly. Please try to calm down. When you get back and get settled, call me. I have a few things I want to discuss with you, but it can wait till later." She agreed to call him and disconnected. She couldn't think about what he wanted. It was obviously about Eric, but she didn't want to deal with that now. She just wanted to pack her bag and get on the road.

23

Thirty minutes later Holly was headed north. After switching stations several times she turned the radio off. She didn't want to listen to cheerful music or talk radio. She just wanted to bridge the distance between herself and Mr. Johnson and Mrs. Kingsley as quickly as possible.

She saw the sign for Camden and checked her dashboard clock. Eight forty-two. She had made good time, stopping twice to stretch her legs and get something to drink. As she pulled onto Terwilliger Place she noticed a car parked across the street with a man inside. As she got out of her car he left his car and started to walk up the driveway toward her.

"Miss Miller? I'm Officer Collins. The sheriff asked me to introduce myself to you when you got here so you didn't get nervous. I'll just be in my car Ma'm if you need anything. Someone will be around later to relieve me but no one will bother you unless there's cause to be alarmed."

"I'm sorry," she said, but why are you here?" The long day was taking its toll and her head was starting to ache.

"Just as a precaution, Ma'm. In case Mr. Copeland shows up."

"Eric?" she asked, the pounding in her head starting to sound like a freight train. "But why? Why are you looking for Eric?" she asked.

"I'm sorry Ma'm. You're going to have to talk to the sheriff about that." He looked up and down the street and then walked back to his car. Holly was still holding the handle of her roller bag and felt suddenly nauseous. She rolled the bag to the steps and pulled it up to the landing. She let herself into the house, which was unusually quiet and dark. There was mail on the front table and a blanket and pillow on the little sofa in the front room. Holly's heart sank. Mrs. Kingsley must be exhausted. She never left without tidying up and Holly suddenly wondered who was watching the store.

She knew she had to shake off the fog that was surrounding her if she was going to be of any use to these two people who meant so much to her. She went to the kitchen, found the bottle of aspirin and washed several down with some water. After a quick trip to her room to change clothes and splash water on her face she was headed back out the door to Memorial Hospital.

The big double door entrance to the hospital opened automatically; Holly walked in and to the information desk. The woman told her which floor and room Mr. Johnson was in, reminded her that visiting hours were over already and gave her the hours for tomorrow. Holly thanked her and moved toward the elevator bank ignoring her caution about visitor's hours. They could ask her to leave if they wanted but she was going to see Walter Johnson first. She needed to see that he was OK with her own eyes.

She got off the elevator at the third floor and saw from the sign on the wall that Mr. Johnson's room was to the left. Reading the numbers on the doors as she went she came to his room and pushed the door open cautiously. She could see the foot of his bed and a chair in the corner of the room occupied by a sleeping Mrs. Kingsley. Holly moved slowly into the room. She approached her sleeping boss and looked down at his bruised face. She reached out and covered his casted left hand with her own. It wasn't until a tear splashed off of his cast that she realized that she was crying. Walter Johnson had been like a father to her since she had moved to Camden and it broke her heart to see him lying here like this.

Mrs. Kingsley moved in the corner and Holly looked over at her as she opened her eyes and felt for her glasses on the little table next to her chair. "Holly? Thank goodness you're home. Are you all right dear?"

"I'm fine, Mrs. Kingsley. I'm so sorry I wasn't here to be with you guys and to help. I just don't understand what's going on." She moved over to her landlady and hugged her. Beatrice held onto Holly for a long time and Holly could tell that this gentle woman had been afraid and worried.

There was a grunt from the bed behind her and as she turned around her boss gave her a tired look and said "I see you have finally decided to grace us with your presence." She went back to his side and held his hand. Searching for the words to tell him how sorry she was for what had happened she started to feel emotional again.

"Don't start cryin' on me. It took me a full day to convince Beatrice that I was fine. I don't have the energy to start all over with you." He gave her a weak smile and she smiled back at him. "Did you bring my car back in one piece?" he asked

"I sure did. She's all gassed up and ready to go. I even vacuumed up all the French fries." She grinned.

"Well the good news is your Jetta is no longer leaking transmission fluid." She started to thank him but he raised his good hand to stop her and continued. "The bad news is your driver's seat is now on the passenger's side." Holly stared at him trying to make sense out of what he just said when she realized what he was telling her. Of course, the car he had been driving when he left work had been hers. The truck had hit her car. She started to open her mouth to ask him a question about the accident when Mrs. Kingsley looked over toward the door to the hospital room and said hello to Sheriff Butler who had just taken off his hat and walked into the room.

"Beatrice, Walter. Hi, Holly," he said. Holly realized that Officer Collins must have informed his boss that she had returned to the house and left shortly after. It wouldn't have been hard to guess where she was going. The question Holly still couldn't answer was why he was so anxious to talk to her. She wouldn't have to wait long for an answer because he asked Walter and Bea if he could borrow her for a few minutes and together they left the room and walked down the hall toward an empty lounge.

"Can I get you anything?" he inquired dropping coins into a coffee machine.

"No thanks," she said and waited. He motioned to a couple of plastic chairs around a circular table and they sat down facing each other.

"I know you've got to be confused Holly because I asked Bea and Walter not to tell you anything until I got a chance to talk to you." She stayed quiet and waited for him to continue.

"Holly, do you know where Eric is right now?"

"He's in New York visiting his college roommate. Why? I don't understand what Eric has to do with Mr. Johnson's accident."

"Well, to be honest with you neither do I. The truck that hit Walter was parked up the road from the store and pulled out just as Walter started to pull out onto Main Street. Walter also remembers that the truck's headlights were out even though it was dark outside." He paused. "Do you understand me so far?"

"You're saying that whoever was driving the truck was waiting for Mr. Johnson?"

"I'm saying it's possible that the crash was intentional but Holly, Walter was driving your car. And you were supposed to be working on Thursday night weren't you?" She nodded as the repercussions of what he was saying sunk in. He believed that Holly was the intended victim of that crash.

"Are you sure the crash wasn't just an accident? Do you know who was driving?"

"Well, you know by the time Walter left most of the businesses on the street were already closed but we got a decent description of the truck from a guy walking his dog. That information led us to the Wilkes property." He took a sip of his coffee. He waited for Holly to comment but she didn't. The truth was she couldn't. Her mind was numb from all that she had heard today. There just didn't seem to be room for any more bad news.

"Sam Waterson, you know, the agent that manages the property for the Wilkes, well he let us look around a little and we found Eric's old pickup in the shed up there looking pretty banged up." He leveled his gaze at her. She nodded her head at him. She wasn't capable of anything else.

24

Holly stared down at her hands clasped on the table. This afternoon sitting on the chief's porch she had felt certain that Eric had been a victim. Now she was being told that he had tried to kill her. The facts were all there in her head but her heart was still unable to accept them. She wanted to believe there was some other explanation, but that seemed unlikely now.

"I'm not sure what I am supposed to do now," she said.

"You could go home. To Ohio, I mean, you would certainly be safer there."

"I can't leave Mr. Johnson. He will need me at the store. And Mrs. Kingsley - she looks exhausted."

"They will both tell you to go home of course. They want you to be safe. But you do what you want. I will keep a man around as much as I can until we get Copeland into custody. After that you should be safe. Why don't you go on and say good night to Walter and take Bea home. We can talk some more tomorrow."

Somehow she walked back to the hospital room and said goodnight to her boss. Walter told her to drive his Bonneville until she could get a rental car. She thanked him and promised to go to the store to check on things in the morning and come visit him afterward.

Holly followed her landlady down the hallway and into the elevator. They were both exhausted and aside from general conversation about the drive home and what was needed from the grocery store, they said very little to each other. They drove home in separate cars and when Holly pulled into her space in the driveway she noticed a different unmarked car parked across the street from the house. She felt a pang of guilt. Her boss was in the hospital and her landlady's home was being guarded from what the sheriff believed to be a dangerous person - Eric. Holly still couldn't reconcile the man she had come to love with the tale of arson in Virginia and the car crash here just two nights ago. Pain and fog started to crowd her thoughts again as the tension headache returned.

The following morning she got up early and left a note for Mrs. Kingsley that she would be back before lunch. She wanted to get to the store and check over everything. Run the inventory lists for Friday and Saturday that hadn't been done while Mr. Johnson was in the hospital. She knew he would be worried and she wanted to be able to tell him everything was caught up when she saw him this afternoon. She worked hard to keep her mind off of Eric and all that had happened. She had called her parents from her cell phone when she knew they would be up and updated them on Mr. Johnson's accident. She left out the details about her trip to Virginia and what the sheriff had told her because she wanted to avoid an argument about going home. She wasn't going to run from what was happening here. Besides she owed it to her boss to keep the store running until he recovered. There were messages on the answering machine from his poker friends wanting to know how he was and volunteering to help out at the store. Holly took down their names and numbers because she knew she would need some help over the next week or two. She made a simple spreadsheet of the hours that the store was open during the week and then called the two people on her list that she knew her boss trusted the most. Once she had their available times filled in on the list she filled the rest of the spots in with her own name. She could see that she would be missing classes over the next two weeks and made a note to herself to go see the dean this week. With the cash register balanced and the credit card machine batched out she gathered her inventory lists and her schedule, tucked them into her satchel and locked up. Mrs. Kingsley would be home from church by now and Holly wanted to talk to her.

An hour later the two women were sitting at the big kitchen table sharing a pot of tea. "I am still not sure what happened after I left," Holly said turning a slice of lemon over in her tea cup.

"Well," started Beatrice, "Walter doesn't remember much after the crash but he remembers pretty much everything leading up to it. He says he pulled out from behind the store and stopped at the corner to turn onto Main Street. There was a truck idling up the street a bit to the side but he didn't pay much attention to it and as soon as he pulled out the driver of the truck stepped on the gas and drove straight at him. It was dark out and there wasn't much light except for the dim street light that was across the street, but he was able to give some detail about the truck. Luckily he had already started to make his turn so the impact was just between the front and back seat on the driver's side, otherwise his injuries could have been much worse." She paused here noticing the pained look on the young woman's face.

"You know that the sheriff thinks it was Eric?" Holly asked. Of course, he would have filled his friend Walter in and Beatrice had probably been there. If not, Mr. Johnson would have told her himself.

"Yes. I know that."

"He thinks it was supposed to be me in that car," she said looking down at her hands.

"Well I am very glad it wasn't," said Mrs. Kingsley "And for that matter, so is Walter."

"I don't know what to believe," Holly whispered. The emotional strain caused pain in her throat and tears pricked at her eyes. She took a deep breath and asked "Do you want me to move out?"

Her landlady stared at her but didn't pretend to be surprised. She knew Holly would be feeling responsible for what happened. She was also heartbroken but hadn't had time to realize it.

"No," Beatrice said firmly. "If I can't convince you to go home to your parents until this mess is sorted out then I want you right here where I can keep my eye on you."

Holly got up from her chair and went around and stood behind her friend. She leaned down, wrapped her arms around the woman's neck and whispered, "I'm so sorry. I can't believe this is happening."

"One way or another, this will work its way out, Holly. Now you go get ready to visit Walter and I'm going to pack a little snack for you to take to him. While I'm at it I think I will make some lunch for that young man sitting out front." Holly smiled to herself as she made her way upstairs. Once the guys at the station heard about Mrs. K's cooking they would be begging for duty in front of the house on Terwilliger Place.

25

Holly decided in the elevator on the way up to see Mr. Johnson that she was going to tell him the truth about her trip to Virginia. She owed him that much. She would also have to tell the sheriff. She should have done so the night before but she had been so shocked that she had forgotten what she had learned in Virginia. She realized that this was going to make the case against Eric stronger but she couldn't do anything about that now. The elevator doors opened and she stepped out carrying the basket that Mrs. Kingsley had sent full of homemade goodies for her boss, her bag carrying the paperwork from the store and a few personal effects he had asked for from his desk. When she opened the door to his room he was sitting up in bed flipping channels on the wall-mounted television. He switched off the TV with the remote and looked at her over the top edge of his glasses.

"I have everything you asked for from the store and..." she held up the basket lined with a checkered dish towel "lunch, compliments of the best cook in Camden." He smiled at this; Holly could tell that the accident had brought Mrs. K and him closer together. Beatrice no longer needed Holly as an excuse to see him and he was eager for her company. She felt cheered that something good had come of this terrible mess. She rolled the tray table over the bed and into place for him to eat his lunch. She ignored his obvious discomfort at being waited on by her and chatted instead about her efforts at the store. He played along with this little game and asked her questions that she answered in detail.

While he ate his lunch she pulled the things she had brought for him out of her bag. She set the copy of Richard

North Patterson's "No Safe Place" on the table beside his bed and beside it the address book he had requested. She went into the bathroom and put the toiletries she had brought him from the small bathroom attached to his office. She smiled as she set his aftershave on the sink. She knew he wouldn't have asked Mrs. Kingsley to bring this to him but she was likely the reason he wanted it. Holly asked him when he was being released and he said that they had told him that barring any complication from his concussion he could go home on Wednesday.

When he had finished eating she cleared the food away and set out the inventory sheets and batch totals she had brought from the store. There wasn't much to these but he could see for himself that everything balanced and she knew that he was relieved that she had done the inventory. It was a small thing and not really necessary unless you were an ex-Marine who did everything by rule. The lack of continuity and organization was worse for someone like Walter than the actual physical injuries that he had suffered. She showed him the schedule she had made and he started to argue that she had herself down for too many hours and couldn't possibly commit that much time. She interrupted him and assured him that it was no problem and under the circumstances it was the least she could do.

"I can't tell you how sorry I am that this happened to you. I can't bear to think that I might be the cause of this," she said gesturing to his arm and the room in general.

"You can stop that right now," he snapped at her. "We don't know for sure what happened and even if it was that Copeland boy it certainly wasn't your fault. Besides if I had to choose between being here and having to tell your father this had happened to you I would be right where I am, thank you very much. I don't suppose you have told your father about this?"

"No. I barely understand what's going on myself," she admitted. "Besides they would worry constantly and beg me to come home..." He opened his mouth to say something but she stopped him. "Which I have no intention of doing. So, it just seems kinder to wait until Eric is back and all this gets straightened out before telling them anything."

"Matt told you last night that they found Eric's truck?" he asked in a voice she knew to be calmer than he felt about the matter. She nodded. He believed that Eric had done this to him and intended it for her. She couldn't stand in front of Walter and defend Eric. With all that she now knew about Eric she couldn't, with conviction, defend him to anyone. They were quiet for a moment then she pulled a plastic chair up next to his bed.

"I have something I want to tell you," she said. "I wasn't in Williamsburg." He stared at her but he didn't say anything, so she went on. "I was in a town not far from there called Chesterfield. It's where Eric grew up." He waited, so she continued. "Before I left we had an argument. I won't go into the details but mostly it was about his refusal to discuss his past or his family, anything really, except what we do together. I was pretty sure we were over and since he was going to New York and I was too miserable to sit around here I decided to take a trip and see if I couldn't at least find out something about him."

"Did you?"

She nodded and took a deep breath and told him about her trip to Virginia. He listened quietly while she explained about her trip to the library, her long talk with Alice, and finally her visit with Chief Sparks. When she got to the part about Eric being questioned about the fire that killed his brother and grandmother he sat up in his bed a little and started to fidget with his reading glasses on the roller table in front of him.

"Does Matt know all of this?" he asked when she was finished.

"No," she answered. "But I didn't keep it from him on purpose. I was just so shocked by what he told me and seeing you here, I didn't even think about it until this morning." She was pulling at a thread sticking out of a button on her sweater. He noticed she looked pale and had dark circles under her eyes. He had never seen her look so unhappy. "Anyway I am going to call him when I leave here and tell him. I just wanted to tell you the truth first. I'm sorry I lied, I just didn't want to talk about

Eric to anyone and I knew you didn't trust him already. And it looks as if you were right after all."

"Well, none of that matters now. When Matt finds him, and he will, at least I will know you're safe and we can start to put all of this behind us." He reached out and patted her hand. "You couldn't have known what he was really like, you know. Not if he was intent on keeping it from you. He fooled everyone, not just you."

"He didn't fool you." She told him how she had found the fax in his office while she was looking for the repair kit for her glasses.

"I never suspected him of anything except being shy until I saw that bicycle. By your own admission your bike was OK when you got to his place and he was the only other person around. The night you went to the hospital, on your birthday, I was beside myself. I wanted to drag him out of that room and make him admit that he had done that to you, but I could see how much you cared about him and I wanted to be wrong." He shook his head, folded his glasses and put them away.

"I can see you're tired. I'm sorry if I have upset you with all of this," she said.

"Well I am tired, but I'm glad you told me. Now there's nothing standing between us and we can get on with putting things back in order." She smiled at him. Putting things in order. She wasn't sure that was a possibility for her for a while. The man she loved had tried to kill her. And he had very nearly succeeded in killing someone she cared very much for. Suddenly she didn't know who Eric Copeland was. He couldn't be the person he had portrayed to her over the last year, because that man would never have tried to hurt her. She was starting to feel nauseous again.

"Are you OK?" Her thoughts returned to the hospital room and the concerned man staring at her. She forced a smile.

"I'm fine. I just need a drink of water." She found a plastic cup, rinsed it out in the bathroom and drank some water. She splashed some on her face and patted it dry with some paper towels from the dispenser.

26

She left Mr. Johnson to take a nap and promised to contact the sheriff right away. He also sent his compliments and thanks to Bea. That reminded her, she was going to have to tell Mrs. Kingsley about her trip to Virginia. She was glad she hadn't told her this afternoon. The stress of the past two days was causing a visible strain on the older woman and Holly hoped that her return would relieve some of the burden. She had phoned the sheriff on her way home and left a message for him to call her. The house was quiet when she arrived and Holly was glad that the owner was getting some much-needed rest. She was looking in the medicine cabinet in the first floor powder room for something to settle her stomach when she heard footsteps on the porch. She hurried to the door before anyone could ring the bell and wake up Mrs. Kingsley. She recognized the sheriff through the curtains in the window of the front door and pulled the door open as he was reaching for the bell. She said hello in a quiet voice. He took the hint and followed her into the house and down the hallway to the kitchen without talking.

Once they were out of earshot of the second floor bedroom she asked, "I take it you got my message?"

"I did, and since I was nearby I decided to stop by and see you in person." She figured there was more to this than he was letting on but she didn't care. There was very little anyone could tell her now that would upset her more than what she had found out yesterday.

"What can I do for you?" he asked, nodding as she gestured at the lemonade pitcher she had just removed from the refrigerator. She poured a glass for each of them and sat down at the table. He followed her lead and took a seat.

"I have something to tell you about Eric." He had been about to take a sip of his drink when he stopped and set the glass back down on the table.

"Has he contacted you?"

"No," she said. "Actually, we had a bit of an argument before he left. I thought that was why he left actually. At any rate I wasn't surprised not to hear from him. Distance is what he was after."

"What is it you wanted to tell me then?"

"I know Mr. Johnson told you I went to Williamsburg for the weekend. That's because that is where I told him I was going." She repeated the story she had told her boss in his hospital room an hour or so before. As she repeated the information she realized that she had to put any doubts she had about Eric aside and accept that he was not a part of her life anymore. The sheriff had taken a pad of paper out of his breast pocket and was taking notes. Holly spoke slowly and tried to make sure she didn't leave anything out. When she was finished he looked both anxious and irritated.

"Why didn't you tell me this last night?" he asked trying not to appear irritated.

"I wasn't trying to keep it from you, I was just overwhelmed and exhausted. I could barely comprehend what you were telling me. I didn't believe he could do those things. I still don't understand."

"Holly, we aren't talking about a hit and run here. Or an angry boyfriend. We're talking about a man who may have already killed two people and tried to kill you!" She nodded and put her hands over her face.

"You say you argued before he left. What was it you argued about?"

She spoke in a dull voice. "His past. His family. He refuses to talk about it. He gets angry or withdrawn if I bring it up."

He was quiet for a moment and then he asked," Did you argue about this around the time you had your bike accident?" he asked.

"Yes," she said, holding his gaze.

"Holly, did Eric know you were going to Virginia? Did you tell him or anyone else why you were going there?"

She thought back to the last morning she had spent with Eric. He had seen the application she was sure, but she didn't know if he had looked through her notebook and seen her lists for her trip.

"He may have known I was going. He certainly knew I was snooping around." She told him about the application and Eric's behavior after finding it.

"Well considering what you found out on your trip it's not a stretch that someone with his history might have tried to keep you from going." Again she nodded.

"Do you know where he is?" she asked.

"Yes. Well, sort of," he answered. "He's on his way back here."

Holly physically tensed.

"He's turning himself in. We left a message at his friend's place in New York and alerted the police in that precinct. He must have gotten the message and contacted his lawyer. They in turn contacted us to say he would be turning himself in Monday morning."

When she didn't say anything he continued. "He's been instructed by his lawyers not to contact you when he returns, so I wouldn't worry about him showing up or calling. I'll have someone out front until he's in custody and you just need to sit tight until tomorrow." He saw the worried look on her face.

"Don't be afraid. I'll have someone watching him from the moment he gets back into town. We will know where he is every minute until he shows up tomorrow morning."

She suddenly felt very tired. The long drive and the emotional strain were taking their toll on her and she longed for a nap. The sheriff left and she watched him walk to the officer in the car across the street and talk to him for a moment. Holly made a quick trip around the house to check that all of the doors and windows were locked and then went upstairs. She was mentally and physically exhausted and she would take a nap.

27

She woke up later to the sound of the phone ringing in the downstairs hallway. She couldn't see the clock because she had set her bag on the dresser in front of it. It was dark outside though and it felt late. She didn't have the energy or the courage to repeat her Virginia story for the third time that day so she took the coward's way out and stayed in her room. This wasn't hard because even though she had slept for what must have been several hours, she was still tired. Holly was hungry however, and as if she could read her mind Mrs. Kingsley tapped on her door a few minutes later. She came in at Holly's invitation carrying a small tray that held half of a sandwich and a glass of milk.

She didn't know why but this simple gesture by her friend brought all of the emotions she had been hiding from to the surface. The fear and the frustration. The terror and heartbreak. Her shoulders began to shake and soon she was face down on her bed crying like a child with a skinned knee. Beatrice Kingsley put the tray down on the chest that served as a coffee table in front of the small sofa, sat on the bed beside Holly and stroked her hair. She didn't interrupt the flow of sobs or offer meaningless comments about how everything was going to be all right. She just waited for Holly to pull herself together. She didn't have to wait long; the crying fit ended as abruptly as it began. Holly sat up, blew her nose on the tissue that Beatrice held out to her and took a drink of the milk.

"Thank you," she said.

"You're welcome. I had a lazy day myself but I would say we were due a little break." Holly smiled. She dabbed at her eyes with a clean spot on the tissue and let out a deep sigh. "Are you sure you don't want to go home for a little while?"

"No, Mr. Johnson needs me at the store and I'm sure the sheriff will want me to stick around to answer any questions," she said, feeling better.

"What about that friend of yours from over at the college? Maybe you could use someone your own age to talk to."

"Actually I tried to call her this morning from the store but I just got her answering machine. I left her a message to call me."

"Well, if you're sure you're all right I've got some things to do downstairs and then I'm going to make an early night of it." Holly noticed that her friend was looking much older. *"Worry does that to you"*, she thought. *"Or more accurately your young tenant's insane boyfriend does that to you."* Beatrice left. Holly got out her notebook and made a list. She always did that when she felt at loose ends. She had picked up this trait from her mother; Elizabeth worked from one constantly revised list. As she planned her activities for the next few days she started to feel more confident. She was also starting to feel something else. Anger. She suddenly realized that she was furious. Eric had hidden his life from her; lied to her about his past; tried to poison her; even sabotaged her bike. He had also injured and almost killed someone she cared about. She had been walking around in a fog since she got back. He had almost managed to turn her into one of those feeble helpless victims that always made her crazy when she watched the women's movie channel on Saturday afternoon with her mom. *"Well, Eric, not this time."* By now she had finished her list, straightened her bed and laid out her clothes for tomorrow morning. She had to open the store tomorrow and she wanted to be there early to get everything ready.

The store was more crowded than usual for a Monday and after several people had stopped to ask about the accident and Mr. Johnson's condition Holly realized that part of the reason for the extra business was simple curiosity. Well, as long as they were spending money she would just keep smiling and telling them that Walter was doing great. He would be furious if he knew he was the center of town gossip. She pleaded ignorance about the details of his accident when asked, claiming truthfully that she had been out of town at the time.

Angie stopped by on the pretext of needing air freshener for the office. Holly knew this was a ploy to get some juicy gossip but she just smiled and gave vague answers to her questions until Angie finally gave up and went away, without any air freshener.

The day passed pretty quickly and sales were good. Holly took a short break during a slow period to eat the lunch Mrs. Kingsley had dropped off earlier and call Walter Johnson. He picked the phone up on the first ring and she felt a pang of guilt when she realized he had been waiting for her call. She went over the inventory she had received and discussed the day's sales. She left out the part about the nosey customers however and he seemed a little cheered that things were going smoothly.

Walter's friend Bill was coming to relieve her at six. She made out a cheat sheet in case he had any problems with the register or the credit card machine. She would stop back at closing time and go through the closing procedures but she would have two and a half hours to herself to get caught up on her laundry and a writing project for school. She hadn't heard from the sheriff all day and she was starting to get a little nervous. As if on cue he walked in the front door of the store. She knew he was there to see her so she pointed to the back of the store toward the workroom and office while she finished ringing out a customer. When the store was empty she walked to the back of the store.

"I was worried when I didn't hear from you," she said.

"Well, we've had a busy day. There are a couple other things going on besides this mess," he said in a mildly sarcastic but friendly manner.

"Eric showed up around lunch time with his attorneys. Now I've spoken with the police in Chesterfield, but despite the concerns about arson and the deaths resulting from the fire, Eric was never formally charged. So for now all we have is the truck. And we don't have a good description of the driver. Just that it was a male that generally fits Eric's description as well as a million other guys."

She stared at him puzzled.

"We can't charge him until we can prove that he was actually in town and driving that vehicle. The prosecutor thinks that without a stronger case that he might get off. I don't want you to worry though; Eric understands that under no circumstances is he allowed to contact you. He could be arrested for trying to intimidate a witness for the prosecution." She wasn't sure if this was true or if the sheriff was just trying to make her feel better. Either way she didn't care. She was not afraid of Eric. Maybe she should be, but she wasn't. Her mouth was dry. He was home. He could even be here in town, eating at Rosa's or at the post office. She closed her eyes and drew a deep breath. The bell rang letting her know there was a customer in the store.

"Are you OK?" the sheriff asked.

"I'm fine."

"No closing up alone. No walking home alone. Understand? Now we're watching him, but that doesn't mean you can get sloppy."

"Don't worry. I'm going to be careful."

"This investigation could go on for a couple of weeks and I can't keep a guard at the house twenty-four seven, but a cruiser will be driving by twice an hour. If you need anything or are concerned at all just call."

The customer traffic had picked up while they were talking and one was now standing at the front register waiting to be rung up. Holly assured the sheriff that she would be fine and hurried to the front counter. As he was leaving Bill arrived and the two men spent a few minutes outside on the sidewalk talking. She ignored them and busied herself with sweeping up between the aisles and answering questions for the remaining customers.

28

Tuesday morning Holly stopped by the store to open up for another one of her boss' poker buddies who was working the first shift. She had just put the small bills and some loose change in the register when the phone on the wall rang.

"Good morning Mr. Johnson," she said in a chirpy voice.

"You can't answer the phone like that," he barked. "What if it had been someone else; a vendor, or a customer?"

"Well, I thought it was a safe guess considering we don't open for another forty-five minutes and you hadn't called yet. Besides, how many vendors would be calling from Memorial Hospital?" He remembered the caller ID on the front phone and grunted.

"Make sure you count the money before you put it in the drawer."

"I just did. And stop worrying please. It's not like I don't know what I'm doing."

Another grunt. She could tell he was tired of being in the hospital. The buzzer on the back door rang.

"I have to go now. There's a delivery around back. But I will call you this afternoon." She hung up and hurried to the back door to let the driver in delivering boxes of inventory for the store.

Once she had her helper Bill, settled and had given him some basic instructions and her phone number she got in Mr. Johnson's Bonneville and headed to campus to speak to the dean about the fact that for the better part of the next two weeks she would not be able to attend classes.

Her meeting went better than she thought it would. She would be allowed to skip lectures as long as she kept up with assignments. As she left the building she attempted to reach Megan again but all she got was the answering machine. She checked her watch and decided she had time to stop by the Psychology building to see if Megan was there. She had never been in that building before and was surprised at how quiet it was compared to the building where she spent most of her on campus time. She asked a few students if they knew Megan. One wiry undergraduate in desperate need of a haircut told her that he knew who she was but hadn't seen her around in a while. She asked him where Professor Fiennes' office was and he gave her directions to the second floor. She made her way down the hallway and up the wide set of stairs and began checking the names on the glass doors until she came to the one marked "S. Fiennes, PhD". The door was partially open and Holly knocked and peeked her head in to see if anyone was there. The tiny outer area that was probably where Megan worked was vacant but she could see the professor leaning back in his chair talking on the phone. He looked up at her as she stepped into the office and motioned for her to come in. She busied herself looking at the various diplomas and citations on the wall. Various framed articles written by and about him covered the walls as well. Holly thought Megan's hero worship of the man might not be misplaced after all. She reached out to straighten a crooked frame when a smooth voice from behind her asked,

"May I help you?"

"I hope so, my name is Holly Miller, and I'm a friend of Megan's."

"Yes?"

"Well, actually, I have been trying to contact her and haven't had any luck. I thought I might find her here."

He looked confused for a moment and then said, "Megan isn't working here right now. In fact I don't think she is taking classes at all for the rest of the semester."

Holly was stunned and it must have shown on her face.

"I don't understand." She sat down on the edge of the chair across from his desk and set her bag on the floor by her feet. "I just had lunch with her last week and she was telling me how hard she was working."

"That's true. She did work very hard for the most part. But she came in last Thursday and said she needed some time off to take care of some personal business. You said your name was Holly?"

"Yes, actually I believe Megan has spoken to you about me, or rather my boyfriend on a few occasions." Holly was slightly embarrassed.

The professor looked puzzled. "I'm sorry, what was it she would have spoken to me about?" he asked leaning forward.

"Megan was concerned about my boyfriend's behavior." Holly briefly described the situation with Eric and the concerns her friend had said the professor had raised. She kept waiting for him to nod in recognition but it soon became obvious that he had never heard anything about either her or Eric. She was suddenly very embarrassed and stood to leave. "I have obviously made a mistake. I'm sorry to have bothered you."

The professor ignored her apology and instead looked at her with a curious expression on his face. "Holly, you said you had lunch with Megan last week. What day was that?"

"Wednesday," she answered.

He motioned for her to sit back down. "Did Megan seem upset at all?"

"Not any more than usual. I expected her to throw a fit when I told her where I was going, but she didn't. She was always encouraging me to stop worrying about Eric's past and find someone else." She shook her head confused. "I really can't believe she would just walk out on school and her job like that. She never even hinted that there was anything wrong. I was so wrapped up in my own problems I didn't even notice."

He didn't respond to this and appeared to be deep in thought.

"Do you know if she went to see her parents in Florida?" Holly asked, interrupting his thoughts.

He gave her a strange look and then simply said, "I couldn't say." Holly was sure there was something he wasn't telling her but she knew he wouldn't divulge personal information about a student to her. "Please don't worry. Megan is a very strong girl. People like her always land on their feet." Then he scratched his head and asked, "What town did you say you went to in Virginia?"

"Chesterfield," she answered. "Why?"

"No reason," he said as he wrote the name of the town on a pad of paper lying on his desk and then stood up. She guessed this was her signal that it was time to go, so she stood also.

"Well, Holly, if I see Megan I will certainly tell her you are looking for her. As for your young man I hope that all works out for you."

"Well, thank you for your time professor." She left his office and retraced her steps down the stairs and out of the building.

After Holly left his office Simon Fiennes walked to the four-drawer filing cabinet in the corner of his office. He unlocked it with a small gold key he kept in his desk drawer. He pulled open the second drawer and thumbed through the files until he reached the one marked *Saunders, Megan*. As he looked through her file his eyes fell on the part of her application that listed her hometown. Chesterfield, Virginia. Confused and a little worried he lifted the handset of the old fashioned black phone on his desk and dialed her number. Little did he know that this phone call would cost him his life.

29

Holly checked her watch and thought that she might just have enough time to swing by Megan's apartment building before she had to head back to the store. She had never been inside but she knew where it was because she had dropped her friend off here after one of their shopping trips together. She made her way slowly down the streets lined with houses and apartments full of students who had fled the dorms for the freedom of off-campus life. She stopped frequently to let groups of young adults weighted down by backpacks cross the street. She pulled up to the square red brick building and found a spot close to the sidewalk that led to the front door of the unit. The building housed eight small apartments offering the tenants a view of either the small parking lot on one side or another apartment building on the other. Holly gave herself a mental pat on the back for choosing to live and work in the next town over from the college. She had enjoyed her undergraduate years but she was happier now fluctuating between life as a student and having a private life of her own away from both school and home. Next year she would start considering what she wanted to do. She was already thinking about doing some freelance writing and possibly putting together a book of short stories. She had considered teaching when she was a sophomore at Miami but had changed her mind. Writing was her passion and she just needed to find a job that would allow her to do that and support herself as well.

She walked through the front door and found herself in a cramped hallway leading immediately to the doors of the four apartments on the first floor. There was a stairway to her right that would take her to the upstairs apartments and a set of mailboxes to her left. She walked over to the mailboxes and started reading the names. When she got to the one for number 202 she saw that the name "Cooper" had a line drawn through it and in pen someone had written "Saunders". Holly went up the stairs and found the second door on the left was number 202. She knocked and waited. She didn't hear anything so she knocked again. She looked down and saw a tattered welcome mat. Leaning against the wall by the door were cardboard boxes that were flattened out. Holly wondered if they were for bringing stuff in or taking stuff out. Had her friend moved out without telling her?

She went back downstairs and out the front door and got into her car. As she was opening her car door she saw Megan getting out of a small Honda Civic. The driver was wearing a ball cap and had a cast over his right forearm and wrist. He also seemed to have some cuts and scratches on his face. Megan closed the door and her friend drove away. Holly walked over to her friend who looked up and stopped dead in her tracks.

"What are you doing here?" Megan asked, not even pretending to be happy to see her friend.

"I was worried about you."

"Well as you can see I'm fine. But I'm late so I'm sorry I can't stay and talk."

"Megan stop! What's going on? I saw the boxes upstairs. Are you going somewhere?"

"My mom is sick in Florida and I am going down to spend some time with her. I'm sorry I haven't been able to talk to you but I have been busy reorganizing my life."

"Is there anything I can do to help?"

"No, thanks though. Look I have to go." She gave Holly a small wave and hurried up the steps and into the building.

Holly for the second time that day was stunned. What had just happened? She wanted to follow Megan upstairs and make her tell her what was going on but she had to get to the store. She couldn't keep volunteers coming in to help if she didn't show up to relieve them when she said she would.

30

Holly stayed busy over the next few days covering the majority of hours at the store and trying to keep up with her writing and research assignments from school. Mr. Johnson had been released from the hospital and showed up at the store randomly to check on things. He was able to answer the phone and entered inventory information into the computer with his one good hand, but he tired easily and generally only stayed for an hour or two.

On Thursday she was sitting up on a stool she had dragged out from the back room so she could work on her laptop at the front desk when the store was quiet. The front bell rang and she looked up to see Sheriff Butler come through the front door. Holly's heart started to beat faster. She had done a pretty good job of staying busy to keep her mind off the events of the past week. She had managed over the last seven days to lose both her boyfriend and her best friend and she still didn't really understand what had happened.

"Hi Holly."

"Hi Sheriff."

"Walter here?" he asked, taking off his hat and setting it on the counter.

"No. He came in this morning for an hour or so, but he had a doctor's appointment and I really don't expect him back today."

"Well, it's you I came to see anyway. I haven't talked to you since Monday and I haven't heard from you so I assume Eric hasn't tried to contact you?"

"No. He hasn't." She sat waiting. She knew she should ask him questions but part of her didn't want to know the answers.

"Well, he hasn't been seen around town from what I can tell so he must be keeping to himself up at the Wilkes place."

Holly nodded then asked, "Anything new?"

"Just that his story about being in New York is holding up. His friend can vouch for most of his time. There are a few segments of time when he was unaccounted for. One of them was during the timeframe of the hit and run, but none of them are long enough for him to drive back here, commit the crime in question and return to the city."

"Does that mean he didn't do it?" she asked, suddenly feeling like the room had tilted.

"It just means we don't have any evidence putting him at the scene and he has a pretty decent alibi. He could have gotten someone else to do it for him. The paint on his bumper matched the paint from your car. So we definitely have our vehicle. We just can't prove his involvement yet."

"Could someone have stolen his truck? Could the accident have been a coincidence?" she asked, feeling naïve under his pitying look.

"Well, I guess anything's possible Holly, but I don't think so. Don't forget about the things that happened in Virginia. People that upset young Mr. Copeland have a way of ending up dead. Walter is lucky to be alive. Frankly considering your escape from that dinner he made you, I would have to say, so are you."

She couldn't argue with him and her heart suddenly felt heavy. He told her to call him if Eric contacted her and to be careful. He left as a young couple came in to the store.

That evening when Holly got home there was a message for her from Chief Sparks in Virginia. He left his number and asked her to call him. She dialed his number, got his voice mail and left a message letting him know she would call back the next day. Friday was a busy day at the store and her help had called in sick so she had to work a twelve-hour shift. When she finally got all of the paperwork done and closed up the store she was exhausted and went home and straight to bed.

Saturday morning she got up early and made herself some breakfast. When she had set the table she dialed the chief's number from the phone in the kitchen and sat down with a glass of juice at the table. After four rings a man's voice answered.

"Hello"

"Hi, I'm calling for Chief Sparks."

"May I ask who's calling?"

She told him who she was and he asked her to hold for a moment. When he came back he asked her what her business was with the chief. She told him she was returning a call when he said "I'm sorry Miss but Chief Sparks is dead." Holly froze. She couldn't speak. Her heart was thudding.

"Miss are you still there?"

"Yes. I'm sorry. I'm just a little shocked."

"Yes Ma'm. We all are."

"May I ask how he died?"

"Well, it looks like a robbery. He was hit from behind coming in the back door. His house was torn up pretty good." He asked for her name and number. She gave it to him and hung up.

It had to be a coincidence. No one knew about her conversation with the chief but the sheriff and Mr. Johnson. But this was one coincidence too many. She picked the phone back up and dialed the number the sheriff had given her. She left a message for him to call her as soon as possible, scraped her full plate into the garbage and walked back upstairs to get ready for work. The phone rang a few minutes later and she answered it on the second ring.

"Holly, are you all right?" Sheriff Butler sounded concerned.

She told him about the message left for her by the chief and her return phone call. When she was finished he was quiet for a moment.

"Damn!" he said.

"Do you think this has something to do with Eric?" she asked.

"I won't know until I talk to whoever is investigating. No matter how this turns out Holly, it wasn't your fault." She didn't answer him.

"You aren't responsible for Eric Copeland's actions. He was messed up long before he met you." Her hand was shaking as she held the receiver. "I'm going to assign someone to keep an eye on you as many shifts as I can afford. You have to be careful. Do you understand me?"

"Yes." She promised she would, thanked him, and hung up the phone. Sitting down on the bed she covered her face with her hands. She must have fallen asleep because she woke up suddenly hearing the kitchen door open and close again. Mrs. Kingsley had come back from her early morning walk at the local mall with her friends. Realizing how late it was she rushed around throwing on clothes and pulling her hair up into a ponytail as she raced out the door to her rental car. Her car had been deemed totaled and was still in the possession of the police as evidence. She would get an insurance check soon and have to buy another car, but she wasn't ready to think about that yet.

31

When she got to the store the lights were on and the OPEN sign was out. Mr. Johnson was at the front counter waiting on a customer. She rushed in and gave him an apologetic look.

"Don't worry," he said. "I've got it all under control." He smiled at her and she realized that the sheriff had probably called him. He hadn't mentioned Eric or the accident to her since he had gotten out of the hospital. She knew he didn't blame her but she couldn't help blaming herself. If Eric hadn't been a part of her life none of this would have happened. She shook her head and went back to hang up her jacket and bag. It was going to be another long day.

When she got home that evening her feet were killing her. The store had been busy all day and she had been standing on her feet for hours. She sat at the kitchen table and talked with Mrs. Kingsley about the store and how everything was going. Anything but Eric.

"I put your mail on the table in your room."

"Thank you. I'll go through it tomorrow," Holly said, taking a bite of the delicious roast. She was starving.

"Have you talked to your parents?" the older woman asked while clearing dishes from the table.

"I talked to Dad today. He wanted to know if I had looked at cars yet. I told him I've been busy. I guess I'll go tomorrow. Thank goodness the store isn't open on Sunday." She didn't know if the car dealers were either, but at least she could look around without being pressured. When Beatrice didn't respond, Holly knew what she really wanted to know was if Holly had confided in her parents about Eric.

"No," Holly said to the unanswered question. "I haven't told them anything more than that Mr. Johnson was test driving my car when he was struck by a hit and run driver in a truck," she said not looking up from her plate. "They would be hysterical and truthfully it is all I can do to keep my own emotions in check. I'm really walking on a thin wire here," she said in a tight voice.

"Well, you do what you have to but I have to say that you might be underestimating them." Beatrice wrapped up the leftovers neatly and put them away.

"I will tell them. I promise. I just need a little time." This sounded lame even to herself but she didn't care. She was emotionally drained and physically exhausted. All she wanted now was a hot bath and a warm bed. She gave her landlady a long hug and went upstairs.

On Sunday morning she made herself a cup of tea and some toast then carried it up to her room to pay some bills and get caught up on her work for school. She had slept in and Mrs. Kingsley hadn't awakened her to go to church. It was nice to have the house to herself. She was sifting through the stack of mail that had accumulated over the last several days and separating it into piles of bills and junk when she came across a manila envelope. Her name and address were on the front in a small masculine-looking print. The postmark was from Virginia. She slit open the top of the envelope with a letter opener. Inside were photocopies of some newspaper articles and a note from Chief Sparks. Her hand started shaking and she realized by the postmark he must have mailed it the day before he was killed. She brushed a tear away and read the note also written in his neat print.

> *"Holly, I came across my files on the Copeland case after you left. I have sent a full copy to Sheriff Butler. He can share with you what he sees fit. I am enclosing anything from the file that is available through archives to the general public. Upon reading the file again after so long I didn't see anything that jumped out at me, but you're welcome to it.*
> *Good luck and be careful.*

Best regards.
Chief Tom Sparks"

She put his letter down and thumbed through the pages he had sent. There were notes on the articles and pages identifying when and where they had come from. Some of them were things she had acquired on her own at the library. There were several however covering the fire at the Copeland house and the resulting investigation into the deaths of Eric's grandmother and brother. There were two with pictures of Eric flanked by his attorneys. He looked young and scared. The last copy was of an article regarding a young woman's claim to the Copeland estate. The headline read "Copeland Heir Keeps His Cash". The case had been thrown out and the entire estate had gone to Eric. There was a picture that had not copied clearly. Holly looked closely at it. It wasn't a woman at all, but a girl maybe seventeen. She had long blonde hair that was held back in a headband but it was blowing in her face. She was brushing it back with her hand when the picture was taken. Two things caught Holly's attention. First was the charm bracelet on the girl's wrist. Second was her face. Even with the slightly fuzzy picture the girl in the picture was clearly Megan Saunders.

32

Holly was starting to feel like she was in some sort of fun house where nothing was what it seemed. For the first time since all of this had happened she felt the urge to talk about it to her parents. She felt like a child who didn't know what to believe and desperately wanted someone to simply tell her what was right and what was wrong. Unfortunately the Millers had left for a barefoot cruise in the Bahamas with a group of old friends. They would be unavailable for the next five days so she was just going to have to work things out for herself. The first thing she needed to do was talk to the sheriff. She called his cell phone and left him a message to call her at home. This was the second time she had called him in two days. He returned her call while she was in the shower and left a message that he was in Virginia talking to the police about the murder of their retired police chief and would be back late that evening. He left a number at the Chesterfield police station and told her if she couldn't wait till Monday to call him there. She tucked the note from Chief Sparks back into the envelope along with the copies of the newspaper articles he had sent her. She considered waiting until tomorrow to let the sheriff know about Megan's attempt to claim the Copeland inheritance but considering he was already in Virginia he might be able to find out more about the situation. She dialed the number he left for her in his message. An operator answered and Holly asked for Sheriff Butler. She was put on hold while the sheriff was located. After almost ten minutes he answered the phone.

"Holly, are you all right?" He sounded anxious.

"Yes, Sheriff, I'm sorry to bother you but something has happened that I thought you should know about." She told him about receiving the envelope from Chief Sparks. He was quiet while she read him the letter he had enclosed with the articles. When she told him about seeing her best friend in the picture he was shocked. Then he asked, "Are you sure it's her Holly? That was several years ago."

"I'm sure Sheriff, it's Megan." She went on to tell him about Megan's hasty decision to leave school and her cold attitude toward Holly last week in the parking lot.

"Well, you were right to let me know. I can get them looking into the Saunders girl right away. This certainly does add a new twist to things." He was quiet for a moment then he said, "Holly, you know that for the time being Eric is still a suspect."

"I know Sheriff. Don't worry, I'm not going to do anything stupid." But she couldn't help hoping that the sheriff would turn up information that would clear Eric, although he probably never wanted to see her again. She said goodbye and put the phone back on its cradle when it rang again. She picked it up quickly.

"Hello," she said.

"Holly," Eric said. She didn't answer. "Holly, please, I know we're not supposed to talk but I can't stand it. Are you OK? Please just tell me that." She moved over to the small chair next to the table where the phone rested and sat down. Her whole body had begun to tremble.

"Holly," he said pleadingly. "I would never do anything to hurt you. I don't know what's going on but damn it I'm going to find out. I love you. You know that." His voice was desperate and strained.

"I know," she said in a faint voice.

"I know I can get through this if you believe in me. I can take anything. I know you went to Virginia. I can imagine what they told you, but I swear to God Holly, I didn't do it. I have lost everyone I ever loved, everyone." He was crying now. "I can't lose you."

"For your own good Eric, I can't talk to you. But you know how I feel. I couldn't change that if I wanted to." She hung up. She was crying now too. He wasn't lost to her after all. Maybe there was still some hope. She couldn't even think what that meant for Megan. She considered going to see Professor Fiennes tomorrow after work, but she knew he wouldn't tell her anything. The professor would talk to the sheriff though. He would have to. She slumped back in the chair and closed her eyes. Some of the tension that had embedded itself into her muscles over the last week started to dissipate. She hadn't let herself even think about the time she had spent with Eric over the last year. Now her mind wandered over the memories and she let the warmth and passion she felt for him wash over her. Eric had to be innocent; it was all a terrible mistake. *"Maybe not a mistake at all,"* she thought. *"What does all of this have to do with Megan? She challenged his estate and lost. But why pretend not to know who he is?"* Holly shook her head as if the physical movement could shake away all of the mental fog. She sighed and decided there was nothing she could do now and she had a lot to do to catch up on her own life before heading back to the store tomorrow morning.

33

The following week went by quickly. Holly hadn't heard anything from either the sheriff or Eric. She kept herself busy working in the store and doing her schoolwork. Mrs. Kingsley told her on Sunday morning that the sheriff would be coming for dinner that evening.

"Walter is coming too," she said almost as an afterthought. Holly wasn't fooled though. Her landlady had spent an especially long time at the beauty shop on Saturday and had gone shopping afterward to boot.

"If you make a list I can run to the store for you," Holly volunteered.

Beatrice Kingsley whipped a piece of paper out of the pocket of her apron and handed it to her. "Thank you dear," she said fussing in her spice cabinet. "Now make sure everything is fresh."

Holly assured her that she would and went upstairs to get her jacket. She was glad to have something to do. The busy week had given her plenty to keep her mind off of Eric. She worked harder at the store than she had to and came home every evening exhausted. Mr. Johnson had taken to coming in and opening up in the morning. This allowed Holly to go to class and keep up with her schoolwork. He tired easily though and couldn't unpack or put away inventory easily with his cast. His friends still came around to help but they didn't do things the way he liked so Holly convinced him to leave the stocking to her. She was grateful for the physical work as it relieved some of the anxiety she felt, but Sunday was different. Before her trip to Virginia she used to spend Sunday with Eric, exploring the wilderness around them or during inclement weather lying around his cottage alternately reading and making love. She longed for those days and wondered if they would ever have a lazy Sunday in bed again. Forcing herself to think about something else she grabbed her keys and jacket from her room and hurried downstairs and out into the crisp October air.

The market was busy with the after church crowd and Holly was happy to take her time and stroll around. She had gotten everything on Mrs. Kingsley's list and was roaming around the produce area looking for some fruit to take to work with her for lunch for the coming week when she heard a voice behind her that stopped her in her tracks.

"Every time I leave the house I expect to see you." Eric was right behind her. She paused a moment to collect herself before turning around.

"Please look at me." She turned and looked into his face. He was pale and looked like he hadn't slept in a week. She wanted to reach out and touch his face but she didn't. If she touched him she might never be able to let him go and she had to do that.

"You look terrible," she said and then quickly said, "I'm sorry. I just meant that you look tired."

"You look beautiful." He never took his eyes from her face. People were starting to stare at them. Eric's name had been in the paper when it had been confirmed that the truck that had hit Walter Johnson had been his. It was a relatively small town and it didn't take long for the stories to start circulating. Holly knew she should leave but her feet seemed rooted to the spot.

"I have to get this back to the house. Mrs. Kingsley is having a dinner tonight," she said lamely.

He nodded and looked down at the basket he carried in his hand. "My attorney thinks I might be cleared soon."

"That's great," she answered. She wanted to throw her arms around him but it wouldn't take long for that story to get back to Walter Johnson who still believed that the man who put him in the hospital was Eric Copeland.

"Can I call you? I mean, when the attorneys say I'm clear."

"Of course. There's a lot for us to talk about." She smiled and forced herself to say goodbye and walk away from him. Her legs were so shaky she didn't know how she was going to make it through the cashier's line and out the door.

When she was sitting in her rental car she closed her eyes and leaned her head back against the seat taking several deep breaths before putting her car in gear and driving home. She hoped the news about her brief conversation did not make its way back to her boss and the sheriff before dinner tonight. It was hard enough to control her feelings about Eric without being grilled at the dinner table about her encounter with him. She knew even if they decided not to press charges against him, Mr. Johnson's feelings would not change. He had never trusted or liked Eric although he had never come right out and said so to her. Walter Johnson was a straightforward guy. There was no mystery or pretense about him. Eric on the other hand was a walking mystery. He wasn't forthcoming about his past and too many accidents happened around him. No, proof or no proof, as far as Walter Johnson was concerned Eric Copeland was trouble. Period. After all that he had been through Holly couldn't flaunt a renewed affection for Eric in front of him. When and if it was possible for them to see each other again she would be as discreet as possible and hope that the truth would come to light in a way that would allow her friend and boss to see Eric the way that she did. Until then she would respect his feelings. She owed him that.

34

By the time she got back to the house Beatrice had already measured out many of the ingredients and had her recipes propped up on special recipe holders. Holly volunteered to help in the kitchen but was asked to set the table instead. She put out the good china and polished any water spots off of the silverware. She went through her collection of CDs and found some classical music that someone had given her for Christmas the year before. She tore off the plastic wrapping and put it in the player for some dinner music.

Dinner was delicious. Mrs. Kingsley had outdone herself. Both Mr. Johnson and Sheriff Butler ate second helpings as well as dessert. Holly was pouring coffee when the sheriff said he had a few things he wanted to discuss with them. She finished pouring, then sat back down in her seat and waited.

"As you all know I spent last weekend in Eric's hometown of Chesterfield." He paused but no one spoke so he continued. "I was working with the police department down there to help determine if the death of their retired police chief had any connections to the events that have been taking place up here." He took a sip of his coffee.

"While I was there I got a call from Holly informing me of a package that was sent to her by the same chief the day before he was killed." While the sheriff described his conversation with Holly, she watched as her landlady and boss shook their heads and turned to her in confusion.

"Why Holly, you never mentioned this to me," Beatrice said, obviously hurt by the seeming lack of confidence.

"Actually Bea, that was my fault," the sheriff said, coming to Holly's defense. "The contents of that envelope and letter could be considered evidence in a crime and I asked Holly to keep the information to herself and drop the envelope off at my office." Holly was relieved as her friend reached over and patted her hand.

"Well, of course, that makes perfect sense." Bea Kingsley said in the direction of Walter Johnson who had yet to utter a word. He simply leaned back in his chair, his cast arm resting on his lap and his right hand turning his coffee cup slowly in circles while he waited for what was coming next.

"The girl in the picture, Holly, is indeed your friend Megan. Her last name however is Summers, not Saunders. She filed a claim to the Copeland estate several years ago but her case was thrown out of court for lack of evidence. According to her and some letters her mother left behind when she died, Megan believes she is the product of a love affair between her mother and Eric's Uncle Patrick." He paused to take another sip of his coffee.

"That's right," Holly said. "Alice, the waitress I spoke with said that Patrick left a string of broken hearts behind when he died. It was a motorcycle accident, I believe."

"Correct. Megan's mother lived on the west side of town in a mobile home community. She worked various jobs as a waitress and she cleaned houses some until she died of ovarian cancer when Megan was twelve. It seems the girl was in and out of foster homes for years until she came upon the letters in a box of her mother's things. When the Copeland estate was in the newspapers regarding Eric's inheritance Megan promised money to an young attorney if she was awarded part of the estate and he filed a claim."

"Is the girl really Patrick's daughter?" Beatrice asked.

"Well, right now, no one knows. The letters alone aren't proof. I suppose some DNA testing could have been possible at the time, but the sitting judge's family had been long time friends of Charles and Eleanor Copeland and he wasn't about to drag their name through the mud again. Frankly, the girl never had a chance. There's a rumor that one of the maids working at the Copeland house witnessed an angry exchange between the girl and Eleanor on the front steps of the house several months before the fire. Eleanor apparently sent her packing in a not so kind way." The sheriff shook his head and looked tired.

"Megan told me her mother lived in Florida," Holly said. "I don't understand why she kept all this a secret. Maybe I could have helped."

Walter spoke for the first time since the topic had been raised. "So who started the fire the night that the grandmother and brother were killed?" Holly looked at him in surprise. A connection between Megan and the fire hadn't even occurred to her.

"That's a good question. Both the current police chief in Chesterfield and I would like to talk to the girl on that subject among others, but she seems to have disappeared."

Holly interjected, "She told me she was going to take care of her mother, but that was a lie too. Did you talk to Professor Fiennes at the college? He might have some idea."

"I left a message for him on Thursday, and I dropped by on Friday when I didn't hear from him. He wasn't there and the couple of people I talked to hadn't seen him."

Holly felt the hairs on her arms and the back of her neck rise.

"What about the Copeland boy?" Walter asked.

"Well, his alibi holds water as far as you're concerned. His lawyers are onto the connection with the Summers girl so for now he's clear. His claim is that his truck was stolen, used in the crash and returned. No doubt they will be pointing the finger at Megan. Although I don't know how the girl could have known where Holly was headed and why."

"Because I told her," Holly said quietly. "I lied to Mr. Johnson about which town I was going to and I didn't want to leave without someone knowing where I was. I told her what I was doing and when I was leaving. She didn't know I was leaving early though." Holly put her hands over her face. How could she have been so stupid? If Megan had been watching Eric then she would have known about his truck. Anyone could get in and out of his place easily if they wanted to.

"Oh dear, none of this is your fault." Beatrice comforted her. "I must say it is an awful mess. To think I had that girl here for dinner in my home and her capable of such things."

"Well, at the moment we don't have anything to tie Megan to the truck, but we will be checking the evidence that was collected and looking at it with fresh eyes," said Sheriff Butler.

"Sheriff, is it likely that the person that hit my car with the truck could have been injured also?"

"Yes, I suppose it's possible. Why?" Holly related the details of her encounter with Megan at her apartment to him, including the young man with the injuries driving the car.

"Megan's students worshiped her. She used to joke that she could get them to do anything if she wanted to."

The sheriff had taken out the notebook that went everywhere with him and made notes about Holly's description of the man and the car. When he was done he put the notebook away and changed the subject. "I suppose as far as you're concerned Holly, Eric is off the hook. Again."

"Humph," Walter commented.

"But I must caution you that until we have answers, you need to be careful."

"Don't worry Sheriff, all of you in fact. I'm not rushing into anything. I have a lot of thinking to do." They all smiled at her good sense but her heart was pounding. She longed to be away from the table so she could go to her room and digest all that she had heard. Eric was free. He wasn't a suspect. Relief flooded her. He had been through so much, lost so much. At last they could talk about his past. It wouldn't be this dark secret between them.

It was late by the time the men left and the dishes were all washed and put away. Mrs. Kingsley settled herself in the chair by the kitchen fire. Holly told her goodnight and slipped off to take a hot bath. For the first time in two weeks she went to bed with a hopeful heart.

35

Walter Johnson's wrist was still in a cast but other than that he seemed to be past the worst of his injuries. He had reverted to his usual work schedule while relying on Holly for help with anything that required two hands. She knew he was itching to take that cast off himself and get back to his planes. She also returned to a somewhat normal schedule except for the time she used to spend with Eric and Megan. She had spoken to Eric on the phone twice that week and they were planning on having dinner at his house on Saturday evening. He had opened up to her somewhat about his family. She knew most of the story already and hesitated to push him because she now understood how painful the loss was. He had confided in her that he blamed himself for not being there to save his brother and grandmother the night they died. He had been so grief-stricken about their deaths that for a while the investigation that seemed to be focused on him didn't seem real. They marveled at Megan's involvement in the whole thing and wondered how much of what had happened was caused by her.

The sheriff stopped by the store on Thursday afternoon and motioned for Holly to follow him to the back room where Walter was in his office. She finished ringing up the customer she was helping and hurried back through the swinging door. She entered the small office to find the sheriff sitting in the chair opposite her boss' desk with his hat in his hand and his head bent. They were obviously waiting for her.

"Matt's got something he wants to tell you Holly. I'll just go keep an eye out front." Walter left, closing the door behind him. Trying not to appear panicked she took her boss' chair because it was the only other place to sit in the small office.

"I'll get right to it Holly. Professor Fiennes was found in his car about a half hour south of here at a rest stop."

"He's dead?" she asked, but she knew already.

"Yes. He's dead. The county has the car and is processing it to see if he died in the car or somewhere else."

"What does this mean? Do you think Megan had something to do with it?"

"Well, Holly, she certainly is a person of interest to us right now on a lot of fronts. I can't say without more information whether she was directly involved in this or not. I do want you to be very careful though. We have reason to believe that Megan has left the state. There's no way to know for sure where she is until we physically locate her, so until then we all have to be on our guard." He studied her for a moment and then went on. "She obviously had some plan that included Eric but we don't know what it is. He claims to know nothing about her past or her claim to be his cousin, which may or may not be true." Holly could understand the sheriff's skepticism but it still irritated her. "She may still harbor some resentment toward you though so you need to be careful, as does Eric, until we are able to question her."

"So you're saying Eric is no longer considered a suspect at all?"

"Until we have the truth I won't absolutely rule anyone out, but for now we are not focusing on Eric for any of the open cases we have." He stood up and put on his hat. "You still have my number. Call if you need me or hear anything."

She nodded and gave him a weak smile. She wanted him to leave so she could sit alone for a moment and process what she had just been told. She was relieved that evidence was moving the focus of attention from Eric, but the thought of Megan doing any of these things made her feel physically sick. Her mind raced over all of the times they had spent together and she searched her memory for any sign that she had missed. She had truly thought they were friends. Megan had always been aloof but Holly hadn't had room in her life for a more intimate or demanding friendship. She had been spending so much time with Eric over the last year that the weekly visits with Megan were all she really wanted. Her head was swimming. Was Megan the one who sabotaged her bike that day? She thought about the figure she had seen in the fading light. Maybe. But what about the allergic reaction? She physically shook her head trying to clear away all of the cobwebs that kept appearing.

"You all right?" The sound of Walter Johnson's voice in the doorway startled her.

"I'm fine. Confused, but fine." She stood up to leave then sat back down again. She asked him, "How could I be so wrong about someone? She seemed so normal."

He took the chair across from his desk that the sheriff had recently vacated and shook his head. "I wish I could tell you. I didn't do any better myself. I have been blaming that boyfriend of yours from day one." He looked and sounded apologetic. The buzzer sounded letting them know that someone had entered the store and they both gratefully took the opportunity to focus on something else. Holly left the office in front of him and went to help the customer.

36

Holly's parents having just arrived home from their cruise had been informed briefly about the events that had transpired over the last few weeks. They were at first angry and upset at being kept in the dark, but their feelings soon gave way to anxiety over their daughter's situation. They were both flying in for the weekend to try to convince themselves that Holly was OK and to attempt to persuade her to come home with them.

The arrival of guests gave Mrs. Kingsley a much-needed diversion. She spent most of Thursday bustling around the already spotless house tidying up. Holly went to the store with a long list of groceries that were needed to prepare the various meals her landlady had planned for her parents' visit. Beatrice had never shown any fear about the ongoing situation to Holly but the worry and the strain was showing in her face. She seemed older lately and she was quieter than usual. Holly's insides twisted when she thought of this. Even though she knew she wasn't to blame for any of the terrible things that had happened she was the one who had introduced Megan into the lives of two people she cared so much for.

After putting the groceries away and asking if there was anything else she could do to help, Holly quickly went upstairs and changed into clean jeans and a sweater. She was meeting Eric for a drink and she was late already.

When she walked in Eric was already seated at a table near the rear of the bar by the pool table. There were four guys playing pool and drinking beer. She noticed the small stack of quarters on the side of the pool table and looked around the room. It was early in the evening and there weren't many people in the bar.

"I guess we're up next?" she inquired as he stood up out of his chair and kissed her.

"You guessed right. I thought it would be fun. We haven't played in a while. Of course it will be us against two of them if they want to keep playing."

He looked great. The deep purple shirt he had on was a great color for him. She had a sudden urge to be somewhere else, anywhere else alone with him. She realized he had caught her staring at him and she blushed. He smiled and then waved at the barman to bring two drinks, a replacement for him and one for her.

"How long have you been here?" she asked.

"Long enough to know we are going to clean those guys' clocks if they ever manage to finish a game." He tossed a piece of popcorn into his mouth and raised his eyebrows at her in a mischievous fashion.

"Did you hear about the professor at the college?" she asked him quietly.

"Yep," he said.

"It's terrible. I just spoke to him last week. I can't imagine what his family must be going through." She looked up at him and found him staring at her.

"You talked to him last week? I didn't even know you knew him." He looked at her intently.

"I was looking for Megan last week after class. He was in the office and we talked for a few minutes."

"What did he say?" He asked this in a casual manner but he was watching her closely.

She told him about her encounter with the professor and her subsequent run-in with Megan in the parking lot of her apartment.

"That girl was a real pain," he said.

"Was? That's more confident than I feel." She laughed at his phrasing. "She could still be one." He didn't answer this. Then she got serious. "I keep hoping that something will happen and this will all turn out to be a big mistake."

He shook his head and smiled at her. "Life isn't neat and clean Holly. It's messy and complicated." She knew he was referring to his own painful past. She saw one of the pool players scratch on his attempt to sink the eight ball and she grabbed the opportunity to change the subject.

"Looks like we're up," she said and hopped out of her chair. Not even a month ago she would have jumped on Eric's sad reference to his past and offered comfort, but things had changed; she had changed. The horrifying experiences of the last few weeks had raised some self-protective walls in her character. Instead she left him to rack the balls as she busied herself with looking for a straight cue stick.

The four men who had been playing before them relinquished the table so it was just the two of them playing. Eric, who seemed to be good at everything, was a natural at pool. He broke, sinking three balls, two of them stripes and the game was on. Holly's dad had bought a table and put it in their finished basement when she was little. She'd been playing with him since she could see over the side of the table. Eric had a head start on her but she soon caught up. The first game went quickly with Eric dropping his last two balls and the eight ball in one turn. The second game lasted longer with Holly continuing to hide the cue ball in places that left him no shot. She beat him soundly and they ordered another round of drinks to start their tie-breaking game. The bar was starting to fill up now and another couple put their quarters on the table. Holly's shot on the eight ball was harder than she had intended. The cue ball followed too closely and went in the hole right after the black eight ball. Eric did a little victory dance and she shook her head at him.

"You can't possibly feel good about winning like that," she said, pretending to be irritated.

"I will take any win you care to give me," he said with exaggerated modesty. She rolled her eyes and went back to their table.

She was starting to feel tipsy now and suggested they order an appetizer before she got too drunk. He gave her a suggestive eyebrow wiggle and she shook her head at him.

"Oh no. Not tonight. My parents are coming in early tomorrow morning and I need to be home when they get there."

He gave her a pathetic look and then shrugged his shoulders.

"I'll see you at dinner tomorrow won't I?" she said. She had left the invitation on his voice mail and he hadn't called back to confirm.

"Not exactly." He was not looking at her.

"Why not exactly?" she asked. The old Holly would have been upset and disappointed. The new Holly had her arms crossed and was giving him a very unpleasant look. She felt empowered somehow. For a while she had lived with the belief that he was out of her life for good and although she had been unhappy she had survived. Now she knew that if she and Eric couldn't make it work she would be OK. Also the mystery was gone. She knew his secret. She had come face to face with the tragedies in his past and the knowledge somehow gave her strength.

"I am meeting the gallery owner at a show for another artist Friday so we can discuss how best to display my work."

Even though she knew if she called the gallery there would in fact be a show on Friday night she was sure he was using it as an excuse. She didn't push it though. If he didn't want to come to dinner with her and her family she wouldn't press him.

To his statement she just shrugged and told him to order something for them to eat, then she dug some quarters out of her purse and headed for the jukebox. When she returned he was toying with his glass.

"You seem different," he said.

"I am different," she replied looking right at him.

He nodded his head as if he understood. Then reaching over and squeezing her hand he said, "I love you."

"I know," she said. She loved him too but she didn't say so. She had uttered those words plenty of times in the past but tonight she left them unsaid. She had told the sheriff and her friends that she would be careful and she intended to be. But it wasn't her life she feared for with Eric, it was her heart she was protecting.

They spent the next hour eating and talking about his show and which paintings he would display. Before all of the recent distressing events had happened Holly had put in her resume to every reputable publisher on the east coast. Just before the trip to Chesterfield she had accepted an offer and was looking forward to a starting a job at a big name publishing house in New York City next year. They spoke easily about their plans and were careful not to mention her trip to Virginia or anything that had transpired since. Both of them had agreed they needed time away from the stress of these events to heal their relationship. For the first time Holly started to understand his aversion to conversation about the past. She also knew that he wasn't coming to dinner because even though he knew no one would push him about Chesterfield or Megan Summers it would be on everyone's mind. She understood him better now but she didn't feel the same need to comfort him or to ease his mind about things. She would be careful from now on. Even with the people she loved. Eric was right; life wasn't neat and clean, it was messy and sometimes dangerous.

It was almost eleven when he walked her out to her rental car and kissed her goodnight. His kiss was gentle but there was an underlying passion in it.

"When do you get rid of this thing?" he said opening the door for her.

"Hopefully this weekend. That's why my parents are coming in so early. Dad wants to go car shopping tomorrow."

"Well, have fun. I'll call you." He stood back and raised his hand in a friendly wave.

She waved back and drove away. She was glad she hadn't gone home with him. She was anxious to put some distance between the recent events and their relationship before it reached the intensity that it had before. She yawned and looked in the rearview mirror. She watched him get smaller then she turned the corner and lost sight of him altogether.

37

Saturday morning came very early. When Holly opened her eyes the light sent sharp pains through her aching head. She felt around the bedside table for the water glass she had put there last night and finding it washed some of the sawdust out of her mouth. *"When will I learn?"* she groaned. Several aspirin and a hot shower later she was padding barefoot down the stairs to the kitchen where the contents of pots and pans were putting out delicious smells. She knew she should have gotten up earlier and volunteered to help Mrs. Kingsley but she was too hung over and besides, Bea Kingsley rarely tolerated anyone's help when she was preparing a meal for company.

"Your parents called while you were in the shower. They were at the airport picking up their luggage. I expect they will be here in a half hour or so." The older woman passed on this information as she bustled around the kitchen setting out plates and napkins. Holly poured herself a cup of juice and made a cup of tea for her landlady.

"Here, sit for a minute and drink this," Holly urged. "Everything is clearly ready and you don't want to be all hot and bothered when they get here." Mrs. Kingsley did sit down with Holly but not without mumbling something about never being hot and bothered about anything in her life. Bea sipped her tea and tucked a few stray gray hairs back into place.

"Dad and I are going to look at new cars this afternoon. If you like I can invite Mom along and you could get in a little nap," Holly offered.

"Goodness Holly! I'm not an invalid and I don't need a nap. Besides I was going to take your mother over to that Christmas craft show that was advertised in the paper."

"She'll love that," Holly said smiling. "Of course she'll have to buy another suitcase to take home everything she buys." They both laughed at this.

The reunion with her parents was less stressful than she had thought it was going to be. They ate a large breakfast and then her father went off to find Walter Johnson. He promised to be back by noon to go car shopping with Holly. Elizabeth and Holly urged Mrs. Kingsley to sit a while in her chair by the fire and talk to them while they did dishes. She refused however, saying she had some things to do upstairs and left Holly and her mother alone. They took turns washing and drying and Holly filled her mother in on the details of the past few weeks that she had withheld over the phone. After a long silence Elizabeth put down her dishtowel and with tears in her eyes she begged Holly to return home with them. Holly had known her mother would be worried for her but she had not expected the fear and pain in her mother's face. In fact she could never in her life remember her mother looking so frightened.

"I'm OK Mom," she said uselessly. The words sounded stupid even to her.

"Holly, that crazy girl is killing people. She killed a police chief for crying out loud. You can't stay here and wait for her to come after you." Elizabeth's voice was shaky. Holly was sure she was on the verge of tears.

"The police are looking for her as we speak, Mom. They think she may be in Florida where her grandmother lives. She wouldn't dare come back here now that she's been exposed," she reasoned feebly.

"She's crazy Holly. Crazy people don't think rationally. What if she blames you for all her problems? You're in danger here." Tears slid down her mother's lovely face.

"If she's determined to get me Mom, I would be in danger even at home. Megan knows where you live. But I don't believe she will come after me. Not now. I think she's a little twisted but I don't think she's suicidal."

Her mother was looking at her. She was staring at her as if seeing her for the first time. "You've changed somehow. You were always independent, but something is different," her mother whispered, getting her emotions under control. Holly handed her a tissue.

"I guess I have in some ways. I'm certainly not the same naïve girl that moved here last year. I accept what has happened but I won't let it ruin my life or make me afraid to live. And I know you and Dad are worried about me, but I'm not about to run home and hide."

Elizabeth Miller reached over and hugged her daughter who was turning out to be a very strong and intelligent woman.

38

Her father returned at noon as promised and together they set out in search of a car to replace Holly's beloved Jetta. Her father didn't require nearly the explanations her mother had this morning and Holly assumed he had already been brought up to date by his friend. They talked about the recent events briefly, then the subject quickly turned to the task at hand and they drove on companionably discussing the merits of this car over that one. The money from the insurance company combined with what she had saved would put a sizeable down payment on a nice car and Holly eventually decided on a new Honda Accord. They picked out colors, interiors, and options and Holly was starting to get excited. The salesman was guiding them back to the finance department so Holly could discuss pay arrangements on the balance when her father cleared his throat and said that wouldn't be necessary.

"Your mother and I discussed it and decided since you managed to get a scholarship to school and there is still money left in your college fund we would cover the balance of the car. There will still be some left over later to help with a down payment should you ever take a real job and decide to buy a place of your own." His face flushed a little and he was clearly embarrassed at admitting that he had saved so much for his only child. Holly flung her arms around him and hugged him with tears in her eyes. "It's not about the car Dad," she said hoarsely.

"I know baby. I know." He hugged her back, thankful that that crazy girl hadn't managed to hurt his precious daughter.

The salesman busied himself straightening brochures while father and daughter took a moment to gather themselves.

And after another twenty minutes, a few signatures, and a personal check from Joe Miller, they were on their way home to share the good news. Her car would be delivered in a week and she couldn't wait to take it for a drive.

They spent the rest of the weekend relaxing and getting caught up. Megan Summers' name was deliberately avoided by all. Dinner Saturday night was wonderful as usual. Walter joined them and sat at the head of the table opposite Bea. He opened the wine and said grace as if he had been playing host to her hostess for years. Afterward Holly finished the dishes in the kitchen while everyone else went to the front room to relax. She noticed that no one had asked where Eric was or expressed disappointment that he wasn't there. Any reminder of the terrible events of the last few weeks would have shattered the light mood of the evening. She noticed that even Mr. Johnson had abandoned his rolled up shirtsleeves and opted for a sweater that covered his cast. She laughed to herself about how easily they had all chosen denial and escape over reality. The phone rang and she picked it up.

"Hi," Eric said.

"Hi yourself. How's the show going?" she asked, forcing herself to sound friendly and carefree. She refused to let him think she was disappointed that he wasn't there.

"Great. If you like modern finger paintings." He sounded bored.

"Ouch. Feeling a little bitchy?" she chided. Eric had never criticized other artists' work before.

"I know. That was petty. But I'm bored and I miss you," he said.

She swallowed the urge to tell him how much she missed him too and simply said, "Thanks. Me too." They talked for a few more minutes while she did dishes and when it was clear he wasn't going to talk her into sneaking away and meeting him at his place later they hung up. She really did long to feel him next to her and to wake up in his bed with the smell of fresh coffee brewing but that would all come. She had always worked the hardest at their relationship and she felt it was his turn to make an effort. He needed to be more open and forthcoming if they were going to have any kind of a future and he wasn't going to open up to her if he didn't have to. So torture seemed the only option. She smiled to herself as she rubbed water spots off of the wine glasses.

39

The rest of the visit with her parents seemed to fly by. They continued to try to talk her into moving back home for a while, but eventually they gave up and left amidst promises that she would be home in a few weeks for Thanksgiving. Holly hadn't reintroduced the topic of traveling home with her parents for the holiday to Eric. Not because she wanted to avoid an argument as she had done in the past, but because she thought the time apart might have enough impact on him that he might volunteer to go home with her for Christmas. The Thanksgiving invitation had been extended to Mrs. Kingsley and Walter Johnson as well but he would not leave the store and she would not leave him. This was not said in so many words but that's what it boiled down to. Holly was excited to see the relationship bloom between these two people that she cared so much for. Mrs. Kingsley no longer used Holly as an excuse to stop by the store with food and Walter showed up for dinner at least one night a week. He was always dressed in a nice shirt and jacket and Holly had noticed that Bea was paying extra attention to which dress she wore and having her hair set regularly at the salon in town.

The week after her parents left Holly waited anxiously for the delivery of her new car. She couldn't wait to hand over the keys to the rental she had been driving and take her first long drive in her new baby. Eric teased her about her excitement but she ignored him and commented that he couldn't possibly understand what she meant since he insisted on driving around in that old car of his or that equally bad truck. There was a moment of silence when she mentioned the truck. The accident that had involved Eric's truck and almost killed her boss was still a sensitive spot for everyone. Holly both looked forward to and dreaded the day when the police located Megan and their questions would all be answered. She didn't look forward to facing her old friend. Well, what she had thought was a friend anyhow. It still hurt to think that all of the time they had spent laughing and talking together may have been just another way for Megan to keep tabs on Eric. Having his name cleared once and for all of any connection to the terrible events in Virginia and here in Camden would be worth it though. She couldn't deny that on some level those terrible days of believing that Eric had killed his brother and grandmother and had tried to kill her had left her with a very cautious attitude toward him. Not just him, everyone. She was doubting her own judgment, and by the way she had misjudged Megan she was right to. She had definitely learned a lesson about trusting people too easily.

"Are you going to ignore me all night?" Eric asked bringing her out of her thoughts and back to the table at Rosa's where she had met him for dinner. She had asked him not to order ahead and he was waiting for her to make up her mind.

"Sorry, just daydreaming I guess."

"Well could you pause just long enough to order because I'm starving." She detected a note of aggravation in his voice. She wondered if he was irritated that she had deviated from their normal routine yet again by telling him she didn't want to share a pizza. Actually, she had. It felt good to express a little independence. She laughed at this a little. They were at the same restaurant after all. She thought that having the power to upset him by changing a routine - that if she remembered correctly, he had established - felt good.

"Now you're laughing at me?"

"You must be hungry." She dismissed his question, reached over and held his hand. "You're awfully cranky." She gave him her sweetest smile and he seemed to relax. He motioned to the waitress that they were ready and she ordered a salad and a glass of wine and he ordered a beer and some pasta. They talked companionably about her new car, his paintings - anything but recent events. After dinner he kissed her warmly outside the front door of Rosa's and then went to his car while she walked the short distance back to the store. She felt happy and content. Their relationship was mending but on different terms. Her terms, to be exact. She wasn't yet ready to invite the kind of intimacy she had once wanted from him. The awful events of the last few weeks had left her feeling very guarded, but she was feeling more confident every day and maybe after a break from each other over the holidays they would be able to put it all behind them. She was looking forward to getting out of Camden for a few days as well. She longed to see her old friends. For the past year she had been so involved that she had put her life and friends in the Midwest on a back burner to focus all of her attention on Eric. Now she wanted to go home, sleep in her room again, and hang out with her college friends, the ones that hadn't moved away to pursue careers or husbands or both.

Her car had arrived a week late but it hadn't mattered because when she finally sat in it for the first time she thought she would never get out. She loved everything about it from the smell of the new leather seats to the sound system as she closed her eyes and listened to her favorite CD. She drove everywhere. When it came time to pack for her trip home Holly was depressed about having to leave her car behind.

Eric had been especially moody during the past week and she wondered if it was because she hadn't reissued the invitation to come home with her that he had been so quick to turn down before her trip to Virginia. She had ignored all of his pouting and gone out of her way to be cheerful. She hadn't asked him what he was going to do for the holiday and she was pretty sure this had irritated him as well. She spent Tuesday night at his cottage and they made dinner, built a fire and played Scrabble in front of the fireplace. She loved being tucked away here with him. And she really was going to miss him while she was gone. She told him this just before they fell asleep. Their lovemaking had been long and tender and she wanted him to know how much she cared for him. He had looked in her eyes for a long time and finally said, "I love you Holly. I have lost everyone in my life that I have ever loved and I won't lose you.

Do you understand me?" He was breathing hard and he was very intense. She was unprepared for this declaration and could do nothing but nod her head and give him some feeble reassurance that she wasn't planning on going anywhere.

She watched him as he slept, wishing he were getting on that plane with her. But she knew it was too early. Too soon to expect him to let down all of the walls he had put up between him and the world that had treated him so cruelly. She wasn't going to ask him again either. She had decided to go out and live her life normally and if he wanted to be with her he would have to come too; otherwise she would leave him behind. It was a hard decision. "Tough love" they called it. Whatever it was she knew she couldn't hide away in his cottage in the woods with him forever.

He drove her to the airport in her new car and kissed her goodbye at the baggage check area as increased security measures since 9/11 meant he couldn't go to the boarding area and wait with her. He was going to park her car at his place and return to the airport on Sunday to pick her up.

When she stepped off the plane at the Dayton airport, Holly was very excited. She had been gone for a year and was suddenly very homesick. Her mother was waiting for her at a prearranged spot and they quickly collected her bags and loaded them into her mother's Volvo station wagon.

"Mom, you don't have to drag me and my soccer friends around everywhere anymore, why don't you get something a little uh, cooler, to drive?"

"I love this car," Elizabeth claimed looking a little hurt. "Besides, you know I am always hauling shrubs and rocks back from various nurseries, how could I do that in some little sports car?"

"You're right. I give. I just want you to have some fun," Holly said, smiling at her beautiful mother.

"Who says I'm not having fun?" Elizabeth asked. "Here's some fun for you; the girls and I are going to Vegas in two weeks." Her mother's "girls" were her pink poker friends. They had a standing game the second Saturday of every month.

The game rotated from house to house and they all brought an hors d'oeuvre and a bottle of wine. Sometimes they had specialty drink nights. Margarita night was a favorite but they tried to keep the drinking to a minimum and keep the game and the companionship at the top of the agenda.

"That's great!" Holly said, truly excited for her mother. "You guys have been talking about this for a long time."

"Too long. Anyway, about you. I know we didn't talk about it at dinner a few weeks ago but what's going on with you and Eric? Has that cooled off?" There was nothing in her mother's voice to give Holly the impression that she was happy about a possible break between her daughter and her boyfriend but somehow Holly knew that it was exactly what Elizabeth wanted.

"Not a cool down so much as both of us being in a prolonged state of shock over the accident and Megan's involvement," Holly answered. "I was also shocked about Eric's family history. It's just taking longer to adjust for me than it is for him; after all, what happened to his brother and grandmother was not news to him. He didn't really know Megan all that well either. The whole thing is just so awful. Eric put up these walls years ago as a buffer between him and all the terrible things that happened, while I just took it right between the eyes." Holly was twisting the strap to her satchel around her finger.

"I'm so sorry for what you have gone through honey. I wish you would come home for a while and let your father and I help you through all of this," Elizabeth said with tears in her eyes. Holly reached over and put her hand over her mother's.

"I know you do, but I love Eric, and even though I am not willing to go back to things the way they were before all of this happened I do want to see if there is some way we can go forward."

Elizabeth agreed to drop the subject. Privately she was amazed at her daughter's strength. Holly had been through so much and yet she refused to compromise her plans or her lifestyle. The two women spent the remainder of the drive home chatting about her parents' upcoming trip, local gossip, the budding relationship between Walter and Bea - anything but Eric Copeland.

40

The Thanksgiving dinner she and her mother prepared was delicious. Holly spent hours with her aunts and uncles and cousins. They asked if she was seeing anyone special and she knew that her parents had kept her relationship and the events that had happened recently in Camden to themselves. They had always protected Holly's privacy when she was growing up and she was very grateful to them now. Eric had called both Wednesday and Thursday nights and she noted that while he made an effort to ask about her family and friends he sounded distracted. Both times he told her he loved her before he hung up and she knew that he did. She hoped it was enough to push him out of his shell a little.

She had planned outings with friends for both Friday and Saturday nights and was spending the days with her parents. She tried several times over the weekend to reach Eric at the cabin and on his cell phone but he hadn't answered. She refused to worry about it though; he was probably holed up in his studio. If anything had gone wrong someone would have called her. She knew for a fact that the sheriff's people were still keeping an eye on Eric. As long as Megan was still free they would be in some danger. Sheriff Butler had phoned her before she left to say that because the death of the chief in Virginia was likely related to the death of the professor and the attempt on Mr. Johnson that the FBI was taking an interest in the case. He had warned her that they would probably want to talk to her when she got back to town. This information had not been shared with her parents. She didn't want them to spend the entire holiday worrying about her safety.

The weekend passed quickly and on Sunday morning her phone rang with Eric's distinctive ring. He had downloaded "People Are Strange" by the *Doors* to her phone so she would know it was he calling. She smiled at his twisted sense of humor and answered.

"I was starting to worry about you," she said.

"I'm sorry; I have been painting like a mad man. I spent the last two nights on the couch in the studio." She knew he didn't take his cell phone to the studio so he wouldn't be bothered when he was working but she still thought this excuse was a little weak. She pretended not to care though. If he wanted to pout because she hadn't stayed home with him she wasn't going to give him any attention over it.

"Well it sounds like you're really making progress," she said brightly. "I on the other hand, have done nothing but eat, shop, and hang out."

"I can't wait to see you tonight. You are staying with me aren't you?" He sounded lonely.

"Of course. Mrs. Kingsley isn't expecting me back until tomorrow morning." She was looking forward to seeing him. Her trip home to Ohio had been refreshing but she had made a life for herself in Camden, at least for now, and she was happy there. Next summer she would start working a job in her field. She would have to start in an entry-level position but eventually she wanted to be an editor. She also wanted to write. Maybe just articles and the occasional column at first, but whatever she did for a living she would always write. She wondered if when she finally did leave Camden and pursue a career somewhere else if Eric would come with her. That thought used to worry her. In fact she had not been as aggressive with her studies over the last year because she felt that somehow leaving Camden behind meant leaving Eric behind, but she didn't worry about that now. She loved him, but she wouldn't give up any more of herself for him.

The flight east was bumpy and Holly spent most of the trip gripping the armrest of her seat. Why hadn't she driven her new car home? She knew why but when you're facing the possibility of a fiery plane crash logging miles on a new car doesn't sound like that big of a deal. The turbulence lasted almost the entire flight. By the time the plane was on the ground her nerves were shot. All she wanted to do was get her luggage and get out of the airport. Eric was standing exactly where he said he would be and when he saw her he waved and gave her a big smile. She waved back and tried to forget the last few hours.

"How was the flight?" he asked, taking her carry-on from her and hugging her with his other arm.

"A little like spending two and a half hours in a martini shaker," she said with a weary smile.

"Poor baby. Let's get out of here." He grabbed her hand, gave it a squeeze and led her to the baggage claim.

They were loading her bags into the trunk of her new Honda when he told her the suitcases felt twice as heavy as they had when he had driven her to the airport last week.

"It's not funny," she said. "They charged me an overage fee because they are so heavy."

"What have you got in here anyway, dumbbells?" He was actually breathing a little heavily carrying, pulling, and shoving her luggage out of the airport and into the car. She laughed and pretended to be insulted.

"That trunk represents many hours of bonding with my family and friends." He gave her a funny look and she continued. "Women bond best at the mall or the salon. So that's where we went." She stuck out a hand and wiggled her pink-tipped nails at him. He kissed her hand and then pulled her over and kissed her mouth.

"Well, I hope you know where everything is in those bags because I hate to have to unload the whole lot tonight and put them back in tomorrow morning."

"Very funny. Everything I need is either at your place already or in that lovely little carry-on I found in a leather shop back home." They held hands and talked while he drove them back to Camden. She told him all about her trip and her friends. He listened as she talked and asked questions here and there. She noticed that he seemed more interested in her life in Ohio than he had ever been before. She leaned her head back and sighed. The tension in her neck and back from the plane trip was starting to ease up and she felt glad to be home. She was also starting to feel a little hopeful that Eric was coming out of his shell.

They called Rosa's from the car on the way home and ordered a pizza. They picked up the pizza and took it to Eric's house. Holly was starving and was half way through her first piece before Eric could get back to the little coffee table in front of the fireplace with their drinks.

After eating two thirds of a large pizza they pushed the table out of the way and stretched out on the big furry rug. They had bought this rug together after seeing a movie where a couple had made love on one just like it. This spot had been the scene of many evenings of passion for them and as they snuggled under a blanket in front of the blazing fire Holly started to feel warm in all the right places. Eric smelled good and his arms were strong and muscular. He made a habit of cutting all of the firewood himself and Holly was always impressed and more than a little turned on by his muscular arms and back. The hours spent in the studio painting left him stiff and achy so he spent most of the time he wasn't working out hiking, biking and climbing around the hills and woods of Camden. As she ran a hand down his broad chest she was thankful that he was so devoted to exercise.

He had his arms behind his head and was staring at her with raw desire in his eyes. His steady gaze gave her butterflies in her stomach and other similar feelings a little lower. She held his stare as she ran her hand slowly down his chest, over his flat stomach, and finally to the place she was looking for. He closed his eyes and groaned. She reached up and traced a nipple with her finger and then gently placed her lips on his. He wrapped both arms around her and pulled her across his body until she was resting on her back and he was leaning over her. His kisses were long and passionate while he held her close to him with his left arm and explored her body with his right. He lowered his head over her breasts and kissed them taking her nipple into his mouth while his fingers probed and massaged her nearly to insanity. When she thought she couldn't stand it anymore he positioned himself over top of her separating her long lovely legs with his own strong ones. He held himself over her for a moment staring into her pleading eyes and held her ravaged gaze as he thrust himself deep inside her. They moved together eyes locked until she cried out as wave after wave of ecstasy overtook her. He continued his deep rhythmic motion and she was gasping and gripping his back with her fingers and manicured nails when he threw his head back and moaned. They collapsed on the tousled blankets and panted, still tangled up in each other's arms and legs. The fire was hot and they lay quietly in front of it for a long time before eventually falling asleep.

41

The air was cold and Holly could see her breath as she dragged her suitcase out of the trunk of the car and up the back steps to the kitchen door at Sixteen Terwilliger Place. The sun was just starting to warm a hole in the frost pattern on the top of her new car and for the first time in weeks she felt happy and optimistic. She was balancing her luggage against her leg on the top step and fumbling for her door key when the door opened, startling her. She stumbled into the warm kitchen smelling the delicious aroma of sausages and eggs. Mrs. Kingsley left her to manage her bags herself and hustled back to her stove where her welcome home meal was sizzling and popping. Holly parked her suitcases in the corner by the fireplace and hung her coat on one of the sturdy hooks by the door.

"Smells delicious," she said, giving her landlady a quick hug hello.

"Your mother called to make sure you got home OK."

"I'll call her after breakfast," Holly said ducking into the little powder room past the pantry to wash her hands. She emerged a few minutes later and began to enquire about how the holiday had gone for her and Mr. Johnson. Holly was tickled as she listened to Beatrice tell her about the wonderful dinner they had made together. Holly noticed that the older woman had begun referring to herself and Walter as "we" as in "We had a lovely dinner." And later, "We sat in the front room and watched a television program," Beatrice said, responding to Holly's hug with a quick pat on the arm so as not to take her eye off of her stove.

The conversation soon turned to her own holiday and Holly went about setting the table and telling her friend about her trip and all of their diversions.

"I can see the trip home was good for you," Beatrice said as she set a platter filled with eggs and sausages on the table. Holly poured juice and coffee for both of them. She was putting the coffee pot back when she noticed that Bea was putting an extra plate at the table

"Are we expecting company?" Holly couldn't help smiling and wiggling her eyebrows at the woman she had come to love like a grandmother.

"Don't be silly. I invited Walter to breakfast. He's driving me to the store today. My car has been acting up and he wants to look at it this afternoon," she said, dismissing Holly with an exasperated hand wave. Holly didn't have time to respond further because there was a quick rap at the door and then Walter Johnson let himself in saying a hello as he hung his hat and coat on the hook next to her own.

Holly poured him a cup of coffee while she related for a second time the events of her few days at home. She left out most of the details about shopping, instead telling him about the small wood shop her father had put into the basement to spend more time with his new hobby of building small furniture pieces. Walter was interested and asked her several questions about which saw her father had bought and whether he had taken his advice about installing a small air compressor.

The trio ate breakfast together at the big table in the kitchen. The fireplace put out ample heat to have Holly and Walter shrug out of their sweaters. They both complimented Bea on the wonderful breakfast. Holly started to clear the dishes but Bea interrupted her and told her to go on and get ready for work.

"We'll take care of these," Beatrice said taking the plate from Holly and handing it to Walter. He nodded as if he had been clearing and washing dishes in this kitchen for years. Holly restrained a grin and pecked the older woman on the cheek before dragging her bag down the hall and up the stairs.

After her shift at the store Holly was sitting on the sofa in the front room reading a book her mother had given her when there was a knock at the front door. She didn't recognize the figure through the lace curtains covering the oval window in the large door. She opened the front door and stood in front of the outer storm door.

"Can I help you?" she asked. He was a tall, attractive, well-built man she guessed to be in his early thirties. The long black overcoat was neat and hung nicely on his straight frame.

"Hello, I'm special agent Dan Hunter with the FBI. Are you Holly Miller?"

Her heart started to beat a little faster. So much for a lazy afternoon. "Yes. Would you like to come in?" She opened the door and stepped back. Standing next to him she noticed that he was taller than she had first thought. He was at least six foot one or two inches tall. She took his coat and hung it in the closet noting the vague smell of a sporty cologne.

He chose a chair in the sunny front room opposite the sofa where she had been reading. She reclaimed her place across from him and waited for him to start.

"Sheriff Butler informed you I would be dropping by didn't he?" He withdrew a business card from his wallet, leaned over the coffee table and handed it to her. She looked at it for a moment and then laid it down on the table next to her book and tea mug.

He had removed a pad of paper from the inside of his overcoat before she hung it up and he now opened the pad and rested it on his right knee. He sat up straight in the chair and while he looked friendly and comfortable she could tell that under the right circumstances he could be a strong and formidable opponent. He began to ask questions about how she came to live in Connecticut and about her studies. He made notes as she told him about her roommate from Miami University and her meeting with Walter Johnson and Beatrice Kingsley. She told him how she had met Eric and he let her continue with her story, stopping her occasionally to ask questions. His manner was easy but methodical.

They had been talking for almost an hour when he asked to use the restroom. She directed him down the hall and when he was out of sight she quickly ran to the small mirror in the front hallway to check her hair. She felt a small pang of guilt as she hurried back to the sofa and took up her position before he returned. When he did he asked if Mrs. Kingsley was at home. Holly told him that she was running errands and would probably be back soon.

"Can you tell me how you met Megan Summers?" he asked. She told him about their meeting at the café off campus and how they had become friends. Holly had known her as Megan Saunders and when he referred to her as Summers it was as if he were talking about someone else. His next question took her completely off guard.

"When you think back to your original meeting was there anything about it that would make you believe that she had planned to meet you?"

Holly took a moment before answering. "Well," she started, "I couldn't say for sure of course but she was always at the restaurant on Tuesdays at the same time I was. I just assumed that we had similar schedules. It wouldn't have been hard though if you were paying attention to realize that I had the same routine every week." This thought was depressing. Not only had her best friend probably been using her for information on her boyfriend but she had also been completely naïve. Holly made a mental note to start varying her schedule. *"Great, now I'm starting to get paranoid."*

"Holly?" Dan Hunter was staring at her. "Are you OK?" His voice was gentle and concerned.

"It's just all very overwhelming. I can't understand how I could have been so stupid," she said, shrugging and taking a sip of her tea. She had offered him something to drink twice now and he had refused both times.

"Please don't look at it that way. You were dealing with someone who was very clever and devious. Most honest people assume that same honesty in the people they meet unless they're given a reason to think otherwise. There really wasn't any reason for you to suspect that Megan's intentions were anything but sincere." She blinked at him. Of all the reassurances she had gotten from her family and friends over the past weeks these words from a total stranger had been exactly what she needed to hear. It was the first time someone had said something that actually made her feel better. Eric went out of his way to pretend none of this was happening. He just wanted things to get back to normal as quickly as possible. It felt good to be able to talk about all of the terrible things with someone objective.

"I thought she was my friend," Holly said, not caring how childish and pathetic she sounded.

"To tell you the truth Holly, from what I have been able to learn about Miss Summers, in her own way she probably thought she was being your friend as well. She certainly appears to have had ulterior motives for meeting you and carrying on the friendship, but that doesn't mean that none of her feelings and communications during the time you were friends were real."

Holly was pretty sure he was just trying to make her feel better but she didn't care. She thanked him and asked him what else he wanted to know.

"Did you know Megan was diabetic?"

"Yes. She told me that after we met. I suggested that we split a dessert and she declined saying that she was diabetic. She had to be careful with her diet. Why?"

He didn't answer right away. It was as if he was deciding whether or not to tell her. "Professor Fiennes died from an overdose of insulin. It was injected into his neck. There was nothing in his medical records or personal effects to indicate he was diabetic."

Her mouth was dry and her hands shook when she took a sip of her tea. "Did Megan kill him?" she asked, wishing her voice didn't sound so shaky.

"Her prints were in his car and on the syringe that was found between the seats of his car."

She took a few deep breaths and regained control of her emotions. He waited patiently for her to calm herself.

"Did Megan ever mention a Derrick Peterman?" he asked her. Holly could tell by the subtle change in his manner that of all the questions he had asked her so far this was the one he was really after.

"No. Was he a student? She tutored a lot of students. Most of them had crushes on her."

"Derrick wasn't a student. He was an attorney. As a law student in Virginia he encouraged Megan to challenge the Copeland estate as a potential heir. She lost of course and her interest in Derrick diminished along with her hopes of inheriting a fortune." He paused as if deciding whether to give her any more information, but she was curious and quickly encouraged him.

"If she hasn't seen him since she was a teenager in Virginia, what makes you think she would have spoken to me about him? She obviously went pretty far out of her way to keep her true identity a secret from me." The shock of Megan's betrayal washed over her again and she put her teacup back on its saucer, not trusting herself to maintain her composure.

"Actually Megan has seen Mr. Peterman recently and while you are right about her desire to maintain her privacy, it is possible that she made some comment unintentionally that could be useful."

"I can't honestly think of anything right now but if I do later I will let you know. I'm sure once you locate this Derrick guy you can ask him yourself. "She tried to sound nonchalant but somewhere down deep she knew where this was going.

"Derrick is dead Holly," Agent Hunter said in a level voice. He never took his eyes from her face. She knew he was watching for her response. He would have been trained to watch her responses to questions to evaluate whether she was telling the truth, but there was something else. Unlike all of the cold FBI agents she had seen in movies and read about in books, Dan Hunter was genuinely concerned about the effect his information was having on her. It was having very little effect as it turned out. Not now anyway. Her hands were cold and she felt somehow numb. Too much had happened over the past few weeks. At this point she was just filing her emotions away to be dealt with later.

"He was the man I found in the woods. Wasn't he?" She asked the question with a tight controlled voice.

"Yes."

"Why?"

"I look forward to asking Megan that question myself."

Holly nodded and looked down at her shoes. She concentrated on her laces for a few moments and mentally reminded herself to breathe in and out. Once she was sure she was able to remain calm she looked up at Agent Hunter and nodded silently.

He turned a page in his notebook and cleared his throat. He asked her several more questions about Eric and then he started a new page of notes on her trip to Virginia. He told her that there were other agents questioning people in Chesterfield but he took a lot of notes anyway. His last questions were about her current relationship with Eric. She answered them as best she could without giving him any intimate details. He thanked her for her time and told her he might need to talk to her again. She assured him that would be fine and gave him her schedule for the week. While he was putting on his coat she finally asked him about Megan.

"Do you have any idea where she is?"

"Well we are certainly keeping an eye out for her in Camden and also around campus, but honestly we believe she has gone south."

"To Florida?" she asked.

"Maybe," he answered vaguely. "She does have a grandmother there as you may have heard from Sheriff Butler. Anyway there have been some reports of her car in the Tampa area and neighbors of her grandmother have reported seeing a woman and car matching her description entering the grandmother's trailer. Our people are watching the trailer park but so far we haven't located her. The grandmother is in the hospital and claims she hasn't seen or heard from her granddaughter. But it's really just a matter of time before we catch up with her."

"So you don't expect her back here?" she asked looking directly into his brown eyes.

"No Holly, we don't think she will come back here. She knows the place is crawling with law enforcement. Until she is found however we will have unmarked cars outside your home, work, and school. Sheriff Butler's budget was a little strapped to maintain that kind of surveillance but now that there is a nationwide manhunt for Megan the FBI is footing the bill." He smiled at her and put his hand on her shoulder. "Don't worry; Megan Summers isn't going to get near you."

He was trying to make her feel safe and he was doing a very good job. Maybe too good. Holly was irritated with herself for reacting to him that way. So he was tall and good-looking. Yes, he had a great body too. But going weak in the knees for an FBI agent who made you feel safe was embarrassing. Besides things were just starting to feel right again with Eric. She said goodbye, closed the door behind him and forced herself not to watch him walk down the steps to his car. She caught her reflection in the mirror and was irritated to note that she looked flushed. She placed a hand to her rosy cheek and felt how warm her skin was. The ring of the telephone on the little table under the mirror startled her and she quickly grabbed it.

"Hello," she said sharply.

"Holly? Is everything OK? You sound upset," Eric said. Her cheeks went from rosy to scarlet as she forced herself to take a deep breath before answering.

"I'm fine. I guess I'm just a little unnerved. An FBI agent just left. He came to ask me about Megan."

"Was his name Hunter?"

"Yes, actually I think it was." She tried to sound nonchalant.

"Yeah, he was here on Friday morning at the crack of dawn. Kind of a hardass if you ask me. Did he upset you?"

Holly was taken aback by his description. Agent Hunter had been very gentle with her. "No, he was fine. The topic in general upsets me. I just want it to be over."

"Don't worry, it will be. I promise." His voice brought back memories of last night and she found herself feeling flushed for a whole other reason. Agent Hottie started to recede from her thoughts and she was back in reality where she belonged. They talked for a few more minutes. She had switched shifts with Mr. Johnson today and for once had Monday evening open. She had planned on a quiet evening to herself but now she wanted to do anything except sit home and think about what Agent Hunter had told her. Her best friend was murdering people. Eric said he had to go into town and run a few errands and suggested they meet for dinner. She accepted his offer and headed upstairs to change.

42

The next week flew by and Holly spent most of her spare time with Eric. Together they had put up the Christmas lights around Mrs. Kingsley's front porch. Walter had picked up the tree and Holly and Eric put the lights on it. The tension between Mr. Johnson and Eric had lessened a little. They weren't ever going to be close but her boss was polite to her boyfriend and Holly figured that was good enough for now.

The whole campus looked picturesque as well under the first significant snowfall of the year. Holly had always loved winter even back home. It was Tuesday and she was heading out of the Arts building and toward the café in town for the first time since she got back from Virginia. She knew her friend would not be there to have lunch with her ever again but she was drawn back there by old memories. The café was crowded with students clamoring for hot coffee and a warm place to congregate. Holly eventually got a small table by the window. She stirred her tea and watched the light snow fall over the neat row of shops adjacent to campus.

"Are you meeting someone or may I sit down?" She looked up to see the tall handsome FBI agent standing next to her table. He was wearing the same dark overcoat over a dark gray cashmere sweater and black slacks. He stuck out in this college hangout like a sore thumb. She smiled and nodded to the seat across from her. "Help yourself Agent Hunter, I'm not expecting anyone."

"Please, call me Dan." He crossed his long legs and waved at the waitress. "Coffee please." He gave the harassed looking waitress a quick smile that had the obvious desired effect. The waitress was suddenly all smiles and pushing stray locks of hair out of her face as she hurried off to get his coffee.

"I'm sorry to interrupt your lunch this way but I wanted to talk to you." His coffee arrived and he stirred it for a moment even though he had not put any cream or sugar in it. Apparently the tough FBI agent liked his coffee black. Holly waited quietly watching him and finally when he had taken a sip and set his cup down he reached in his coat pocket and withdrew his notebook.

"When you went home for Thanksgiving break you said Eric drove you to the airport?"

"Yes, that's correct."

"What car did he drive you in?" he asked. She couldn't see the relevance of the questions but she didn't ask him about them.

"We took my new car. He was to come back to get me on Sunday so he drove the car back to his place and parked it there."

"Any special reason for taking your car?"

"I just recently got it and I love driving it," she said. "Eric said you talked to him on Friday. Didn't he tell you all of this?"

He gave her kind of a guilty grin. "Actually I forgot to ask. I went back to check with him later but he wasn't around."

"He was probably back in his studio painting. He doesn't have a phone back there and he can't hear you knock out front."

"Actually, I went to his studio. There was no sign of him. There was also no sign of your car."

"Well then he must have run an errand or something. Forgive me but I don't see what my car has to do with the search for Megan?"

"Most likely nothing," the agent said in an easy manner. "I just have to have a complete time line for everyone involved for the file. The bureau likes paperwork." He flipped his notebook closed.

"How did you know where to find me?" she asked. He pointed out the window to a black Ford Taurus parked just down the street. There was a man sitting in the front seat of the car.

"Has he been following me?" she asked in amazement.

"Sometimes him, sometimes someone else. I mentioned that to you last week."

"Yes, but I just assumed they were in front of the house and at work. I didn't realize they were following me everywhere."

"It's just a precaution. They will probably be called off in the next day or so anyway." He looked at her as he took another sip of his coffee.

"Why? Has something happened?" Her hand started to shake slightly. He reached over and took the teacup out of it and set it on the table before she spilled it. He covered her shaking hand with his own.

"A trailer in Megan's grandmother's park was burned to the ground last weekend. A body was found inside but could not be immediately identified. It turns out the trailer was being leased to a salesman who spends most of his time on the road. The owner of the trailer turned out to be Megan's grandmother. She apparently owns a few of them and rents them out for additional income. The salesman, who had been out of town, was eventually found alive and well. We got a rush report on the DNA yesterday. The body in the trailer was in fact Megan Summers."

She felt the room start to spin. She could hear him telling her to breathe and when she finally opened her eyes he was on his knees next to her.

"I'm sorry I shouldn't have told you here." He sounded irritated with himself. She was feeling better and assured him that she was fine, just a little shocked. He took his seat across from her but seemed prepared to reach out and grab her if necessary.

"I know Megan has done some terrible things. I should hate her. But I never knew that side of her. I only remember her as my friend." There were tears rolling slowly down her cheeks now and her hands were trembling. He handed her his napkin and leaned forward so he could talk to her privately.

"Hate is a wasted emotion Holly. If anything Megan was to be pitied."

She started to feel stronger and asked, "How did the fire start?" She sat upright and put her traitorous hands in her lap. Agent Hunter looked closely at her, obviously trying to decide if she had heard enough for one day.

"Please." She urged him in the most confident voice she could muster. "I need to know."

"The point of origin appears to be where the body was found. It may be a suicide. There was also evidence of a syringe near the body. Considering how the professor was killed Megan may have injected herself with an insulin overdose and started the fire."

"You don't sound like you believe that," she said looking at him.

"I have always been suspicious of overkill situations." He ringed his coffee cup with his finger. "If Megan was going to kill herself with insulin why start the fire?"

"That sounds logical. Is the bureau thinking there was foul play in her death?" she asked, physically controlling her tone of voice so he wouldn't notice the panic she was feeling.

"Not especially. Considering the fire in Virginia that killed Eric's grandmother and brother it may be that Megan is something of a firebug. People with those tendencies don't generally abandon them."

"What does that mean? Is your case closed?"

"I will probably be around for a few days tying up loose ends. Your bodyguards will get the order to back off maybe as soon as tomorrow."

"So, it's over?" she asked.

"Well it won't be official for a day or two. But as far as you are concerned I guess the answer is yes." His voice was calm but she thought he was still not satisfied. He had probably wanted to catch Megan himself. In all of the books she had read, law enforcement types moved up through the ranks by making the big collar. It must be deflating when your suspect kills herself.

"Well, if you are sure you're all right I had better be going. I have a lot of paperwork to finish."

"I'm fine. Thank you for telling me. It will be nice to get on with my life without constantly wondering where she is and what she's going to do next." He nodded but didn't say anything.

He put his overcoat on and reached out to shake her hand. "If you have any questions or concerns about this case you can always reach me at the numbers on the card I gave you. Do you still have that?"

"Yes. Thank you. But I am looking forward to putting this behind me."

"Well, good luck." And he was gone.

She sat for a while staring out the window as the snow continued to fall. There was something very anticlimactic about the way things had ended up. She didn't care though. It was over. That's all that mattered. Megan couldn't hurt anyone she loved anymore.

43

There was a message from Eric to call him. Holly was pretty sure he had heard the news about Megan either directly or from his lawyers. She knew he would understand how she must feel and so there was no triumph in his voice when she returned his call.

"You heard," she said flatly.

"I heard. Are you OK?" he asked.

"Yes. I'm fine. It's just a little weird that's all."

"Well, I'm sure you don't want to talk about it. Did Sheriff Butler call you?"

"You mean you don't want to talk about it," she thought. Eric never liked to talk about anything emotional or unpleasant. What if she had wanted to talk about it? That's where Megan usually came in. Holly felt her stomach twist a little.

"No. Agent Hunter showed up at the café when I was having lunch. He told me." *"Stick that in your pipe and smoke it,"* she thought with a bit of truculence.

"Leave it to a jerk like him to come and give you upsetting news in a public place. I can't wait for that guy to leave town." She could have told him that Dan Hunter had been a perfect gentleman, but she didn't. Instead she said nothing while he waited for her to confirm the FBI agent's status as an insensitive brute. Which she didn't. After a few awkward moments he cleared his throat and continued.

"Anyway, I was wondering if you were up to a ski trip. Your boss is back to his old self more or less. I thought it might be nice to spend some quality time alone together."

"Stuck on a painting?" she teased him.

"No, smartass. I just finished one and thought it would be a good time to take a little R&R before starting again. But hey, if you're not interested..."

"Kidding. I was just kidding. It sounds great. When?"

"How about we leave Friday? You could work the early shift and we could leave as soon as you get off. We could check into a bed and breakfast. Have a nice quiet dinner. That would give us all day Saturday and Sunday morning to hit the slopes before we drive home."

"Sounds great. Where are we going?" She knew he had already planned the whole thing. Eric never left anything to chance. She was suddenly feeling more lighthearted than she had felt all day.

"Mohawk Mountain. It's in Cornwall about and hour and a half from here." He sounded excited.

"It's a date," she said and told him goodbye.

Her spirits were lifted and she went about the rest of her day without the heavy sense of dread she had been cloaked in for weeks. She would eventually have to deal with her feelings about Megan. There were a lot of them and they were very complex. But for now she wanted to put some distance between herself and the deaths of Chief Sparks and Professor Fiennes. A sense of guilt had plagued her since they had both been killed shortly after talking with her. It might even take professional help to sort out her own feelings of responsibility. But for now a little happiness and a lot of snow was the preferred therapy.

She finished her errands and hurried to the store to relieve Mr. Johnson. He had a doctor's appointment to get his arm X-rayed and she didn't want to be the reason he was late. When she walked into the front of the store she didn't see him. She walked through the neatly organized rows of shelving carrying every imaginable type of nut, bolt, and screw toward the swinging door at the back of the sales floor to hang up her coat and bag when the door pushed open and out bustled Beatrice Kingsley. Holly was surprised to see her and stopped in her tracks. Mrs. Kingsley noted the look on her face.

"What's wrong dear?"

"Is everything all right?" Holly whispered, worried that something had happened to her boss.

"Oh for heaven's sake of course everything's all right. I'm going along to his appointment so I can hear for myself what the doctor says."

She shook her head as if she were a schoolteacher dealing with a trying child. "I think he is doing far too much with that arm and I want to hear an expert's advice with my own two ears." With that she tossed the end of her scarf around her neck, walked purposefully to the front door and stood there waiting. A few seconds later Walter Johnson emerged from the back room, said hello to Holly and gave her a few instructions about inventory. He made no mention of his appointment or any reference at all to the determined woman standing with arms crossed at the front of his store. As he turned to leave she could have sworn she heard him mumble something that sounded dangerously close to "interfering woman", but when he reached the front door he held it open for Mrs. Kingsley and followed her down the walk and around the corner to his car. Holly couldn't help smiling to herself. If there were ever two people who belonged together it was those two and she congratulated herself on being the one to bring them together.

The rest of the evening passed uneventfully, as did the next few days. Holly didn't see Agent Hunter again but she knew he had left town because the sheriff stopped by to talk to Mr. Johnson saying that they had wrapped up most of their investigation in Camden and happily the FBI was out of his hair.

Thursday night Holly packed for her trip the following day. Mr. Johnson had gotten one of his friends to come in on Saturday to help at the store and they were closed Sunday so she didn't have to worry about things at home. She could enjoy her trip and her boyfriend for two glorious days. She had packed plenty of warm clothes for the hours on the ski slopes and some not-so-warm clothes for the hours back at the bed and breakfast in front of the fire in their room. Eric was great at planning trips and she knew that he would have a very special room reserved. He never talked about his money and he certainly lived very modestly day-to-day, but when it came to his time with her he was very generous. The gentle manners she had been attracted to when she had first started dating him were no doubt acquired from years of growing up with his refined and somewhat domineering grandmother. Holly found herself trying to imagine Eric's life in Chesterfield. His had certainly been a privileged childhood. She imagined him and his brother changing into clean pants and shirts with their hair combed and coming down to dinner in the dining room of that beautiful house she had stood and gaped at just weeks ago. Eric had told her very little about his brother but she knew from the few conversations they did have that he had cared for Lucas. Losing his brother must have been a terrible blow after the loss of his parents. She forced the thoughts from her mind and sat on her suitcase so she could get the locks closed. It was only a two day trip but cold weather clothes were bulky and it was best to layer.

44

Friday morning seemed to drag on forever. Holly found herself watching the clock and cleaning the same surfaces over and over again. She actually had plenty of work for her class that she could do but she hadn't brought her laptop and she really didn't feel like sitting still and writing now anyhow. She was anxious to get on the road. At two forty-five Walter Johnson came into the store taking his hat off and shaking the snowflakes onto the mat while he stomped his feet. It had just started snowing about a half hour ago and the sight of the big fluffy flakes just made her all the more anxious.

"Everything going OK?" her boss asked as he moved around the front counter and started to thumb through the receipts. Holly was on her knees sliding new identification tags into the little slots on the front of the plastic containers that held different styles and sizes of door hinges. The old ones were torn and smeared and she had been replacing a row of them each time she worked.

"A little slow. But then things should pick up this evening it being payday and all." She worked a tattered tag out of its slot with her fingernail. The pink polish that had been so carefully applied at her mother's salon last weekend had been replaced earlier today with a deep red that would go perfectly with a certain nightgown she had packed.

"Your date's here," Walter said as he carried some receipts in one hand and his hat and jacket in the other and headed toward the back of the store. She stood up and looked out the large plate glass window in front of the store and around the painted letters advertising the week's specials. She saw Eric parallel parking her new car in a spot in front of the store. He had picked up her car last night so he could fill it up and check all of the fluids before they left today. He must have stopped by the house already and gotten her bag. She had left it in the kitchen by the back door and Mrs. Kingsley had assured her that she would be there when he came to pick it up. Her landlady had said very little about Eric since the discovery of Megan Summers' involvement in the deaths of the professor and the police chief in Virginia. Holly was sure there had been some private conversations between Beatrice and Walter on the subject. The two had become intertwined into each other's lives in a way that was subtle but very specific. They didn't wander around town holding hands or go out to romantic dinners together. Their relationship was one that would look to an outsider as if they had been a couple for many years and were now settled and comfortable with each other. Holly had the occasional urge to ask one or the other about any future intentions they might have but she appreciated the privacy that they had always extended to her in her relationship with Eric and kept her curiosity in check.

Holly gathered her little pile of tags and returned them to the counter, checking quickly to make sure everything was in place. She didn't want her boss to have to work a busy Friday night shift alone and not be able to find anything. Walter had always seemed to be one of those guys who were larger than life. He was tough but caring, he could fix anything, and he never complained about his life or circumstances to anyone. He reminded her a lot of her father. His accident had been a shock to her. That sense of security she had always felt at home as a child and a young girl had been extended into her adult life by the presence of Walter Johnson. His injuries and subsequent fragile state had opened her eyes to her childish point of view. Part of the recent change in her attitude toward Eric, who had suffered far more than she had, was a need to protect herself. She knew she couldn't always rely on the men in her life to see that she was safe. She had to get smart and start looking out for herself.

Eric was stomping the snow off of his hiking boots on the rug at the front door. He took off his gloves and stuffed them in the pockets of his worn leather jacket. Holly noticed for the first time that the jacket was probably very expensive. Its worn look fit with Eric's understated way of life; he had worn that jacket often and the leather was soft and supple. Her boyfriend had never given the outward impression that he had a great deal of money, but if you looked past the older model car and the cottage life he led, you might be surprised. When she and Eric had been having dinner a few days previously Holly had asked him the time. When she saw he had a different watch than he usually wore she looked more closely and recognized that it was a Tag Heuer. The polished steel case and electric blue dial were half hidden behind the cuff of Eric's striped rugby shirt. Her brain registered the fifteen hundred dollar value of his new trinket but her only comment was that she liked his new watch. He told her he had showered in his old one too many times and he had been forced to replace it.

"We better hit the road before we get snowed in here," he said bringing her out of her thoughts. She gave him a quick kiss and brushed some of the snow out of his hair with a grin.

"I'll just grab my coat and tell Mr. Johnson I'm leaving," she said hurrying to the back of the store. Shrugging into her jacket she stuck her head into the small office where her boss was bent over his receipts loading them into his computer system. He had developed his own method of tracking inventory and liked entering everything himself.

"I'm off, can I get you anything before I go?" she asked.

"No, I'm just about done here. You go on ahead," he said taking off his glasses and looking at her thoughtfully.

"I suppose he took the car to the station and gave it the once over?" he asked.

"Yes sir," she said smiling at him.

"Well you kids have a good time. Take your time driving in this stuff." He motioned to the air around him in reference to the snow falling outside. "There's no reason to hurry." He gave her a quick smile before he put his glasses on and returned to his paperwork. She promised him they would be careful and left him to his work. As she walked toward the front of the store where Eric was waiting for her with a crooked smile on his face, she felt as if her world that had tilted a few weeks ago was suddenly right again.

"And just what are you smiling at?" she asked as he held the door open for her. She walked out into the snow and started toward her car when she was yanked backward and spun around. In one quick movement he had pulled her against him and was looking into her eyes. She was taken off guard and breathless. Before she could ask him what was going on his mouth closed on hers hungrily. Forgetting that they were on a public street and in front of her place of employment, she reached her arms up and wrapped them around his neck and met his lusty kiss with one of her own. Eric had pulled the loose fabric tie that held back her ponytail releasing it to blow in the wind. He grabbed a handful of her thick hair tilting her head back while his mouth smothered hers. They stayed locked in their embrace for only a few seconds but when they released each other Holly knew without looking they had just provided Angie with a hot topic to pass around this weekend.

She made a few idle attempts at chitchat that drew little more from him than the occasional glance. The sexual tension in the car was thick. Eventually she gave up attempts at conversation and contented herself with looking out the window at the snow-covered scenery racing by her window.

"Umm, where are we staying?" she asked, searching around for conversation.

"You've never been there." The corners of his mouth resisted a smile.

"How do you know? Maybe I have been with my other boyfriend." This drew a raised eyebrow but no response.

Deciding not to play his game any longer she reached in her satchel for her iPod, leaned her seat back and pretended to ignore him.

45

The Wake Robin Inn rested on a hilltop giving its occupants beautiful vistas. Three stories of white painted brick rose up before them as they made their way up the main driveway.

"Eric, it's beautiful!" she exclaimed pulling the earphones from her ears and sitting up in her seat.

"I take it this is your first visit to this particular inn then?" he teased, with a smile on his face.

She gave him a playful swat and returned her attention to the window. "You know I was kidding," she said, still looking out the window.

"Too late, you're going to have to pay for that 'other boyfriend' comment." She looked at him, but he had already put the car in Park and was getting out. He came around and opened her door while she was packing her things back into her satchel. When she stepped out of the car he took her hand and brought it to his lips.

"I can't wait to get to our room," he whispered looking directly into her eyes.

She felt the butterflies start to flutter in her stomach. How did he do that? After all this time he could turn her knees to noodles. She wondered how exactly she was going to have to "pay" for her earlier comment. Smiling, she decided that this particular penalty could turn out to be quite enjoyable.

The lobby was well appointed and comfortable for an inn and while Eric went to register she looked around. Along with the obvious winter thrill seekers there were also several sets of parents with children in uniforms. This was apparently a preferred place for visiting parents of children attending the nearby private schools.

"Let's go," Eric said from behind her. He grabbed her hand and led her up the carpeted stairs to their room on the second floor. The room turned out to be a beautiful suite with a four-poster bed and a working fireplace.

"Eric, it's wonderful. Maybe we should skip the skiing and just stay here all weekend."

"I'll go along with that," he said wrapping his arms around her and kissing her forehead. She raised her arms up around his neck and reached up for a kiss. He pretended not to notice this gesture and turned his attentions to the fireplace instead. She noted the fresh flowers and the giant fruit basket on the table and knew that these were not the normal amenities offered by the establishment. Eric had made special requests. Smiling to herself she pretended not to have noticed.

"Is there a restaurant here?" She looked around the room for a leaflet or brochure identifying the inn's amenities.

"No, there's an Irish pub that's open until nine. We can go down for a drink if you like. I've made reservations at *The Boat House*. I believe they have a sushi bar." He was still messing with the fireplace, which was fortunate because when she caught her reflection in the mirror she realized her mouth was open. He never ceased to amaze her.

"Well, it's still pretty early. Shall we freshen up and then have a drink at the pub before dinner?"

"Sounds like a plan. You go ahead; I'm going to veg for a moment." He lay back on the big bed clasping his hands behind his head and closing his eyes. Strike two. She picked up her overnight bag, headed into the combination dressing room and bathroom and closed the door. The accommodations in the suite were lovely and she could imagine this set of rooms had been very expensive. There were probably only a few suites in the inn.

Half an hour later she emerged dressed in wool slacks and a cashmere sweater. Her long hair was held in a delicate knot by a pair of antique silver combs she had found in a shop over the summer. She fastened the simple diamond studs her father had given her for Christmas last year in her ears and put on the necklace Eric had given her for her birthday. Eric had also changed and was wearing black slacks and a grey sweater. He looked handsome and smelled great but she kept her demeanor light and airy. He had started this game but she could play it as well as anyone.

Eric carried her jacket over his arm and opened the door for her. Michael Bryan's pub lived up to its name and had a pleasant casual atmosphere. Eric ordered a Guinness and Holly opted for a glass of wine. They talked with another couple for a time and the bartender related the history of the inn.

After a while Eric checked his watch and paid the bar tab leaving a generous tip. He helped Holly into her jacket and they left to find their restaurant.

46

Holly was using chopsticks to dip her tuna roll into a little dish of soy sauce, wasabi, and pickled ginger when she looked up and caught Eric staring at her. Self-consciously she lowered her chopsticks and returned his stare.

"I like your hair like that," he said.

"Thank you. I keep waiting for it to fall down." She smiled back at him and took a sip of her wine.

They took their time eating, talking, ordering small courses, enjoying the atmosphere and each other's company. The sexual tension was building but neither one acknowledged it.

They drove slowly back to the inn enjoying the snow-covered landscape as it shimmered off the headlights of the car.

"Have you skied here before?" she asked.

"No, but I hear it's great. Are you ready?" There was a quiet challenge in his voice.

"I will be after a good night's sleep," she returned noting the slight twitch at the corners of his mouth.

They parked the car and walked with her arm through his across the grounds and up the steps to the entrance of the inn. Their room was as they had left it except that the bed had been turned down. Eric busied himself with the fireplace once again as she dropped herself into a wingback chair and closed her eyes. He sat on the floor by her feet and leaned his head into her lap.

"Dinner was lovely, thank you," she said.

"You look tired, maybe you had better get started on that 'good night's sleep' so you can keep up with me tomorrow."

"Maybe you're right." She got up, went in to the bathroom and closed the door. When she emerged a few minutes later she was wearing a long red satin gown trimmed in cream lace that clung lightly to her curves. Her hair was still held up in the silver combs exposing her long lovely neck. The delicate scent of Asian spices followed her into the room. Speechless, Eric instinctively moved toward her. She paused a few inches from him and then turned away toward her side of the bed when he caught her wrist and pulled her to him.

She started to make a half-hearted protest when her words were cut off by his mouth crushing down on her own. His strong hands moved over her satin-clad body. He gently pulled the combs out of her hair and let it fall over his hands. He buried his left hand in her thick dark hair and pulled her head back kissing her scented neck as his other hand explored her breasts and body hungrily. He slowly moved her to the edge of the bed and sat her down in front of him while he pulled the sweater off and removed his slacks. Pulling her to her feet again he reached down and started to slide the gown up over her hips and then over her head and shoulders until she was standing naked before him in the glow of the firelight. He kissed her mouth and neck as his hands explored her body. She closed her eyes and tilted her head back as his fingers and lips brought pleading moans. When she was just sure her legs would come out from under her she pulled him down on the bed with her and begged him with her eyes to finish what he had started. She opened herself to him and he obliged her over and over again.

47

The morning sun peeked through a crack in the drapes and Holly raised her head over Eric's sleeping body to peer at the clock. She traced the line of his jaw with her finger and kissed his shoulder as he started to stir. An hour later they were showered and dressed and headed downstairs for breakfast. Holly was stirring cream into her coffee at a small table in the breakfast buffet room while Eric was piling fruit and warm croissants onto his plate. They spent half an hour nibbling on Eric's plate of food and skimming the various newspapers provided by the inn for its clientele. By ten o'clock they were dressed in their ski gear and back in her Honda headed for Mohawk Mountain. The lodge was a flattened A-frame building constructed of concrete blocks with windows ground to peak, painted gray with orange trim. While the main building wasn't terribly attractive the three hundred and fifty acres of forested land that contained the hundred plus acres of ski trails were breathtakingly beautiful. Eric unloaded their gear from Holly's car and they made their way into the lodge to purchase their lift passes. While Eric waited in line for assistance Holly perused the ski shop. He found her trying on crazy ski hats. He rolled his eyes and coaxed her out of the shop.

They spent the rest of the day trying out several of the resort's twenty-four trails. Eric was a natural athlete and skied effortlessly down the more difficult runs. Holly was not as experienced, but what she lacked in practice she made up for in sheer determination. They raced each other down the hills, stopping only in the afternoon for a late lunch in the lodge. The runs were beautiful under the evening lights with fresh snow that had been falling on and off over the last few days. Only half of the runs were open at night. Holly stopped for a cup of hot cocoa and tried to pick Eric out of the many skiers making their way down the slopes. She spotted his blue and black ski jacket as he was half way down the hill. He glided effortlessly in and out of the other skiers as if he had been born on skis. Holly's own legs were so tired from trying to match his pace that she wasn't sure if she was going to feel like skiing tomorrow at all. Her own energy usually matched his but lately she seemed to tire faster. She was sure it had something to do with the stress of the last few weeks and the fact that she and Eric hadn't been keeping up their usual athletic pace.

By the time they had their gear loaded back into their car they were both famished. They stopped on the way back to the inn at a recommended local favorite that served American cuisine. Holly ordered a cheeseburger and Eric ordered pasta. They talked and laughed about their excursion until their food came, at which point there was very little talking while they both dug in. Holly imagined this place did very well serving starved skiers. She looked around her and recognized the various hats and jackets of the skiing crowd. They passed on dessert, too full from their entrees to even consider more, and settled for coffee.

"What if we skip skiing tomorrow and do a little sight seeing?" Eric said turning his coffee cup in circles with his hand.

"Really?" she replied, trying to keep the relief out of her voice.

"I saw you eyeing all those antique and gift shops on the way here," he teased. Before she could open her mouth to argue with him he cut her off. "Besides, when that little kid crashed in front of me I think I pulled a muscle trying not to hit him."

"Well, in that case I guess shopping it is." She smiled at him wondering if he was making it up about the sore muscle but she was so relieved that she didn't care. She had never felt so exhausted in her life.

The following morning after another leisurely breakfast in the dining area of the inn they packed their bags into the trunk of the car and headed out armed with a list of must see places provided by the lady working at the front desk. She had even suggested a place to stop for lunch. The snow-covered landscape was soft and serene. They wove through rolling hillsides, stopping in little towns on their hand drawn map to roam through their shops.

They stopped at several small antique shops and Holly bought a few Christmas gifts and some candles for her room. They were browsing in one particularly crowded shop and she was glad she had left her parka and satchel in the car because it was difficult to navigate through the narrow aisles.

Holly was looking at jewelry in the display cases of an antique shop when she spotted several silver spoons. Beatrice Kingsley had a glass-covered cherry wall display that held antique silver spoons. Holly asked the elderly woman who apparently owned the store if she could remove the spoons from the case for closer review. *Helen*, according to the name embroidered on her sweatshirt, got up from the wicker chair where she had been watching a program on a small portable television set, slid the glass door of the display case open and retrieved the spoons. She unfolded an old leather portfolio that was lined with felt and laid the spoons out on it for her. Holly examined them with a serious look on her face although she knew absolutely nothing about collecting silver spoons. She chose one that was delicately carved and appeared to be very old.

"You have a good eye," Helen said with a rough voice acquired from years of chain smoking. "You picked the most valuable one." Holly had noticed that the spoons weren't marked with a price tag and she figured that it wouldn't have mattered which one she had chosen Helen would have declared it the most valuable. Eric had lost interest and had moved off to look at some carved wooden boxes leaving Holly to haggle with the woman over the price of the spoon. When they had agreed upon a price and Holly had paid for her purchase Helen wrapped the small spoon in paper and stuck it in a plastic bag for her. Holly made her way over to Eric and was about to ask if he was ready to leave when she spotted a porcelain music box up on a shelf. She handed the little bag with the spoon in it to

Eric and he tucked it into a pocket on the inside of his leather jacket. The music box was heavier than it looked as she stood on tiptoe and lifted it off of its shelf with two hands. She had collected music boxes growing up and had a beautiful display cabinet in her bedroom at home with her precious collection in it. The carousel was hand painted and each horse was different. She turned the knob on the bottom gently and set the box down on a table to see how well it worked. She kneeled down so she was at eye level with the box and inspected it for flaws as it slowly rotated playing a song that she recognized but couldn't name. Satisfied that it was in good condition she carried her treasure up to the desk and interrupted Helen again. Eric went out to warm up the car and pull it to the front door while Holly paid for and supervised the wrapping of the music box. While Helen looked around for a cardboard box to keep her purchase from rolling around the back seat of the car during the trip home, Holly felt a rare pang of homesickness. Her parents had taken several vacations without Holly when she was a child and had always come home with gifts for her in their suitcases. Her mother would buy her necklaces made of shells and other treats and her father, whenever he could find one, would bring her a music box. Maybe it was the lovely holiday she had just spent with them that made their separation so poignant right now. It was unlike Holly to feel emotional. Eric honked the horn to let her know he had arrived with the car. Holly tucked her purchase protectively under her arm since a box hadn't been located and headed out the door and down the steps.

They ate lunch at a restaurant suggested by the innkeeper and Holly was ravenous once again. Eric teased her that she was going to lose her girlish figure if she kept eating like that. It was sometime between the turkey club and the chilled dish of sherbet that the truth hit her like the proverbial ton of bricks.

48

Eric was playing with the radio and driving while Holly was backtracking through her PDA checking the dates. How could this have happened? She closed her eyes, leaned her head back against the seat and tried to remember if she had had a period this month. No. With all of the craziness and then her trip home she hadn't even realized that she had missed it. The last one she had noted was in early October. Her heart was pounding. She took several deep breaths and told herself to relax. The stress and anxiety of recent events could easily have caused her to miss a period. Her cycle had always been like clockwork though. She looked at Eric who had finally found a station he liked and was watching the road while his fingers tapped out the beat to the Green Day song coming out of the radio. He looked over at her and winked. She smiled and then closed her eyes, leaned her head back against her seat and pretended to rest while she fought to hold back the tears. This event should be in their future; something to be excited about and anticipated. She knew she couldn't talk to him without giving away her distress so she forced herself to relax and try to sleep. Eric changed the station again to something softer and she gave in to the exhaustion that had been hovering over her all day.

Holly slept most of the way home and awoke as they were pulling onto the street where she lived with Mrs. Kingsley. Eric was holding her hand and glanced at her with a quiet smile. She wondered if he knew but she quickly dismissed the thought as paranoid.

"You snore," he said trying to control the twitching corners of his mouth. She gave him a playful punch in the arm and started to gather her things together. Eric carried her bag to the back porch and waited for her to open the door. Mrs. Kingsley was out and the kitchen was dark except for a small light in the little alcove leading to the bathroom.

"Do you want to come in and have something to drink?" she asked as she set her bag down on the stone floor by the fireplace.

"No. I think I'll get back and spend a few hours in the studio tonight. All that exercise and fresh air has my creative juices flowing again." He gripped her arms gently and pulled her into him for a kiss. As he was turning to leave he looked down at her heavy leather bag and seemed to pause for a moment. He picked up the bag and headed through the room calling over his shoulder "I may as well put this in your room for you before I go."

Holly was speechless, not because of his attentiveness but because she sensed that his actions were more deliberate than his usual casual courtesy. She stood in the same spot until she heard him coming down the stairs and then busied herself with pouring a glass of tea. He hugged her briefly kissing her forehead, another new gesture, and then hurried out the back door pulling it closed behind him. Holly pulled out a chair at the kitchen table and sat down with her tea trying to absorb in her heart what her brain knew to be true. She lowered her head down onto her arms and closed her eyes. Some time later she heard a car door and voices that had to belong to Mrs. Kingsley and Mr. Johnson. Not wanting to get drawn into a group discussion about her trip she quickly moved upstairs, closed her door and turned on her radio to a classical station. She spent the next half hour putting her things away and when she did open her door to put her toiletries back in her bathroom she no longer heard voices. She took the tea glass and headed down stairs. Beatrice Kingsley was sitting in her favorite chair by the front picture window with her slippered feet propped up on the old tufted hassock. She opened her eyes and smiled at Holly inquiring if she had had a good time. Holly told her it was great and headed toward the kitchen to put her glass away and escape any further questions.

"That FBI fellow called for you on Friday evening. Said to have you call him at the number he gave you when you got back." The elderly woman said all this with her head tipped back and her eyes closed. If she was concerned about the FBI agent's continued interest in her young friend she didn't show it.

"Did he say what he wanted?" Holly asked

"No, just said to have you call." This time she leveled her sharp eyes at Holly but didn't comment further. "Don't worry dear, I'm sure there are a lot of loose ends to tie up in a mess like that one."

Holly nodded her head but didn't respond. Instead she told Mrs. Kingsley that she was tired from the trip and was going to bed early. When she got to her room she went to the book she had finished reading and pulled the business card out of the space it had occupied between the pages since he had given it to her. She picked up the phone on the side table and dialed the cell phone number he had written on the back of it.

"Hello." His voice was smooth and relaxed.

"Agent Hunter?"

"Hi Holly, how was your ski trip?"

"Great. I'm exhausted but it was fun."

"That's good. Hey, I just wanted to ask you a question. You said Megan always wore the charm bracelet that was her mother's. Do you ever remembering seeing her without it?"

"No. Never. Why do you ask?"

"She wasn't wearing it when we found her. It wasn't found among her things either. Initially it would have helped to identify her until DNA tests came back, but the bracelet was never recovered."

"Is that important? I mean maybe she put it somewhere before she killed herself."

"Megan didn't kill herself Holly. She was murdered." Holly's hand reached out and felt for the chair she knew was behind her.

"I don't understand, I thought you said she set the trailer on fire killing herself."

"The autopsy report along with other lab reports indicates that the amount of insulin in her system would have rendered her unable to set that fire Holly. Also the lack of smoke in her lungs indicates she was dead before the fire."

"Who...? I don't understand. How can that be?"

"We're still looking into it Holly, that's all I can say right now. I'm just glad to hear you're all right."

"Does Eric know? I mean, do his lawyers know?

"No, and I have to ask you to keep this information to yourself. I only told you so I could convince you to be cautious."

"Do you have another suspect? What could this possibly have to do with me?"

"I'm not saying this has anything to do with you, I just want you to be careful. That's all." His voice was concerned. It occurred to her that he had told her more than he should have in his position and trusted her not to spread the information. She couldn't bring herself to ask him if Eric was a suspect again. She knew his alibi was solid and she had a new reason now to need him to be innocent.

"I may stop by and see you tomorrow morning at the store if that's OK," he said.

"You're here? I thought you were leaving on Friday."

"So did I, but things have changed so I will be around for a few more days."

She said goodbye to him and placed the phone back on its stand. Wanting a bath but not wanting to sit and drive herself crazy with her thoughts she opted for a quick hot shower and warm pajamas. She had been so surprised that Dan was still in town that it hadn't occurred to her to ask why he wanted to see her. As she lay in her bed and welcomed sleep her hand moved slowly over her abdomen and a sense of fear crept over her. Her life had taken some dangerous turns lately. She had someone else to protect now. She made herself a mental promise to be careful from now on and fell asleep before she could ask herself whom she should be careful of.

49

Holly awoke Monday morning to the smell of sausages frying in the kitchen downstairs. Usually not a big morning eater her mouth was watering. The clock on her bedside table said seven-twenty. She stretched, put her feet over the edge of the bed and felt around with her toes for her slippers. She pulled her favorite terry robe on and tied the belt. Just then she remembered the silver spoon she had purchased for Mrs. Kingsley and then remembered Eric putting it in his jacket. She would have time to stop by his place before work this morning. Then she could give it to Mrs. Kingsley at dinner tonight. Mr. Johnson had been coming to a late supper on Monday nights and a few others as well, but Holly was looking forward to a quiet dinner with these two. She padded downstairs and surprised Mrs. Kingsley with a hug. She poured herself a glass of orange juice foregoing the coffee and started setting the table for the two of them.

"Is Mr. Johnson coming for dinner tonight?"

"Yes, and I'm making crab cakes." Holly made the appropriate appreciative noises and did a little happy dance in her head. She had always been a good eater but her appetite had increased and she found herself drooling over dinner before she had eaten breakfast.

She helped clean up after they had finished eating the sausages and scrambled eggs and hurried upstairs to get dressed. She spent a few extra minutes on her hair and make up and then chastised herself when she realized it was her meeting with Agent Hunter that had her primping and not her quick stop at Eric's on the way. She tossed a few things in her bag, checked her image in the mirror one last time and headed down the stairs.

Her car was covered with a light dusting of snow and she turned it on to warm up while she used the brush end of her scraper to scatter the powdery snow from her windows. As she did this she noticed a small blue tag stuck down in the corner of the front windshield on the driver's side. She reached in with her hand and worked the square out with her fingernail. She held it up and looked at it. It looked like some sort of parking ticket. Midwest. She hadn't had the car very long and she didn't recall being anywhere called Midwest. She pocketed the tag and headed out.

The road that led up to the Wilkes estate was clear except for the light snow that had fallen overnight and Holly's car had no trouble navigating the twists and turns up the hill. She parked near the cottage, walked to the front door and knocked as she turned the handle. The door was locked and when no one answered she felt along the molding at the top of the door until her fingers touched the key Eric kept there. She opened the door and called his name as she stomped her feet on the foyer rug and set her bag down by the little table. She called his name again as she walked through the hallway and into the bedroom. His bag was there but the bed didn't appear to have been slept in. He had probably spent the night in the studio as he had on many occasions when he was painting late into the night. She went out the back door by the little kitchen and walked across the clearing to the outbuilding that Eric had converted into a studio.

The studio door was closed but not locked and she opened it quietly so she wouldn't scare him if he were sleeping. She stepped into the room that was warmed by the potbellied stove in the corner. The slipcovered sofa against the far wall had a blanket and a throw pillow tossed across it as if someone had been sleeping there. He had probably gone out hiking. If he had gone for wood she would have seen him at the woodpile when she parked her car near it. Besides there was still a pile of wood next to the little stove. She checked her watch and decided she had a few minutes to wait for him. She spotted his leather jacket draped across the chair of the small table where he sometimes sketched out his ideas. She lifted the jacket off of the chair and felt in the inside lining for the pocket where he had stored the bag with her spoon in it. She felt the spoon, pulled it out of the pocket, stuck it into her own pocket and returned the jacket to its place on the back of the chair. Eric must have worn his ski jacket to go out and she could see his hiking boots were missing from the mat next to the door where they usually rested. She walked around the room looking at the canvases, many of which she had only seen as sketches or in the beginning stages of a painting. His work was beautiful - powerful, to be honest. His signature brooding skies were found in varying stages amongst the different landscapes. She spotted a beautiful miniature landscape that she had never seen before propped up on a shelf where he kept various books and supplies. She moved over to it, picked it up and held it between her hands. She didn't recognize the scenery and she had walked every inch of these hills and woods with Eric a hundred times. She placed the painting back in its place and as she did her eyes fell on a beautifully carved wooden box tucked between a pottery vase and a stack of art history books. She stepped on a wooden stool and reached up to take down the box. She ran her hand over the carving on it and wondered where he had found it. She didn't recall ever seeing it before. She lifted the lid and inside was a tray made of the same wood lined with a dark burgundy felt. There were a few miscellaneous coins and an old pocket watch in the tray that looked familiar though she couldn't place where she had seen it before. She lifted the tray and found a couple of folded sheets of paper that appeared to be letters. She lifted them out of the box and before she could open them up her eyes were drawn to something in the bottom of the box.

Suddenly she was very cold and her heart was pounding wildly. Her hand moved independently of her paralyzed body as she reached into the box and lifted out a silver charm bracelet. Her mind was racing trying to make sense of what she was seeing. She held the bracelet up and stared at the familiar trinkets dangling between the silver links. Still clasping the bracelet she unfolded the pages and ran her eyes down the first one. She could feel the blood rushing through her head and there was a clanging sound in her ears. The letters were from Megan and they were addressed to Eric. Holly skimmed the other pages, her shaking hands making reading almost impossible. They were written at different times but they were all requesting the same thing. Money. Megan had been blackmailing him. Tears filled her eyes and the words blurred as they swam on the page in front of her. She began to fold the letters back up when she heard the latch click as the door to the studio closed softly behind her. When had it opened? Her body was between him and the box but there was no way she could hide what she had found. She stood still and didn't turn around while she tried to calm herself.

"It was stupid of me to keep that stuff," he said quietly.

She said nothing, but slowly moved around to the other side of the table, keeping it between herself and him. He was standing in front of the door in his jacket and boots. His hair was windblown and he looked as handsome as she had ever seen him. But there was something in his face now that she had never noticed before. The aloofness that she had always thought of as sadness wasn't sadness at all but more of a vacancy. He was beautiful, that was certain, but his eyes weren't sad, they were empty. There was no worry or concern in his face at all. His body language was almost casual. She realized that she was terrified of him.

"You killed her." It was more of a statement than a question.

"I put her out of her misery. Mine too for that matter," he said in a nonchalant manner.

"How? She was in Florida."

"The same way I get everywhere. Plane. If that FBI agent were half as smart as he thinks he is, he would have found out that I got my pilot's license when I was a sophomore in college. I have a small plane that is registered to a company that is heavily invested in by my trust." He was still standing a few feet from the door. "Private plane travel is fast, easy, and difficult to track."

"What about the professor?"

"Megan called and said he was on to her. He apparently learned enough from your unfortunate conversation with him to realize she was tied up with me somehow. He advised Megan to go to the police and that he was going to see them himself." His face showed no expression at all except maybe contempt. "We couldn't have that now, could we?"

"And the accident with my car. That was you?"

"I wasn't trying to kill you Holly; I was going to follow you and try to find some way to keep you from going to Virginia. When I saw the old man in the car and realized you were already gone I just lost it. It was stupid, but it all worked out in the end."

Who had it worked out for? Eric of course. She had to think. To keep him talking while she figured out how to get out of this room alive.

"Midwest. The ticket in my car. That's where you keep your plane?"

He eased into the chair and gave her a crooked smile. He was playing with her. He was like a cat toying with a helpless mouse. His complete lack of concern infuriated her. He waited a moment then said, "Careless. I guess I forgot to take it out when I got back. I will have to be more careful next time. You didn't show that ticket to anyone now did you?"

"I...I gave it to Agent Hunter," she lied.

"You never were a very good liar." He said this casually, but she could see a vein starting to pulse at his temple. He was close to losing his temper. He knew she was lying but her mention of the FBI agent seemed to aggravate him.

She felt nauseous. This wasn't happening. No one knew where she was. She looked around without moving her head for something to use to defend herself. He certainly wasn't going to let her just walk out of here.

"My bike? And the mushrooms in the sauce?"

He let the chair legs rock back to the ground hard. The game was getting old.

"It was that *MEDDLING BITCH* Megan's stupid way of trying to get you away from me," he snarled. "She wanted my money but she also wanted you to stay away. I finally convinced her that if she pulled any more stunts like that it would cost her more than her share of the family fortune."

Holly bought time by asking, "What about Chief Sparks?" The watch. That's where she had seen it. He had pulled it out of his pocket and checked it the day she had visited him at his house. Obviously Eric had been there also.

"Your visit gave that old guy just the reason he needed to dig that mess up again. Once he started he wouldn't stop. You can only blame yourself for that one." He leaned forward with his elbows on his knees. She could tell that the whole question and answer thing was starting to wear thin and she still hadn't found what she was looking for. He rose slowly out of his chair and zipped up his jacket.

"There's a baby," she said.

"Yeah, I know. That would have been nice." He looked genuinely disappointed and she felt a chill run up her spine. He was going to kill her.

He took a step toward her and held out his hand.

"Come on. Let's go for a walk. Just like old times." But she knew this time he would come back alone. She was looking for something, anything that she could use as a weapon when her eyes stopped on the clear plastic container of fluid on the worktable next to her. It was the paint thinner that he used to clean his brushes. She stood still waiting for him to come to her.

"Don't make this difficult Holly." His condescending tone angered her. Did he really believe she would just walk into the woods with him to die without a fight?

He took another step toward her and scanned the area with his eyes trying to determine what she had been looking for. Thankfully he didn't pay attention to the container of fluid and she had been careful not to look at it again.

Even though she had expected it his lunge startled her. He reached for her, managed to grab her left wrist and twist it behind her. She grabbed the container with her right hand and threw it over her shoulder directly into his face. He yelled and covered his eyes with his hands and she quickly shoved the table out of her way knocking it over and ran for the door.

She yanked the door handle so hard that her hand slipped off of it when it didn't budge. He must have locked it when he came in. Looking behind her as she fumbled with the lock she saw him wiping his face with one of the many rags that were lying everywhere. The door swung open as he kicked the table out of his way and charged after her. She was afraid to lose time trying to get back into the cottage. If he had locked the door she would be trapped. She pulled the door shut behind her having turned the lock again after she had opened the door. It would only take him a second to open it but it was time she needed. Instead she turned right out of the studio and ran, stumbled mostly, down the slope into the woods. The trails had been to the left of the door and if he wasn't watching her tracks, which he probably would be, he would think she had gone that way. She ran flat out thankful that she had worn her tennis shoes today instead of flats. She could hear him behind her and knew he had not been deceived by her choice of directions, at least not for long. Her jacket was white and she pulled the hood over her head so her dark hair wouldn't stand out against the snow. She had been in these woods many times and she tried desperately to get an idea of where she was. Eric was more familiar with them than she was, but if she could make it to the thicker fir trees she might have a chance. She made it to a dense group of trees and ran into them as far as she could stand it until her side was killing her. She hid behind a cluster of Boston firs and stopped to catch her breath. Her footprints would be difficult to track here because the trees were so thick that the snow hadn't covered the ground. She strained to listen and thought she heard footsteps coming from about fifty feet behind her. She stood still and tried to control her breathing and make as little noise as possible.

From about a hundred yards away and to her west she was certain she heard a stick snap. Eric must have heard it too because he was quiet for a few seconds and when there was another sound from that direction she could hear him starting to move toward it. She waited until he was far enough away that she could move without being immediately detected, then she started making her way in the opposite direction. She was looking behind her to make sure he hadn't circled back when she felt the ground giving way beneath her. She was sliding, no tumbling, down a rocky embankment when she hit the bottom and a pile of rocks. Her head slammed hard against what she could only guess was a large boulder. When she came to a stop she tried to look around but she was having trouble focusing her eyes. There was also a terrible pain in her upper right side. She raised her left hand to her head and when she brought it back in front of her eyes she could make out her red fingers, but not very well.

Snow and dirt started tumbling down the embankment and when she raised her eyes to it she saw Eric looking down at her. She still couldn't focus very well and his blue and black jacket came in and out of her constantly changing field of vision as he made his way down the embankment toward her. She closed her eyes and attempted to turn her head away from the dirt and rocks that followed him down the embankment and rained over her. When she focused her eyes again he was standing directly over her with his hands on his hips and she could feel herself starting to lose consciousness. The pain in her side took her breath away when she tried to move. She was completely helpless and at the mercy of a murderer. She prayed that God would forgive her for putting her unborn baby in the path of this maniac and hoped that she would pass out before he did whatever he was going to do to her. She drew a deep breath and tried to focus her concentration on him one last time, hoping to plead for the baby's life. He squatted down and reached toward her but instead of touching her he picked up a large rock and stood back up.

"The baby," she whispered. It was all she could get out. The pain in her side was crushing.

"I know," he said soothingly. "I might have made a good father. Who knows? It just didn't work out that way."

He raised the rock over her head and she closed her eyes in preparation for the impact. There was a loud cracking sound and for a split second she wondered if it was the rock against her skull, but she didn't feel any different and when she opened her eyes again Eric was falling backward. The rock slipped from his hands and fell to his feet as he went over.

Holly struggled to look around and when she looked up she saw Dan Hunter put his gun back in the holster under his arm and begin making his way down the slope toward her.

"Hold on Holly. I'm coming."

"Is he...?" she couldn't get anymore out.

"He's dead Holly. Don't worry. He won't be getting back up."

He had reached her side and was down on his knees next to her. She heard him say something to her in a gentle and concerned voice about not moving and then she didn't hear anything else.

50

Holly opened her eyes to find Mrs. Kingsley leaning over her and patting her hand. She looked around her at the hospital room very much like the one she had visited her boss in not long ago and winced at the pain in her head when she moved it.

"Now, you just stay still. Walter, go on and get that nurse and tell her she's awake."

There were machines beeping out of her sight and she could see an IV line that started at her right arm and descended out of her field of vision. Mr. Johnson must have been sitting in a chair in the corner of the hospital room because until he stood up to go get the nurse Holly didn't see him.

"What's wrong with me?" she asked. She wanted to ask about the baby but she would wait until she was alone with the doctor.

"You got a pretty nasty bump on the head and a concussion. Also a couple of broken ribs. But nothing that won't mend. You just lie still now and rest. I called your parents and they will be here in a few hours."

Holly was relieved. Tears streamed out of her eyes and slid down the sides of her head to her ears.

"Poor baby." These words, although unbeknownst to Mrs. Kingsley, mirrored her thoughts exactly. She had been in love with and was now carrying the baby of a murderer. At least she hoped she was still carrying it. The nurse came in and shuffled her visitors out saying that she had paged the doctor and he would want to examine her in private.

"We'll be just down the hall getting some coffee Holly. "C'mon Walter," Beatrice Kingsley ordered. And they were gone.

The next two days were spent sleeping off the constant exhaustion and depression she felt and enjoying visits from her parents. They both had looked terrified when they first saw her, but after several reassurances by both Holly and the hospital staff that she was doing well, they relaxed a bit and took turns pampering her.

She was dressed and sitting on the side of her hospital bed waiting for the nurse to come in with her release instructions when there was a knock at the door.

"You decent?" Agent Hunter asked.

"Yes. Come in, I was hoping you would show up."

"How's the head?" he asked, looking sincerely concerned.

"Still in one piece thanks to you," she said and motioned for him to sit down.

"No one has told me what happened and frankly I was hoping to hear it from you. I remember that you shot him, I just don't know how you got to be there." She leveled her gaze at him and placed her hands on the bed on either side of her as if to brace herself for what he would say.

"I stopped by the Wilkes place to ask Eric a few questions before coming to see you at the store. I wanted to see his reaction when he heard about Megan. His ownership of a private plane had been uncovered by the agents in Virginia and he was back to being a prime suspect. That is what I was going to tell you on Monday morning. You were already at the Kingsley place so I figured you were safe for the time being. That was my mistake and I am sorry. I was planning on trying to convince you in person to go back to Ohio until we could get Eric in custody." He stood up and looked out the window for a moment and then turned and leaned against the sill.

"I saw your car when I got there and when I didn't get any answer at the cottage I got a bad feeling. I went back to the studio and saw the open door and the table knocked over. I was terrified I was too late." She realized that he had truly been scared for her.

"I followed both sets of footprints into the woods. I realized he was on your trail so I moved around you and made some noise to distract him. I didn't know if he was armed and I was afraid to shoot in case I hit you so I couldn't just run him down shooting." He paused but when she continued to stare at him he went on.

"He started toward where I was hiding behind a clump of trees but then you fell and he took off after you. I ran after him and when I finally got there he had the rock up. I wasn't sure if I just wounded him what he would do with the rock so I had to kill him."

"He would have killed me. I'm sure of that." Holly said. "And he probably would have forced you to kill him. Eric would never have given himself up." She closed her eyes as shame and anger overwhelmed her.

"He was very clever Holly. He was in control of this sick game of his from the very beginning."

"He never fooled you though, that's why you didn't leave, isn't it?"

"I wasn't in love with him Holly. But no, I never believed it was anyone but him. The evidence pointed to Megan though and I had to follow the evidence."

"The bracelet. It's in his studio."

"We found it. And the blackmail letters. Megan had made a habit of watching the family she felt she should have been a part of. She was watching the night Eric set the house on fire killing his brother and grandmother. When she couldn't get part of the estate legally she started blackmailing him." He was quiet for a moment and then he went on.

"I don't know if this helps at all but from what she wrote Megan cared for you and begged Eric to leave you alone. She wanted the money but she didn't want you to get hurt."

Holly nodded, tears welling in her eyes. This information at least meant she hadn't been completely wrong about her friend.

"What about Derrick Peterman? Who killed him?"

"Probably Eric. Derrick had befriended Megan in the past. It isn't hard to believe that he would approach Eric again to plead her case. Maybe he thought that would win her favor in some way. He couldn't have known the kind of man he was dealing with though."

"It's over then?"

"For the most part. The cottage and the studio have been thoroughly searched and Eric's attorney is handling the removal of his things. As far as you're concerned you might be asked to answer a few questions. Other than that, it's pretty much a closed book. What about you? Are you going home with your parents?"

"Yes. I am going to go home with my mom next week. Dad's leaving tomorrow. I will decide after Christmas where to go from there." He wished her luck, holding her hand in his longer than he should have and then left. She watched him leave and suddenly felt very tired. Her hand went involuntarily to her stomach. The doctor had assured her that the baby was fine and that she shouldn't worry. She decided that she would tell her parents about the baby at Christmas. She wasn't going to let Eric take away one more moment of excitement or happiness about the impending birth of her baby. She was determined to move forward with her life and never look back.

51

Her thoughts were interrupted by another knock at the door. This time a stranger wearing what appeared to be an expensive suit entered, removing his hat.

"Ms. Miller?"

"I'm Holly Miller. Can I help you?"

"I hate to interrupt you Ms. Miller but I have some information that I would like to share with you in private before you go home."

She motioned him to the chair and felt her heart start to pound.

"My name is Sam Langford, Ms. Miller. I am one of the attorneys that handled the Copeland estate."

"Is it appropriate for you to be here?" she asked.

"Yes, under the circumstances, I believe it is. I think once you hear what I have to say you will understand why I wanted to speak to you alone. I doubt that will be possible once you leave the hospital with your family."

She nodded for him to continue.

"We received a letter from Mr. Copeland late last week. It was brought to my attention and forwarded to me while I was here working to resolve Mr. Copeland's local assets." He swallowed audibly. Holly could tell he was very uncomfortable. She didn't do or say anything to assist him in his distress.

"The letter was dated and witnessed by Mr. Copeland and two others from the bank where he did his business. Basically Ms. Miller, Mr. Copeland – Eric – wanted to add a codicil to his will stating that if there were any living or impending children at the time of his death that his estate should be transferred in trust to that child. His instructions directed us in the event of his untimely death to speak to you. Do you understand what I am getting at?"

She nodded again but said nothing.

"In that case I will leave you my card and when you are quite healed up and feel like talking you can call me." He handed her his business card, which she took without looking at it. He rose to leave offering her his hand, which she ignored.

"I am truly sorry for all that you have been through Ms. Miller. Please contact me if I can be of any service to you." With that he left the room closing the door behind him.

Holly stared down at the card in her hand briefly before slipping it into her pocket. A moment later the door opened again admitting her mother followed by an orderly pushing a wheelchair. She knew there would be a time when she would have to come to terms with all that had happened. She would have to accept the horror and the betrayal. But for now she would deal with none of it. Whatever lies had been intertwined in her relationships with Eric and Megan, this baby was not part of it. Her baby was real and he was safe. And she was grateful for that. For now that was enough.